SEASONS OF LIGHT AND DARK

A NOVEL

JANET GILSDORF

Epicenter Press Inc.
Alaska Book Adventures™

KENMORE, WA

6524 NE 181st St., Suite 2, Kenmore, WA 98028

Epicenter Press is a regional press publishing nonfiction books about the arts, history, environment, and diverse cultures and lifestyles of Alaska and the Pacific Northwest. For more information, visit www.EpicenterPress.com

Seasons of Light and Dark
Copyright © 2026 by Janet Gilsdorf

Cover design: Scott Book
Interior design: Melissa Vail Coffman

Library of Congress Control Number: 2025948305

ISBN: 978-1-684923-37-3 (Trade Paperback)
ISBN: 978-1-684923-38-0 (Ebook)

To Jim,
In spite of Lake Dezadeash

Author's Note

ALASKA IS TRULY A MAGICAL PLACE. During my year in Bethel as a member of its medical community at the height of the Vietnam War, I was both an outsider and yet an insider. The Native people, Athabascan Indians and Yup'ik Eskimos, were inventive, resourceful, warm, and welcoming, and no group is kinder to its children. The land is stunningly beautiful, as seen in the wilderness-in-miniature of the tundra, the brilliant sunrises and sunsets, the rivers and bogs that feed the living creatures, and the dance of the northern lights. The tales depicted in *Seasons of Light and Dark* reflect the complexities of the place and its people and portray the practice of medicine and the wonder of living in that far-away wonderland at that unique time.

—Janet Gilsdorf

PROLOGUE

Nᴇᴀʀ ᴛʜᴇ ᴛᴏᴘ ᴏꜰ ᴛʜᴇ Eᴀʀᴛʜ, when the country was at war in the far away jungles of Southeast Asia, two men squatted beside their driftwood fire, their backs to both the river and the icy breeze that blew off it. Luther Uttereyuk handed his brother Morris a piece of last year's dried salmon that he had found in the tent there at fish camp.

"Chilly," Luther muttered and then bit into another chunk of salmon with his back teeth, twisting it away from the rest of the fish.

"Ee," Morris said, nodding in agreement.

The dog sniffed Luther's hands. He swatted him away. The dog moved to Morris. "Get outta here, Sport," he yelled.

"Did you tell Uncle Abe we're here?" Morris asked.

"Ee. He's happy we're getting along," Luther said, "and glad we're helping with the fish."

"Ee. He's bothered me about not doing our share." Morris pulled a paper wrapper from his jacket pocket. He unfolded it, held up a round of pilot bread, and asked his brother, "Want some?"

"Where'd you get that?"

"From a friend." Morris broke the hard-tack in half, laid the pieces on the knee of his jeans and refolded the paper.

"What friend?"

"Just a friend."

"Friend from here or from Bethel?" Luther sat up straight and pounded his right fist against his left palm. "Uncle Abe would want you to tell me so I don't get mad and hit you."

"From wherever that friend is."

Luther shrugged and took his half. He bit off a chunk, chewed, then swallowed. "We could come back in a couple days to haul in more fish."

"Ee. We could. Uncle Abe would like that."

The wind picked up and set the willows that dotted the riverbank asway. A veil of gray mist hung over the tundra, hiding both the sun and the warmth its rays would otherwise pour upon them. "Didn't Uncle Abe leave some stinkheads around here somewhere?" Luther asked as he zipped his jacket tighter around his neck.

"Ee. Somewhere."

Luther took a swig from his half empty bottle of Old Overholt rye whiskey and burped. Then he rose to his feet and wandered around the outside of the tent. He kicked at several clumps of weeds and a charred piece of driftwood and then wandered back to the fire. "Couldn't find where he buried it."

Morris rose and headed to the drying rack, where thirty or so splayed salmon hung like meaty laundry from the wooden bars. He walked around the boat they had beached on the shore, stepped over a pile of weathered carpet squares, pulled several lingonberries from a clump growing in the lichen and moss, and popped them into his mouth. When he neared the open patch where Uncle Abe stored his spare gas can, his extra oar, and a rusty popcorn tub, he stopped.

A piece of plastic, fluttering in the breeze like a trapped blackbird, caught his eye. He pulled at the wrinkled garbage bag. It was stuck in the tundra soil. He kicked a hole in the weeds above the bag and dug deeper into the hole with the end of the oar. Finally, he was able to yank the bag free from the nearly frozen dirt and carried it back to the fire.

He squatted beside his brother and untied the knot at the top of the sack.

Luther sniffed, caught the unmistakable odor of stinkheads, and looked up. "That's it. Gimme some." He extended his open palm to his brother. "Uncle Abe will be glad that we shared."

Morris scooped a wad from the greasy mass of fermented fish heads inside the bag and passed the sack to his brother. Luther took a handful, stuffed it into his mouth, chewed, swallowed, and said, "Uncle Abe makes the best stinkheads."

"Ee," Morris said.

"The women'll be here, tomorrow, right?"

"Right."

The next day, after hauling in a net full of salmon, the brothers watched as their mother, aunt, and sisters chopped the heads off the fish, boned them, tossed the guts into a stream that bumped over the rocks and down to the river, sliced parallel slashes into the fish flesh with their ulus, and hung each set of fillets, connected at the tail-end like salmon butterfly wings, over the rails of the drying rack. They chattered like seals while they worked, and they laughed.

As the women climbed into their boat to return to Nunapitchuk later that afternoon, the clouds overhead grew gray. Then darker gray. Soon raindrops pelted Morris and Luther, and they raced for the tent.

"Stay outside," Morris yelled at Sport when the dog tried to nose his way into the canvas doorway.

Huddled inside, they sipped at the bottle of Old Overholt and hoped the weather would clear soon so the salmon would dry right.

That night, as Luther and Morris slept, a moose padded through the fish camp and tripped over a stake that anchored their tent to the ground. He huffed and attacked one of the tie-down ropes with his antlers. "Lay still," Luther muttered to Morris and socked his brother's arm. "You're wiggling too much."

The next morning they saw that one side of the tent had collapsed, and Morris spotted moose tracks in the mud.

"He could of gored us," Morris said.

"Yup, he could of," Luther answered as he pet his dog Sport.

"Why'd you sock me in the middle of the night? Morris asked. "Are you trying to start a fight?"

"Naw. Remember, we're not fighting anymore."

"Ee."

That afternoon, Morris sat beside the fire, pulled his pant-leg up over his knee and examined his red, swollen calf. He'd ripped the skin open when, earlier in the morning, he reached for the net, fell, and landed on a nail protruding from a piece of driftwood. It still hurt. "Damn nail," he said to Luther. "It's making my eyes funny."

Luther said, "My eyes are funny too. I think it's because I didn't take a shit for a while."

Morris shrugged. He blew on the gash in his sore calf and left the pant-leg gathered around his knee.

Two days later, their Uncle Abe Achee settled into his kayak in Nunapitchuk, Alaska, and paddled toward the family's fish camp several miles downstream on Johnsons Slough. The water below was smooth as liquid glass, and the sun above reminded him of a golden balloon dangling in the clear sky. *Good weather for drying salmon*, he thought.

He beached his boat in front of the tent, and stepped onto the muddy shore. Something was wrong with the tent. It was lopsided. It had never been like that since he and his cousin first set it up about 15 years ago. "Morris?" he called. "Luther?" His voice seemed to disappear into the vast tundra. *What'd those boys do to the tent?* he wondered. Probably had a fight in there. Those two were always trying to out-do each other.

The wind whistled through the willow leaves, and the river water lapped the end of his beached kayak. He stuck his head into the tent. The wall-to-wall-cots were all empty. He walked over to the drying rack. "Where are you guys?" he called. His only answer was the throaty, staccato mating call of a ptarmigan.

The salmon on the racks were drying nicely; he was proud of his nephews for catching so many fish. The boys—he called them boys even though they were twenty-two and twenty-four—were his youngest sister's sons. She had done a good job of teaching them the native ways. No canned meat for them. Near the cold embers and dusty ashes of the fire pit he spotted an empty Old Overholt bottle and a black plastic sack. They'd found his stink-heads, he thought, shaking his head. They'd probably drunk themselves silly, and who knows what they might have done and where they might have gone.

Abe heard the bushes rustle. He turned toward the sound and watched as Sport wandered toward him. "Where'd the boys go?" he asked the dog. Sport aimed his muzzle at Abe's crotch. Abe patted the mongrel's head. "They wouldn't leave you here alone."

He walked around the tent and, several yards beyond the back, he spotted a heap on the ground. He couldn't remember leaving a pile of rags out there. He stepped closer and decided the rags were pants and a flannel shirt. He stepped even closer and saw that the heap was Morris, curled up in the weeds, with his left pant-leg pulled up to his knee and a long, deep gash in his calf. Abe stood over his nephew and called his name. The young man didn't move. Had the boy drunk himself into a stupor? That sounded more like Luther than Morris. Abe tapped Morris's shoulder with the toe of his boot. Nothing. Abe stooped, pried open Morris's right eyelid, and quickly sank backward.

He scrambled to his feet. Morris was dead.

Abe yelled for Luther. Again, no one called back. Their boat was still overturned on the mud, so Luther must still be around. Maybe he had wandered into the willows.

Abe shouted Luther's name as he roamed the shore and into the shrubs. Had Luther stabbed his brother, he wondered as he walked. Luther was the more hot-headed one of the two, short on sense, long on anger. He recalled how Morris used to tease Luther about his girlfriends, and Luther would answer with his fists. Had they gotten into a fight?

Finally he found Luther, slumped on the ground among the willows several yards upriver. His eyes were half open and his mouth held a grimace. He too was dead.

CHAPTER 1

July 1971

IN THE QUIET OF THE EVENINGS, during the months before they moved, Jennifer tried to imagine living in Bethel. She had read in a *National Geographic* that the town was small, isolated, and rustic, south of the Arctic Circle, north of the Aleutian Peninsula. *How small*, she wondered. *How rustic?* It would be frigid and dark all day in the winter, chilly and light all night in the summer, but how cold and how dark? She wondered if the native people spoke English, if she would have any friends, if their twin sons would have any playmates.

When John first suggested he take the Indian Health Service position in Bethel, he'd sensed her hesitation, "*I've wanted to live in Alaska since I read People of the Deer when I was eleven,*" he'd said. "*I've wanted to live among the native people, to learn from them how to exist in harmony with nature. And, now, I can make a difference in their health.*" John's commitment to the IHS was for two years. Jennifer figured that for him it would be two years of long-awaited enchantment. How about her?

She'd lived in California her entire life; in fact, until she went to college, she'd lived in the same house. She hadn't traveled much, except for trips to Oregon and Las Vegas as a teen with her parents. She hadn't even traveled around California much, although she and friends had camped in Yosemite and hiked to the top of the Pinnacles several times.

She knew little about native peoples and even less about Eskimos. One of the girls in her college dorm was a Miwok Indian, but Jennifer didn't know her well. The girl had kept to herself and returned to her hometown after only one year.

The questions about her future in Alaska—where they would live, how the twins would adjust, how she would spend her days— cluttered her mind like piles of dirty laundry. The place was far away, hard to reach, and different from everything familiar to her. Jennifer knew that, for her, their two years in Bethel would be twenty-four months of endless, unimaginable challenges.

As THE WEEKS ROLLED BY AND Jennifer thought more and more about the upcoming move, she tried to consider that it could be positive for her: new people, new food, new weather, a new way of existing. That might be exciting. And yet, it would probably result in a U-turn in her professional tomorrows.

She hadn't completed her PhD in microbiology yet. Chapters one through four of her thesis, as well as chapter six titled "Future Directions" were pretty much set, but chapter five—her favorite, the one she tentatively called "Surface proteins shape the population dynamics of *E. coli* in human hosts"—was not complete. She needed to do a few more experiments, needed to correlate the various adhesive proteins, which protruded away from the bacterial cell membrane and latched onto human cells, with their prevalence among isolates from men and women, from adults and children, from urine, blood, and fecal samples.

She'd worked very hard toward that degree—five years of her life had already been devoted to the classwork, the lab work, the fretting, the occasional rewards. She was so close and yet so far.

"It'll be only a two-year break," John said, trying to reassure her. "When it's over, you'll return with new investigative vigor. You can also continue to work on it, some, in Bethel, can't you?"

"Well . . ." She had answered in her hesitant voice. "I can tweak a few things, but I can't finish it." Bethel had no science library, although she could probably order articles from U.C. Davis. It wouldn't have a lab like hers in California to complete those few remaining experiments, although it would have a clinical laboratory. She would have no microbiology colleagues to discuss her ideas with. Rather than time to finish her thesis, two years in Alaska could be a hole kicked into the previously verdant promise of her professional future.

They debated back and forth, sometimes far into the evenings after their sons had gone to bed. "Your career may be enriched in Alaska, and mine will surely be stunted," she moaned to her husband.

"You and the kids could stay here in California while I serve in Vietnam. That's the alternative. Would you prefer that?"

She shook her head and wiped her tears. "Women's careers always take the back burner so a man's career can shine," she said.

"Not always."

"Give me an example." She cross her arms over her chest.

He paused.

"Just one lousy example."

He changed the subject.

Another evening, she complained about being only the cook and chief bottle-washer in their family. "I want more than that," she said, fighting the sob that was stuck in her throat.

"Of course you do," John said. "We'll see what you can do on that thesis while in Bethel."

"That is so patronizing, John. I'd bet the house that I'll continue in the homemaker role as long as we're married."

"Not necessarily . . ." he began.

"Sure. Not if we're millionaires and can hire people to cook and clean and plan and babysit."

He'd brushed her hair away from her face and given her a big kiss. "You'll make it work. You're one of the most practical people I know."

Later, when he spotted the cartons of scientific papers and textbooks that she piled on their living room floor and planned to haul to Alaska, John had groaned, "We won't have room for all that stuff."

"I'll make it fit," she answered.

The discussion of whether to bring Ginger to Alaska was a long, lively one. John wanted to hunt with the dog; Jennifer thought the VW van would be crowded enough without a big golden retriever and the dog crate. John thought it would be hard on their twins to leave Ginger. Jennifer said, "They're only three and a half. They'll adjust. Besides, my sister will be happy to keep the dog while we're gone."

"Ginger will be ruined as a hunting dog if she spends two years chained up in your sister's back yard."

"Besides hauling the dog and crate all the way up there, we'll have to haul enough food to feed her during the trip." Jennifer was firm. Bringing Ginger along was too much.

"I'll make room. Should we ask the twins? They should have a vote here."

She knew what the kids would say. The vote would be a resounding three to one.

When they started out from Central California, Jennifer saw herself as a modern Tamsen Donner of the infamous Donner party, the woman who ended up stranded in the snow at Alder Creek and ultimately died at her ill husband's side while waiting for the rescuers to arrive. John and Jennifer's VW van, filled to the roof, was a Conestoga wagon to her, and the Alaska-Canada Highway would be the Oregon Trail.

Stowed inside the van were a Tupperware bucket-full of granola for breakfasts and snacks, several jars of pickled eggs, six cans of tuna fish, sacks of apples, potatoes, and oranges, and the greenest of the bananas at Safeway, which, Jennifer figured, would ripen during the trip. The cooler was loaded with a huge tub of potato salad, frozen hot dogs, bags of frozen vegetables, and a frozen chicken. John had, indeed, found room in the back of the van for Ginger, her crate, and her food, and Jennifer had piled the microbiology papers and textbooks on top of the crate. Beside the books she'd slipped a small Styrofoam box containing the *E. coli* strains she'd need to finish the experiments for her thesis.

As they pulled out of town, Jennifer could see in John's posture and his mood that he was utterly thrilled. Everyone's childhood dreams should come true, she thought, but they rarely did, which wasn't always a bad thing. Jennifer's youthful dream was to become a movie star like Eva Marie Saint in *North by Northwest*, but what she had become was so much better: a scientist, a mother, a wife, a curious person. She admired adventurous, courageous people and strived to be one. But, the upcoming venture might require more courage than she possessed. Did she have enough? Would her inquisitiveness carry her through? Would she gain anything from it?

On I-5, just north of Sacramento, Jeff demanded to ride in Ginger's box. John chuckled, pulled into a rest stop, let Ginger out of the crate, and Jeff crawled in.

Thirty miles ahead, at the turn-off to Arbuckle, Jeff wanted out. John pulled off the road, helped Jeff out of the crate and pushed Ginger back inside while Brian, chewing on a strawberry fruit leather, sat silent in the back seat where he had been watching the world pass by through the window.

Half hour later, Jeff begged to go back in the box. John stopped and helped Ginger and Jeff trade places. About forty miles further, as Ginger slept on the floor at Brian's feet in the back seat, Jeff yelled to get out.

"I'm done stopping," John called over his shoulder. "At this rate, we'll never get to Alaska. You have to stay in there a while longer."

Jeff shouted and shook the wire sides of the crate. "Out. Now. Out."

"Quit it, buddy," John yelled. "You wanted in, so stay in."

Jeff kept up the racket. "Honey, let him out," Jennifer said.

"No. I'm not stopping every fifteen minutes."

"Let him out and then leave him out." Jennifer was sometimes amazed that her physician husband couldn't solve some of the simplest problems.

"He begged to go in, and he's staying in."

Jennifer sighed. "John, what if a highway patrolman spots a child screaming in a cage in the back of a VW van? We'll end up in prison rather than in Alaska."

Once again John pulled over to the side of the highway and let his son out of the crate. "That's Ginger's house," he yelled at Jeff. "You're not going in again."

THEY TRAVELED THROUGH THE REDWOODS OF northern California, then forested Oregon, then bustling Seattle and on through upstate Washington and way north into Canada.

"Let's count the tall poles," Brian said to his brother, meaning the telephone posts that flanked the highway. "Yeah," Jeff hollered. When they reached ten, they started over.

At night, inside the tent, deep in a provincial park somewhere up in Canada, with John in his sleeping bag at her side and the kids at their feet, Jennifer listened to the night sounds: the hooty owls, the breeze in the trees, the calls of coyotes, the occasional plunk of a pinecone on the canvas roof. *What are we doing?* she asked herself.

Finally, they reached the beginning of the many days' drive ahead on the Alaska-Canada Highway, which was, in reality, a rut-filled gravel road that wound up high hills and down deep valleys through the seemingly endless forest. She thumbed through the *Milepost* book John had bought to keep track of where they were. At Dawson Creek, she asked him to stop so she could snap a photo of Milepost 0.

"What's so interesting about that?" he asked.

"It marks the beginning of the ALCAN," she said. "Beginnings are always interesting. And hopefully, the corresponding endings are equally as interesting."

At Mile 51.3, they stopped to read the sign on the monument at Charlie Lake. "In memory of the 12 Americans soldiers who drowned May 14, 1942, when their pontoon boat sank while crossing the lake in a storm." Jennifer gazed across the choppy water and thought of the terror of those men as they struggled against the frigid waves. She thought of their wives-turned-to-widows and their poor, orphaned children.

They had the road mostly to themselves; they encountered an on-coming vehicle about once every hour. With pine-dappled sunlight streaming through the van's dusty windows she played "guess what I'm thinking" with the boys and worked on a wool cap she was crocheting for John. Near Mile 342, a huge lumber truck, kicking up debris from the road, barreled toward them. Suddenly a rock shot upward in front of the van. She shut her eyes and turned her face to the side. It hit with a crack.

"Shit," John yelled.

"Shit," Jeff yelled from the back seat.

She opened her eyes. The windshield was intact. The van still ran.

"Watch your mouth, young man," she called to Jeff.

John pulled to the side of the road, and they climbed out. The headlights were fine, but the grille was dented. "Whew," John said. "That was lucky."

The kids, with their puzzles and coloring books, tolerated the hours of travel well, but Jennifer grew more anxious with each passing day. They were well-prepared, with two spare tires, three extra air filters, a plastic jerry can from her lab filled with water, and plenty of food for all of them, including Ginger. Still she worried. About running out of gas with no filling stations for many,

many miles, about one of the kids getting sick, about both kids getting bored, about blowing all their tires on any of the billions of potholes, about bears breaking into the van for food or into the tent while they slept. For sure, though, they wouldn't get lost, as no Ys and no intersections interrupted the relentless forward momentum of the road. Jennifer, however, tucked the possibility of a wrong turn onto the back shelf in her mind, the place where she stored all the anxieties she couldn't control.

At Mile 437.7, they pulled into the Strawberry Flats Campground and set up the tent for the night. The *Milepost* book described the place perfectly: "Fifteen sites on rocky lake shore, picnic tables, garbage containers. *CAUTION: Bears in the area.*" The place was beautiful, and the only problem was when Brian refused to pee in the woods. Jeff, on the other hand, gleefully sprayed a patch of wild blueberries. Finally, she watched John walk Brian a few feet further into the trees and heard him dare their son to squirt on a jagged rock. "Do it the way we Jetters men do it. Paint that baby yellow, my son." His voice, the loudest sound at the campsite, seemed to ricochet off the trunks of the surrounding pines. Brian's giggle followed the words of his father.

WHEN THEY FINALLY REACHED ANCHORAGE, EIGHT days after Jennifer took the photo at Milepost 0, they stopped at the Alaska Native Hospital's shipping dock and loaded empty IV fluid cartons—boxes to pack freezable food—into the van. They then drove to Elmendorf Air Force Base to buy meat for the next year. Just past the entrance, a fighter jet roared over the roof of the van, sending John's cup of cold coffee from the dashboard to the floor. Brian covered his ears with his hands. Jeff yelled, "GAZOOOOOMMMMM."

At the Base Exchange, they purchased three rolls of Scotch Heavy Duty Packaging Tape and two shopping carts full of chicken, beef, pork, and frozen pizzas. No fish. John told her the Kuskokwim River, which ran beside Bethel, was alive with salmon.

He'd packed his fishing pole and hand-carved lures along with his waders and tackle box, assuring her they'd have plenty of seafood. Standing in the windy parking lot, they loaded the meat into the IV fluid boxes, taped them shut, addressed them to themselves at IHS Hospital, Bethel, Alaska, and then drove them to the Wein Air Alaska office, frozen freight division.

For the rest of the food, they had followed the instructions sent by the Native Alaska Health Service and had ordered two years' worth of canned goods, dried noodles, rice, dog food, soap, and toilet paper from a warehouse in Seattle. The shipment was scheduled to leave Washington for Bethel on the second barge of the season and was expected to arrive a few weeks later, but that was only a maybe. If their order didn't make it on the second barge, it would be assigned to the third barge, which might or might not arrive before the river froze over for the winter. If their shipment missed that second barge and freeze-up was early, they'd have no food. Again, she tried to file those worries on that mental back shelf. She didn't have the strength right then to work through alternatives.

Out the window of the Wein Air Alaska plane, past the wingtip and the whirring propeller, and past the dumpling clouds, Jennifer saw only white; white where the sky should be above, white on the snowy ground below. If she squinted, she thought she could see the faint jagged line of the horizon. "I thought there were no roads to Bethel," she said.

"There aren't," her husband said.

She jabbed her finger against the window. "Well, John, what's that?" She pointed toward a smooth stretch of glistening white that curved like a lazy S through the mountain tops below.

"It's a glacier."

The airplane bounced like a basketball on the gravel runway in Bethel. Out the plane's window, Jennifer saw that the green-gray tundra stretched to the far beyond. No woodlands, no bushes, only gently rolling ground covered with what looked like moss. The plane chugged to a stop near a log cabin. "Welcome to Bethel, Alaska, where the time is 2:00 p.m., and the temperature is 56° Fahrenheit," called the pilot.

Fifty-six on an afternoon in mid-July. Jennifer shuddered, reset the knit cap on Brian's head, and buttoned Jeff's jacket up to the top. When they left California two long weeks ago, the temperature was in the nineties, but after they arrived in chilly Anchorage, she had dug through the twins' bags and dressed them in their cool-weather garb.

The wind stung her cheeks as she walked across the tarmac with the twins in tow. It was a crystalline, fresh-air wind, not a hint of plane exhaust nor city stink. Rather, it carried a faint scent of mushrooms. Far off to the left she could see Bethel, a scatter of gray, one-story buildings in a very small town. She glanced at John. A glow of pure delight spread across her husband's face. He was living his pipedream, and his eyes, sparkling like tinsel in the sun, reflected the joy in that.

Moving to Bethel had been 98% his idea—his and the United States government's—and 2% hers. The job there would fulfill his military obligation—he, along with many other American physicians, was a victim of the doctor-draft—and, as a bonus, would satisfy his life-long yearning to live among the Eskimos. As far as the government was concerned, John's choices were brutal and binary: Bethel or Vietnam. Hardly a choice.

It was an immoral war. She couldn't bear the thought of John patching up wounded soldiers in the heat of the jungle. Her brother had enlisted as a conscientious objector and drove the maimed and barely breathing combatants from the battlefields to the field hospital at Chu Lai. His stories were beyond gruesome. Her cousin Mike left his right leg there. Another cousin left his soul. John's medical school friend Gary left his life.

Now, John would finally get to live in the wilds, where he would hunt moose and caribou, feel the freedom of the tundra beneath his feet, and fish the Kuskokwim. He'd talked about chum, sock-eye, coho, and chinook salmon, and she didn't know one from the other. As a physician, he would provide medical care to Arctic native people on the fringes of society. "On the fringes of *our* society," John had told her. "They are square in the middle of *their* society." When he had told her how he hoped to learn a lot more about them, about their unique medical problems, their land, their food, their ways of being, it all seemed like a fantasy. Now, they were actually there.

Inside the dinky airplane terminal, a tall man with a pony-tail who wore a bolo tie topped by a beaded slide introduced himself as Leonard Kills Squirrels. He was the hospital administrator. They later learned that he wasn't a native Alaskan, but rather a Hunkpapa Sioux from a reservation in South Dakota. To Jennifer, his grin seemed forced as he gripped their hands in his huge, calloused palms and asked the kids if they enjoyed the plane ride. Brian buried his head in his mother's coat, and Jeff yelled, "Yeah."

Jennifer glanced around her, at the wrinkled calendar nailed to the terminal's log wall, at the broken windowpane patched with duct-tape, at the clusters of round-faced Alaskan natives. Jennifer and John's fair-haired, blue-eyed family were the only white people in the room.

Leonard asked about their trip from California and their introductory session in Anchorage. "You made it to the BX at Elmendorf for meat, right?"

"Right," John answered.

"That meat'll probably come on the frozen-freight plane in a week or so," Leonard said.

Jennifer looked out the terminal's window to the town in the distance. She wondered if one of the gray buildings housed a grocery store. What would they eat until the meat came? Until the canned vegetables and boxes of rice and dehydrated pota-toes arrived from Seattle? What would they eat if the barge didn't come at all?

Suddenly, frantic barking tore into the quiet of the terminal. A man in a Wein Air Alaska jacket rolled a metal cage atop a well-worn dolly across the room. Jeff pulled away from Jennifer and yelled, "Ginger. You're here." He stuck his fingers through the cage's wire wall and patted the dog's nose. "Hi Ginger."

Jennifer surveyed the terminal for their luggage. No baggage carrousel, not a suitcase in sight.

Leonard led them to a van with the IHS logo painted on the side. John and the twins hoisted Ginger and the crate into the back.

"Our luggage?" Jennifer asked. "Where would that be?"

"Oh, yeah. On the rack."

He started the van and drove to a distant edge of the tarmac, to a rickety wooden structure that leaned away from the wind. Sitting all alone on the weathered boards were their four suitcases.

"You left your car with one of the hospital employees in Anchorage?" Leonard kept one hand on the steering wheel and waved the other in the air as he talked.

"We did," John said. "The Chief of Pharmacy. Great guy. He said we could use it anytime we come back to Anchorage. 'Just give me a call, and I'll meet you at the airport,' he said."

They'd spent ten days traveling in that VW van. Jennifer had grown attached to it and would kind of miss it. She hoped the two-year long, vehicle-share arrangement with a stranger in far-away Anchorage was a good idea. How about living in Bethel with no car? How would they get around? Was there any place to go?

As Leonard drove them away from the Bethel airport, Jennifer stared at the open land, at the gray-green hillocks that rolled, gentle as a lullaby, off into the distance for as far as she could see. She hadn't known what to expect but had never considered that Bethel would have no trees. None at all. In California they grew oranges, plums, walnuts, and apricots in their backyard; flowering jasmine by the front door; pink camellias beside the waterspout behind the garage; and a field of red roses between their lot and the one next door. Two years in this barren place, frozen-for-eight-months-at-a-stretch, lay ahead of her. At the end, the twins would be almost six years old, she'd be twenty-nine. Or maybe a hundred and nine. She closed her eyes, shook her head.

Leonard pulled the van to a stop in a puddle just off the muddy road that ran along a series of fourplexes. Each building stood on thick wooden posts that rose at least six feet above the ground. He walked them up the stairs. Inside the entry, he pointed to the door on the right. "This is my place." He then pointed to the left. "This one's yours." Straight ahead, beside a washer and drier, a furnace belched behind a wall of chicken wire. "CAREFUL, HOT" read a sign stapled to the wooden frame of the wire door above a barrel bolt with a sturdy padlock. He pushed open the door to their apartment and stepped into the kitchen.

"Keys?" Jennifer asked.

"No need for keys," he said.

She gasped. "No keys?"

"Naw, people kept losing them, and no one used them anyway, so we don't bother."

While John showed the boys where they would put Ginger's bed, Jennifer and Leonard toured the apartment. A large plywood bookcase covered one wall in the living room. Leonard rapped his knuckles on the top and said, "The former occupants who just finished their tour of duty here thought you might be able to use this." The couch was upholstered with orange-blossoms-on-muddy-gold fabric, and the curtains—"specially designed to keep out the cold," Leonard Kills Squirrels said—were made of rubber-backed, slubby, electric blue rayon. It was the ugliest color she had ever seen.

They wandered down the hallway. "Bedroom 1," he said waving into a room with a double bed, a chair, a dresser, and a black rotary phone. "The building tends to shift with the changing seasons so the doors either won't open or won't stay shut. Most of us keep them propped open. And that window . . ." he pointed toward the far side of the room. "It froze open last January. Jerry—the doc who just left this apartment—stuffed a towel between the sill and the sash to keep out most of the cold air."

Open bedroom window. All winter. This might be harder than she realized. Hopefully, the boys' room stayed warm. Again, she filed the thought of the frozen-open window onto the worry shelf.

"Oh, and the hospital phone is here." Leonard pointed to the rotary dial instrument on the dresser. "There is no phone service in Bethel. This is a hospital phone. You can make satellite calls back to the lower forty-eight in case of a family emergency. They are very expensive and, of course, we have to monitor their use."

Jennifer took a deep breath. That meant no calls back to her advisor in California about her progress on the thesis.

"Bedrooms 2 and 3 are down there." He pointed to the far end of the hallway. "And here's the storeroom for your food." He reached inside and flipped the light switch. It was huge, with a giant freezer beside the door and shelves from floor to ceiling on the other three walls.

"Bathroom," Leonard said. It smelled of Pine-Sol, and the faucet in the tub dribbled a slow drip . . . drip . . . drip . . .

"Leaky faucet," Jennifer said.

"Yeah, we let 'er leak. The running water will keep the pipes from freezing this winter."

Her head was spinning.

Back in the living room, Brian and Jeff lay on the floor with their heads on Ginger's belly. "Do you like our new house?" Brian asked the dog. Jeff grabbed Ginger's snout, shook it up and down, and growled, "Yeah," in his best canine voice.

"Pretty cool, huh, Jenny?" John still carried his grin. "This is going to be so great."

The twins were wrestling with Ginger in a dynamic pile of dog hair, T-shirts, OshKosh-B'gosh overalls, and muddy sneakers. They called to each other in their own language, the words they used when speaking together, the utterings that neither she nor John understood. Jeff yelled, "Bliney" and Brian, giggling, answered, "Grimpy." She wished she knew what they were saying. Their secret language was yet another step in their quest to ultimately leave her and move to their own far-away, foreign lives. More foreign to her than Alaska.

She thought a moment. No house keys, treeless tundra, 360° horizon, windows frozen open, no phone. She was surrounded by foreign.

LATER THAT AFTERNOON, THEY HIKED THE wooden boardwalk across the tundra into town to Swanson's Trading Store, a dilapidated building with no windows. Inside, the light was dim, the aisles were narrow, and the shelves overloaded with clothes, food, cans of WD40, cases of Coca-Cola, and piles of snowsuits. They bought rubber mud boots for the boys and food to hold them over until the meat came on the frozen-freight plane and the canned goods arrived on the barge.

For dinner, Jennifer warmed up Dinty-Moore beef stew and made a salad from wilted lettuce leaves that had cost a fortune. "Enjoy it now," she told John and the kids. "That may be the last fresh salad we have until we leave."

It was 6:30 when Jennifer, John, and the twins walked across the parking lot to the hospital. John couldn't wait to see the place and introduce himself to whoever was there at that time of night. Jennifer wanted to see the lab.

One of the nurses showed them the clinic rooms, the radio room, and the wards. "How about the laboratory?" Jennifer asked. The nurse guided them to a small room containing a microscope, a tiny incubator, a desk covered with papers, no centrifuge, no freezer, no lab glassware, no autoclave. With each step, her heart sank further toward the floor. There was no way she could do any of her remaining experiments here.

At eight o'clock, they ushered the boys into their bedroom. The sun shone like fire from the west into the window. Jennifer pulled the curtain, which didn't do much to keep out the light, and John told the boys made-up tales of hunting caribou in Alaska.

"Don't get them riled up with scary stories," Jennifer warned.

"Daddy, tell us more," Jeff yelled. "About a bear. GRRRRR."

In bed that evening—it was almost midnight—Jennifer stared out the window as the orange sun settled into the tundra. Back in California, she'd only seen the sun set behind buildings: the two-story house behind their home, the chemistry building across the street from the lab where she worked, the skyscrapers of the city. Then she remembered the sun sinking into the Pacific when they'd been on the beach. The ocean was as vast and flat as the tundra, but oh so different.

Her mind tried to itemize the newness of Bethel. She listened to the dripping faucet in the bathtub, looked through the window that might soon be frozen open, wondered if their food order would actually make in onto the second barge. Her future as a microbiologist was likely shattered. The grant that had supported her salary would end in a year and likely her mentor wouldn't have extra money for her to finish the work. All she could do was hope, and hope some more. Hope seemed terribly inadequate.

CHAPTER 2

"THIS IS DR. JOHN JETTERS AT IHS Hospital Bethel signing in. Over."

Static from the short-wave radio flickered through the dim room like a horde of angry wasps, and the little lights on the face of the equipment blinked red and yellow. This was the end of the first week of John's first stint in the radio room. So far, the cases were straightforward, no crises, no head-scratchers. In fact, they had been incredibly mundane.

He'd expected more action from those radio calls. He'd imagined himself as an Albert Schweitzer of the Arctic, saving lives all day long. In a week, he'd saved no one's life. Not even close.

The clock over the file cabinet read 9:45. John had learned from the clinic aide that it was chronically wrong. He glanced at his wristwatch. 10:06. Six minutes past the official radio clinic start time.

The radio squawked. "Dr. Jetters. This is Evelina Tobeluk in Chefornak. Do you receive? Over."

Her quiet, monotonic voice was as still as a pond, and her words rolled with clipped syllables, gentle pauses, and rounded vowels. He enjoyed the sound of Yup'ik-tinted English. He picked up the ball-point pen, gave it a shake, and jotted the date, time, and "Chefornak station" in the logbook. "Go ahead, Evelina. Over."

"Anna Roehl's blood pressures are better on her new medicine. Last week it was 140/94. This morning it was 130/85. And her sugars are good too. Over."

"Yes, that's better. We might be able to get it down even more. Take her pressure every day for another week and get back to us. We might have to increase the hydrochlorothiazide dose. Over."

"Good. We'll do that. And I'll tell her to eat less salt. Over and off."

A pause. More static. If you could see the static, John thought, it'd look like a fistful of sparklers. He took a gulp from his coffee cup. Evelina had implied Anna Roehl's salt intake caused her hypertension. He couldn't imagine too much salt in any Eskimo's diet. Dried salmon from the Kuskokwim, boiled blackfish, seal oil, bearberries—none of that had much salt. Maybe Mrs. Roehl had the means to buy gussuk food. Potato chips or canned corn could crank up a person's sodium reserve pretty quickly.

The radio squawked again, and the lights blinked.

"Dr. Jetters, this is Tammy Alexie from Nunapitchuk. Over."

"Go ahead, Tammy. Over."

"Abe Achee is here again, this time complaining of pain in his pinky toe. Started about three days ago. It's not red or swollen. No sores. His temperature is normal, and he walks fine. Over."

As she spoke, he continued jotting in the logbook. "Any red streaks up his leg or tenderness in his calf? Over."

"No. And he can wiggle the toe fine. The rest of him is fine too. Over."

"How about his boots? Are they new or too tight or something? Over."

The Nunapitchuk connection paused. The static sputtered. Then Tammy's voice returned. "Ee . . ."

John enjoyed the Yup'ik word for yes. It reminded him of a nursery rhyme from his childhood that he'd forgotten.

"... Mr. Achee said his boots are new and maybe a little too tight. And he's lonely, so lonely after his wife died. She had cancer. And then he found those two fellows, his nephews, dead at fish camp a month ago. He's very sad. Over."

"What's fish camp?" *So much new here*, John thought. *So much to learn.* "And how did they die? Over."

"Fish camp is where people go in the summer to catch and dry fish. Mr. Achee's family camps on a slough a little way from town. We don't know what happened to Luther and Morris. Mr. Achee found them dead on the ground, one behind the tent and the other in the willows near the river's edge. He said they hadn't been shot or nothing like that. Over."

"Hmm. Well, give Mr. Achee some Tylenol and have him check back at sick call in two days or so. Let me know what happens with his toe. Over."

"Okay. The whole town is wondering what happened to those guys and worrying who will be next. Over."

"Sounds pretty scary, all right. Over."

"Okay. Over and off."

Two men dead at fish camp sounded to John like the title of a trashy mystery novel. Strange. He wondered what that was about. Achee probably could have seen if they had been shot or stabbed. Did people shoot people out there? Stab each other? Heart attacks? Strokes? Two young men having heart attacks or strokes at the same time in the same place would be odd. Very odd.

The radio was quiet. His thoughts wandered further, back to that rainy evening several weeks after he signed up for the Indian Health Service. He was lounging on the couch in his California living room and paging through a medical journal when an article about the Radio Medical Traffic in Alaska caught his eye. The author described the radio clinic, the types of medical problems the docs encountered, and the rudimentary training of the village health aides, who, under the direction of the far-away docs at the Bethel Hospital, delivered medical care in their communities. It sounded very primitive to him. When he told his fellow interns about the article, he'd said, "I bet the Eskimos are dying in droves out in those villages."

He figured he'd be at the forefront of treating the native people. So far, it wasn't like that. The illnesses were very minor, their treatments simple. Tylenol. Reassurance. Lots of reassurance. Nevertheless, the alternative for his compulsory military service was Vietnam. Nothing would be worse than caring for dying soldiers in those stinking jungles.

He expected more clinic aides to check in that morning, but it was different every day. If the health aides had nothing to report, they didn't call in. While he waited, he paged through the dog-eared notebook of Arctic medicine hints. *Always think of frost-bite. The native diet, while short on vegetables, is surprisingly well-balanced.*

The radio grumbled yet again. "Dr. Jetters. This is Katie Tanabe in Emmonak. I have trouble here. Over."

He didn't like the knife-edge urgency in her voice and sat up straight in his chair. "What's up? Over."

"Little Nick Nook—he's only three months old—has a fever for two days and is fussy. He just had a seizure. Over."

Oh, boy, John thought. *This could be bad.* "Is he breathing okay? What's his blood pressure and his heart rate? Over."

"Ee, he's breathing okay. Hang on, and I'll check the vitals. Over." Her voice was breathy; she was anxious too.

More static fizzed from the receiver. He paged through the Radio Medical Traffic Manual to see which medications were in the clinics. It was variable. What was taking her so long? He took another swig from his cup. The coffee was now barely lukewarm.

Finally, she returned. "I don't have a baby blood pressure cuff, but his heart rate is 116, and his temperature is 103°. He just vomited. Oh, and his soft spot is pooching out from the top of his head. Over."

Of course her little clinic wouldn't have a baby cuff. He should have guessed that. Fever. Fussy. Seizure. Vomiting. Protuberant fontanel. Could be bad. Very, very bad. "Thanks, Katie. We need to get him to Bethel ASAP. I'll call for a plane. Over."

The possibilities, none good, ran through his mind like a prairie fire, but all together it sounded like meningitis. The kid needed treatment, stat, needed to get to Bethel. Flashes of transport trouble shot through his brain. Maybe a plane wasn't available. Maybe a pilot couldn't be located. Maybe the weather was too crummy to fly. In that windowless radio room, he couldn't see the sky. When he'd walked to the hospital that morning, it was cloudy but nothing that would stop a plane from flying. Hard to know about the weather in Emmonak.

Just a week ago a guy developed what might have been a stroke or some neurologic problem out in Kipnuk. The plane got there but couldn't return for two days. The poor man died out there in the village. That could happen to this little fellow in Emmonak. Meningitis, if that's what he had, could be deadly. Without treatment he'd likely have more seizures, quit breathing, and then his heart would stop rock-stone still.

"Tell the baby's parents he might be very sick and needs to come to the hospital right away. Give him a shot of 100,000 units of procaine penicillin in his butt muscle immediately. Got that?" He spoke slowly, enunciated his words carefully. "100,000 . . . units . . . procaine . . . penicillin. Also, give him one and a half milliliters acetaminophen drops. Understand? Do you have the Tylenol for babies there? Over."

"Ee. Over."

"Okay. I'll be here in the radio room for the next two hours or so." He tried to envision a baby with meningitis in that far-away place, attended by a well-meaning aide who was not trained to deal with that kind of an emergency. It wasn't good. "On second thought," he said, "I'll try to get on the plane to Emmonak myself. If anything else happens, call the radio clinic again. One of my colleagues will cover the calls for me. What's the weather like there? Over."

"It's good. Over."

"Okay. I'm on my way. Over and off."

He ran his eyes over the CONTACTS sheet pinned to the wall until he spotted the number for the bush plane service. He dialed it on the satellite phone.

"Only one plane available this afternoon," said the guy who answered. "But I don't have a pilot right now."

"This is a medical emergency," John said. "A little kid is very sick in Emmonak and needs to get to the hospital here immediately."

"What do you expect me to do?" the guy asked. "Call a dead pilot back from heaven? I don't have a guy to fly that plane right now."

John winced at the man's comment about heaven. "When do you expect one to be available?"

"Depends."

"On what?"

"When one of the currently deployed pilots returns."

"Will that be today?"

"Hope so."

The knot that had twisted in John's stomach grew tighter. The kid needed to get to Bethel. He'd already been sick for a couple days. "Call me when you learn anything about a pilot. Please. Again, it's Dr. Jetters at the hospital."

"Will do."

John wondered what Albert Schweitzer would do in this circumstance. The parallels didn't hang together. No planes in that part of Africa, he was sure. Probably no phone lines, either.

John found one of the other doctors in the staff room and told him the story. "Could you cover the radio clinic while I go to Emmonak?"

"Sure."

"Thanks. I'll see a couple of the walk-in patients for you while I wait for a pilot to show up," John said.

"It's a deal."

Before going down the hall to the clinic area, John unfolded the wax paper from his lunch. Tuna salad, again, on two slabs of pilot bread. He fingered the bread. It looked like a thick, flat, round saltine and tasted like the cardboard box it came in. This was the third day straight for tuna. He had asked Jennifer for something different, and she'd said, "The choices are tuna, Spam, Velveeta, or peanut butter and grape jelly. Or we could go high class and have salmon salad. But you have to catch another salmon, first." He pried open the Tupperware container of Del Monte fruit cocktail and spooned it into his mouth with a tongue blade. They'd ordered three cases of the soggy, sugary fruit, and in two weeks, had finished five cans from Swanson's store. He longed for the crunch of a fresh apple.

No call about the pilot yet. John wished he could manufacture one. Or, fly the damn plane himself. He called the health aide in Emmonak and explained the delay. "How's the baby doing? Over."

"He just had another seizure. A little one. Otherwise, no change. Over."

The clinic nurses' aide handed him a chart. "It's Mrs. Epchook from Tuntutuliak. Her son brought her up the river."

"That's where you're from, right?" John asked.

"Ee. I've known Mrs. Epchook since I was a little girl."

He knocked with three raps and, before he heard a response, opened the door to the exam room. He stepped inside. It was windowless and stuffy and smelled of rubbing alcohol mixed with dirty socks. "Hello, Mrs. Epchook. I'm Dr. Jetters. I don't believe we've met." He smiled at the weather-beaten, somber face of the lady perched on the edge of the exam table. Her head was bowed and her feet, wrapped in sealskin mukluks, dangled beneath the hem of her kuspuk. As did most Eskimos, she looked like a stack of two spheres—a small one (her head) sitting on top of the larger one (her body swaddled in warm, loose clothes). "What's bothering you today?"

Her head remained bowed, and she muttered into the neck of her kuspuk. "My duck fell out."

"I'm sorry." He leaned toward her. "Could you say that again?"

"My duck fell out."

What on earth was she talking about? Her duck? Was that Yup'ik for something? He glanced at the face sheet of her chart; she was 73 years old. Maybe her mind was going.

"Could you show me?"

She blushed and hung her head lower.

"Mrs. Epchook, I want to help you, but I have to understand the problem. I need to see what fell out." He handed her a hospital johnny and stepped out of the room while she undressed.

He called down the hallway to the nurses' aide. "Any word about a pilot to Emmonak?"

"Not yet."

He returned to Mrs. Epchook's room. Seated on the exam table in her hospital johnny she looked completely different. Now she was a small sphere (her head with its round face) perched on a wrinkled, skinny body. He was amazed at the ability of Eskimo clothes to bulk-up a person.

"Your duck?" he asked. It felt odd to say the word. "May I see it?"

She slipped off the examining table, turned away from him, and bent forward at the waist. The overlapping back edges of the johnny fell apart, revealing her pale, creased rear end. She placed her fingers on her butt cheeks, pulled the sagging skin apart, and grunted. Between her glutei a bright red, shiny, fleshy protuberance slid at least five inches out of her anus. She reached backward with her right hand, and a bony, outstretched finger pointed to the mass. "There."

Her rectum. It was prolapsed. "Okay," he said. "I see the problem." She pushed the prolapsed tissue back inside and climbed back on the table. He then asked about pain (a little), stool leakage (some), constipation (yes), number of pregnancies (seven). Finally, he said, "Mrs. Epchook, there's only one way to fix your duck so it doesn't fall out anymore. Should we get your son so he can hear about it?"

She nodded.

Her son, a rugged, solemn Yup'ik man, declined the chair John offered and stood beside his mother with his arms crossed over his belly and his feet wide apart. He tipped his head as his mother spoke to him in their native language. John heard the word duck. The son blushed.

"The only way to fix your problem is with an operation," John said to Mrs. Epchook. "We can't do that operation here in Bethel, so you'll have to go to Anchorage."

She shook her head. "No."

"It's not an emergency, so you don't have to go right away, but we shouldn't wait more than a couple weeks. The sooner it's fixed, the sooner you'll feel better," John said. "I will speak with the surgeons in Anchorage to arrange the operation."

She shook her head again. Her son stepped closer to his mother and spoke to her in Yup'ik. She continued to shake her head and to utter a few Yup'ik words. He continued to talk to her in a soft, gentle voice. Finally, she bowed her head, and her son said, "She'll do it, doctor."

After Mrs. Epchook and her son left the clinic, John said to the nurses' aide, "I just learned the Yup'ik word for rectum."

She shot him a puzzled look.

"Duck," he said, triumphantly.

She started to snigger and then to giggle. She set her hand on the wall to brace herself and to catch her breath as she laughed. "No, Dr. Jetters. You just learned the Yup'ik word for asshole. Our language doesn't have a word for rectum."

STILL NO INFORMATION ABOUT A PILOT. John gathered equipment and supplies for the trip: a baby blood pressure cuff, several

22-gauge needles, a couple 23-gauge butterfly needles, tape, three syringes, a vial of sterile saline, and a vial of reconstituted chloramphenicol.

It was the middle of the afternoon when the airplane guy called back about a pilot.

"Found one," he said. "Do you still need to go?"

John sighed. "Yes. Of course. That sick baby needs to get here soon." He explained that he would go too and bring the baby back to Bethel.

"Okay, we'll refuel and be ready for takeoff in about twenty minutes."

"I'm leaving now."

He called the health aide in Emmonak with the update and took one of the so-called taxis—a rusty, battered old Ford with TAXI painted on the side—in the hospital parking lot to the airport.

The wind was minimal and the ride smooth. Out the plane's window, John watched the tundra below. The land was spotted with patches of water that seemed to link together like a giant, wet web.

"I guess we're lucky it's still light out. What do you guys do at night?" John asked.

The pilot chuckled. "Well, usually we don't go. If it's a dire emergency, we have all the vehicles in the village—most are snow-mobiles—line up along the runway—or on the river if it's the winter—with their headlights on."

"That sounds kind of dodgy."

"Yup. It is."

John wondered how the baby was doing. Would they get there and back before he experienced more serious symptoms of meningitis? Or, worst of all, died?

Further along, John saw a large river snaking through the tundra. "Is that the Yukon?"

"Sure is."

It looked different from the Kuskokwim: wider, with fewer

oxbows and surrounded by rolling hills with snow-capped mountains in the distance.

The plane approached the ground as it circled Emonnak once and then bounced to a stop. John climbed out the passenger-side door. A lone man stood in the weeds just off the gravel landing strip. "I'm Melvin Sunnyboy," he said. "I'll take you to the clinic." He pointed to a wooden building nearby.

The pilot leaned out the window of the plane. "I'll be right here when you're ready to leave."

"It won't be long, I imagine."

Inside the clinic, the health aide stood beside the mother who held the baby in her arms. The aide spoke in Yup'ik to the mother, who then rose to her feet and lay the baby on the exam table.

"This is Nick Nook, right?" John asked. He tried to use his gentle voice, hoping that his worried voice didn't slip through.

"Ee."

"Let's see what we have, here." John undressed the baby and took his blood pressure. "Eighty over fifty. That's okay for a fellow this size." He stroked the baby's skin. Good turgor; the baby wasn't badly dehydrated. He listened to his heart and lungs. Normal.

When John poked his little belly, the baby began to whimper like a sick cat. John quickly peeked into the child's half-open mouth but couldn't see much. The boy's soft spot was, indeed, raised. John cradled the child's head in his hands and tried to tip it forward. The baby's neck was rigid as a stick, and his head wouldn't move. For sure this was meningitis.

"Please tell Nick's mother that I'm going to put a little needle in his vein and give him some medicine. She may wish to wait outside."

The Yup'ik words flew back and forth between the aide and the mother. "She'll stay here," the aide said.

The mother, tears crawling down her high-boned cheeks, stepped away from the exam table but John could almost feel her eyes riveted to his back through the entire procedure. He drew five milliliters from the vial of saline into a syringe and then one and a quarter milliliters from the chloramphenicol vial into a second syringe. He passed the two syringes to the aide. "Hold these for a sec, please." Then he slipped a butterfly needle into a vein on the back of the baby's hand and secured it with several strips of tape. He retrieved the syringe with pale yellow liquid from the aide and injected the antibiotic very slowly into the butterfly's IV tubing.

While he paused between each little push of the syringe's plunger, he watched the baby. Beautiful child. Thick, straight black hair. Round face the color of weak tea. Nothing like his own fair-skinned, blond-haired sons at that age. They had always been healthy. What might happen with this little fellow? He might continue to have seizures. He might become deaf, blind, spastic, or slow to learn. He might die. Or he might be normal. Hard to know. Time would tell.

When the chloramphenicol syringe was empty, he replaced it with the syringe of saline and flushed the tubing. Now the antibiotic was flowing throughout Nick's body and up to his brain, where it would do battle with the bacteria causing his illness.

By early evening, the baby was settled in his hospital crib in Bethel, with more antibiotic dripping into the IV in his right hand and his mother seated at his side. John wandered toward the radio room. When he passed the evening nurse in the hallway, he said, "Have you heard anything about two guys dying at fish camp near Nunapitchuk?" He hadn't been able to shake that weird story.

"Yeah. Two brothers. Kind of strange. They weren't all that old."

"Any idea what happened?"

She shrugged. "Some people think they were poisoned."

"Poisoned?"

"Ee. One of them—Luther Utteryuk—was in trouble a lot. He was permanently kicked out of Swanson's store for stealing cigarettes."

"Do you think someone purposely poisoned them, then?"

She shrugged again. "Dunno."

"What do the police think?"

She laughed. "Police? You mean the state troopers? It was just two guys who died out at fish camp. No one called the troopers. Those fellows weren't shot. They just died."

When he reached the radio clinic room, he sank into the desk chair. He was alone in the dark, and the radio was silent. He leaned his head against the back of the chair. Everything had gone as planned; the system had worked for Nick Nook. He, John, had made a difference. That poor little child, so young, so sick, hadn't been left to die out there in the village with no medical care. How about the guys at fish camp? They hadn't been so fortunate.

CHAPTER 3

T HE ARCTIC SKY ROSE OVER THE tundra, as majestic as the endless ceiling of a huge cathedral. Dr. Stephen Steinberg gazed into the quiet, vast beyond. Today was the anniversary of Sandra's leaving. As he watched a cloud float like a fluff of cotton over the horizon, he contemplated the dynamics of their lives as a couple, the way each phase of their relationship had run in one-year cycles: dating, then engagement, then marriage and living in Philadelphia, finally marriage and living in Bethel. That rhythm had been broken like a shattered vase when Sandra left. They had now been unmarried for one year, and that would go on indefinitely.

Stephen slowly drew his oars through the water. His dinghy slid forward, slicing the Kuskokwim River with the ease of a bird in flight. Stroke after stroke. He liked the tempo of rowing, liked to hear the gentle slap of the ripples against the boat.

A shadow passed overhead. He looked up at the tail end of a goose whose cackle sounded like that of a mad witch as it flew by. He stared at it, at the dark brown body and the white patch under its tail. Up front was its tar-black head. A Black Brant goose.

He maneuvered his dinghy into a creek that branched off the river downstream from Oscarville. The sun, bright as an exploding flashbulb high in the cadet blue sky, was shrouded now and again by lazy clouds. The one directly overhead looked like a crab with two wispy claws leading the way. He took a deep breath, drew the tundra-scented air into his lungs, and watched the soft waves from the boat as it glided along the water. It was a perfect day for ptarmigan hunting.

When the creek had narrowed to about three feet, he beached the boat in the willows along the bank. "Okay, Soldier," he said, "we're here. Out." His dog, a long-legged mutt, leaped onto the mossy shelf beside the creek and sampled the air for bird scent. Stephen pulled his shotgun and walking stick from under the seat and climbed out.

He'd bought the boat for only two hundred bucks from Vernon George in Kwethluk. It was small, perfect for him and Soldier. Vernon was also the guy who taught him to shoot. They used empty Clorox jugs hung from the clothesline behind Vernon's house as practice targets. That was a few months before Sandra left. She didn't like the boat, didn't like the gun, didn't like Soldier. In short, she hadn't liked anything about Stephen anymore.

It wasn't always that way. They met at Robin's Bookstore in Philadelphia, and on their second date, she told him she liked—although she had said "cherished"—his taste in literature, his sense of humor, the way his mouth curled when he smiled. They enjoyed the plays at the Walnut Street Theater and concerts by the Philadelphia Orchestra. Back then she didn't seem to mind that his work as a pediatrician at the Children's Hospital interfered a lot with their social life. She kept busy with her many friends, her job as an analyst in the mayor's office, and her volunteer duties at the Philadelphia Botanical Gardens Club. Her mother had been president of that club, and Sandra was poised to assume that position in a few years.

Stephen stepped away from the dinghy. At the thought of Sandra and the Botanical Gardens Club and her complaints about her inability to plant anything in Bethel, he thrust his walking stick into the permafrost. She was a lot like her mother: same trim figure and keen fashion sense, same quick intellect, same love of the French language, same need for adoration. And, her mother was, indeed, adored by Sandra's father. Stephen could tell by the way his father-in-law's smiling, banker eyes followed his wife when she worked the room at parties, and the way he acquiesced to her requests for . . . everything.

Before they moved to Alaska, neither Sandra nor Stephen had been west of West Philadelphia, ever. Sandra's family had a summer home on the Maine coast and Stephen's on Long Island. For vacations they headed east, to London, Paris, or Madrid. So, when Stephen's draft number came up, and he arranged to sit out the Vietnam War at the Native Alaska Hospital in Bethel, both he and Sandra knew it would be an adjustment.

"No problem," she had said as she tossed her milky blond hair. "How hard can a couple years in the far north be?"

He had liked her spunky attitude about the move and thought she might do better than he would. He had no hobbies back in Philly, focused his complete attention on medicine, and was less resilient, he thought, than Sandra.

She had tried to like Bethel, at first. She took drawing lessons at the regional high school until she became bored. She took Yup'ik lessons from the lady that ran the hospital gift shop, but it was nothing like French. He'd taken her on walks on the tundra, and she hated the mosquitoes, the hidden bogs, the monotonous landscape. She especially loathed the long, dark, biting cold winter.

Now he gazed over the rolling tundra looking for ptarmigan. Their brown and black speckled backs could be hard to spot among the ground plants, although this time of year blotches of the remaining white winter feathers on their bellies would stand out like flares against the weeds. The horizon stretched before him; its line, straight as a ruler but somewhat blurry, separated the land from the sky. He slowly turned completely around, and the view was the same from every angle: hillocks that rose and fell in a soft boil stretching from his feet to the distant beyond, firmament that disappeared into the endless universe, and sedge grass that danced in the wind.

He didn't see any ptarmigan but knew the birds were out there. He hooked his shotgun over his shoulder and headed away from the creek. The ground was spongy as usual. Hiking the tundra was like walking on piles of marshmallows. Every several steps, one of his boots sank into a buried puddle. He blocked those stumbles with his walking stick. It was slow going. He wasn't in a hurry. Step over step.

Step over step. Routine. Predictable. Almost as rhythmic as his life's plan, which had been dictated by the Steinberg family values, had been. One: Graduate from college. Two: Graduate from medical school. Three: Complete a pediatric residency. Four: Join his father's upscale pediatric practice in Philadelphia and hob-nob with the folks of his parents' social set. Between steps three and four, however, his plan had swerved, as directed by the United States government. Like so many other physicians, he had been caught in the doctor draft and, unlike those sent to Hawaii; the National Institutes of Health; or Myrtle Beach, South Carolina, he was assigned to Bethel for his service commitment.

Shortly after arriving in Alaska, something strange had happened to Stephen. He fell deeply in love with the peace of the place; with the intelligent, gentle patients and his fun-loving colleagues at the hospital; with the most serene orange and purple sunsets imaginable; and with the mats of low growing foliage that covered the terrain and were lumpy and bumpy from the heaving permafrost. When he was on his knees and eye to eye with the tundra plants, they reminded him of a miniature, mystic woodland. When he thought of Philadelphia, his mind imagined traffic jams, unending noise, exhaust stink, and insincere, inane comments from their friends.

He stooped to the ground and ran his hand over the tangle of berry bushes, lichen, moss, and fuzzy willow shoots that crowded the earth beside his right boot. Most of the berries in this patch were gone—undoubtedly picked by the children of Oscarville or gobbled by local birds or bears—but he found a few red ones hidden beneath the leathery leaves. He pulled several from the plant and inspected them. Must be bearberries. He popped them into his mouth. They were, as he expected, mealy, with little flavor. Off to his left he spotted a couple of mushrooms, tan little umbrellas on sturdy white stems that rose from the helter-skelter blades of grass. He didn't know if they were edible so he left them there.

Further ahead, he spotted the petite branches of evergreen needles tucked into a patch of bog cottongrass. Tundra tea. He was nearly out. He pulled several handfuls from the soggy soil and stuffed them into his pocket. Tonight, after his hoped-for dinner of pan-fried, fresh ptarmigan, he'd have tundra tea and a cigar.

Sandra hated the cigars and made him smoke them outside on the steps of their fourplex, even in the dead of winter. She thought tundra tea tasted like forest floor. "Well, in some ways, it *is* forest floor, without the trees," he had answered.

She had sneered at him. "Quit being a jerk. I don't like snide men."

He was sipping on tundra tea that summer night when she screamed, "I can't take this any longer." She sobbed as she threw a spatula across the kitchen. And then a saucepan. "I need to be with real people. I want to go to a play, to hear a live orchestra. I can't bear the thought of another goddamn winter in this God-forsaken hellhole." Two days later, she boarded the Wein Air Alaska plane to Anchorage, and then on to Philadelphia.

Soldier, who was ranging off to Stephen's left, suddenly froze, his shaggy tail rigid behind him and his snout pointed straight ahead. He smelled a bird. The tiny shrubs rustled, and a ptarmigan took off, calling, as it flew, in its staccato clucks that reminded Stephen of the road runner in a Loony Tunes show. He raised the gun to his shoulder, aimed, and fired. The bird fell, and Soldier raced toward it. Moments later, the dead ptarmigan lay on the ground at Stephen's feet. "Good dog." He stroked Soldier's neck. "Good, good dog."

The word that always echoed through his mind when Stephen wandered the tundra was "freedom." Freedom from the crowds that had smothered him in Philadelphia without his being aware of it; freedom from their society norms that now seemed ridiculous; freedom from the formality of everyday life back there. Out on the tundra with the breeze sifting through his shoulder-length hair, he was chained to nothing. Certainly not to Sandra anymore. Yet, something about the boggy land and the tiny plants brought her to mind.

He didn't think of her anymore when he was at work and only rarely while he was at home. Sometimes, though, he'd spot something she had left behind, and memories of their lives together would flood over him like a torrent of muddy water. Under their bed, he found her old pink fuzzy slippers with imprints of her bare feet. Her red barrette, with several strands of her creamy hair caught in the clasp, was still in the medicine cabinet in the bathroom. She'd insisted on buying a case of anchovies when they ordered their food from the warehouse in Seattle, and all but one tin remained in its box beside the unused fondue pot in the storeroom. And she'd left a bottle of vodka in the freezer. He didn't know how she'd gotten the booze. Bethel was dry, but rumor had it the Wein Air Alaska planes were sometimes loaded with cartons of black-market alcohol. Vodka had apparently been her antidote to loneliness.

Swinging his walking stick, he rambled back toward the creek. Near a rise in the distance, something moved. Several things moved. Slowly. Deliberately as if choosing their footfalls carefully, they marched across the tundra. Cranes. Graceful as a sonata. He studied their markings. They were sandhill cranes.

Soldier bounded out into the tundra and now returned with something strange dangling from his mouth.

"Here, buddy," Stephen called. The dog stared at his master. The strange thing Stephen still hadn't identified hung like a rag from between his teeth. "Bring that here." Stephen reached for the dog's snout. He couldn't tell what it was. About the size of half a dried salmon. Covered with mud. It didn't smell fishy. Stephen stiffened. "Soldier, give."

The dog resisted.

"Give."

Finally, he wrenched the mystery thing away from Soldier's jaws and turned it over in his hands. Might be a piece of leather. Maybe old sealskin? Or bear hide? He sniffed again. No odor, nothing that smelled toxic. The dog seemed okay, other than wanting his toy back. Stephen kicked a shallow hole into the tundra and buried Soldier's gift. "Sorry, pal," he said. "Don't get sick on me. You're all I have now."

When he got back to his boat, he shoved the dead ptarmigan along with his shotgun and his walking stick under the seat, dragged the dinghy to the edge of the water, and ordered Soldier to get in. Then he shoved off and headed down the creek toward the Kuskokwim River.

STEPHEN WAS OUT OF DURKEE'S FAMOUS Dressing. He needed it for his ptarmigan dinner. Swanson's carried it, because he'd asked them to order it, so he put on his jacket and headed down the boardwalk toward town.

Standing in one of the store's narrow aisles, he stared at the jars on the shelf. Heinz Yellow Mustard. Hellmann's Blue Ribbon Mayonnaise, Skippy Peanut Butter. Where was the Durkee's? It was there a couple weeks ago. He stepped back to get a broader look and rammed into something. He turned around. A young woman, who apparently had been searching for something in the cleaning supplies section immediately behind him, stared back.

"Sorry, ma'am." Stephen stuttered. "I can't seem to find the Durkee's sauce."

"It's right here." She stepped in front of him and pointed to his left. There it was, nestled between the cooking oil and the white vinegar.

"Thanks," he said and grabbed a bottle.

"Now you can help me find the Pine-Sol," she said.

"Hmm. Surely it's here somewhere." Who was she? He hadn't seen her before. He held out his hand. "I'm Stephen," he said. "And you are . . ?"

"Jackie," she said.

Swanson's had no Pine-Sol. "That's strange," he said. "Must have sold out. People here use it for everything. There are no evergreens in Bethel, but the whole place reeks of pine. How about this?" He directed her to the Lysol. She thanked him.

On his way to the check-out, he stopped at the rack of periodicals and pulled a copy of *MAD* magazine from among the *Archie* and *Superman* comic books, Old *Farmer's Almanacs*, and a months-old copy of *Ladies' Home Journal*. He read through the first several pages, chuckling the whole time, before replacing it.

Outside, he started across the muddy lot and spotted Jackie ahead of him. She carried two bulging shopping bags, a mop, and a plastic bucket. She stopped, apparently resting, and set the bags on the hood of a truck. "Need any help?" he asked when he reached her. "How far are you going?"

"To the high school," she said. Her smile was strained. "I guess I underestimated the weight of my purchases."

He grabbed one of the shopping bags and the mop and followed her on the boardwalk toward the education compound. As they walked, she explained that she was the new high school social worker and had just arrived in Bethel. "I was really unlucky," she said, again flashing a strained smile. "The only available housing is one of the old shipping containers. It's a dump."

When they reached her place, a rusty, sulfur colored steel box, she pushed open the door, and he stepped inside. The gloomy room smelled of rotten food and dead mammals. He set the grocery bag on a table. Someone had cut a small window into the steel high on one wall, so a thin ray of daylight streamed in; some of the container boxes where other people lived were windowless. A bed sat at one end of the room, and a shower curtain surrounded what he assumed was a wooden toilet seat built over the honey bucket. Jackie set her packages on the table, sank into the wooden chair, and turned toward him. Her eyes grew misty. "They say several trailers will come on the barge next summer. Until then, this is where I'm supposed to live."

LATER THAT WEEK, HE SAW HER again at Swanson's. She'd come for another jug of Lysol.

"I've decided to return to Atlanta." The frown on her face was resolute. "I can't stand to spend the next ten months, or longer, in that steel box."

"Give it a bit more time," he said.

OVER THE NEXT SEVERAL WEEKS, STEPHEN tried to show her the beauty of the place. When he took her for a ride in his boat, she seemed to enjoy watching the birds as he identified them for her. He taught her how to walk on the lumpy tundra, and when she stepped into one of those water-filled holes hidden beneath the weeds, he caught her by the arm before she landed in the muck.

While on a trip to the Bethel Library, a moldy room at the back of an old warehouse, Jackie tripped going down the wet, wooden steps and twisted her ankle. Stephen held her elbow as she limped on the boardwalk toward her shipping container. She started crying.

"It really hurts, huh?" he asked.

"Yes, but mostly I'm just miserable. I can't stand that box. It's so gloomy. You've been very kind, and I appreciate that, but now, I really *am* going back to Atlanta."

Indeed, she *looked* miserable: gimpy and glum, with a tint of melancholy coloring her whole being. He was moved. "Jackie, the kids at the high school need you. Most of them are boarders and are lonesome for their families back in the villages. Lonesome breeds bad behavior, as you undoubtedly know." He paused, then said, "Come over to my place and we'll talk about your situation here. I'll then get you a ride home in one of the town taxis so you don't have to limp on that ankle."

"Bethel has cabs?" Jackie asked.

"That's what they call them. They're really old wrecks with TAXI painted on their sides. We should be able to find one in the hospital parking lot." His arm was her crutch as she hobbled toward the hospital complex.

At his apartment, she settled into the easy chair while he made two cups of tundra tea. Then she continued to itemize the ways in which she was miserable: the steel box that still smelled of dead mice, the coming cold, the long nights, the bleak town. She missed the peach trees in Georgia, a view out a window, and the luxury of a bath. She'd never lived alone before. "Since I left my parents' home, I've always had roommates. Until now."

Poor kid, he thought. He wasn't sure how old she was, but she'd said something about recently finishing social work school, so probably she was only twenty-three or twenty-four. Indeed, she was merely a kid. And lonely herself.

"Jackie, I have an idea. My place here has two extra bedrooms, a bathtub, and plenty of windows, although the view isn't spectacular. It's warm in the winter, and I'd enjoy some company. We could give it a try for a month or so and see how it goes."

Her mouth fell open, and she stared at him as if she'd seen a ghost. "Ahh . . ."

He laughed. "I mean it. You can have the back bedroom, the one nearest the bathroom. It'll be quiet and private. One month. Rent free. Kind of like probation."

She giggled.

Maybe she was worried about appearances and unflattering gossip. He shrugged and said, "As far as I'm concerned, it's no one else's business if you stay here for a while. You can decide how you want to handle telling the school."

"I guess it'll be okay. For a month." She crossed her legs. "I doubt anyone at school will notice that I'm not in that awful shipping container. If someone asks, I'll just tell them I've made alternative arrangements for a short while."

IT WAS LATE IN THE AFTERNOON when Stephen received word that Leonard Kills Squirrels wanted to see him in his office. He had no idea what it was about.

Kills Squirrels looked like a mad hatter but without the hat. He didn't make eye contact; his mouth worked sideways but no words came out; his tar-black, tightly braided hair pulled his eyes toward his temples. He twirled a pencil between his fingertips. "Please sit," he said, pointing to two folding chairs.

Stephen sat.

"I understand you have a girlfriend living at your apartment. Unwed couples co-habiting on hospital property is against the Indian Health Service rules."

"What on earth are you talking about?" Stephen shifted on his chair. The man was nuts.

"That woman living in your apartment. She's not your wife. That's illegal. She must move out."

Stephen couldn't believe what Kills Squirrels had just said. "That's a pile of garbage," he said. "Show me those IHS rules." Nothing like that had appeared in the housing contract he'd signed upon arriving in Bethel. Stephen stared at the picture of a tomahawk on the wall behind Kills Squirrels' head. Of course, he'd been married when he signed the contract. It was possible he'd paid no attention to such a clause.

"She has a week to leave, or you have to produce a marriage certificate to prove she is your spouse."

"Nonsense. If you demand to see a marriage certificate from me, you'll have to demand one from every other member of the medical staff."

Kills Squirrels pursed his lips. He pulled back his shoulders. He blinked his eyes. "You've heard my words. You may now leave."

News of Stephen's meeting with Kills Squirrels spread among the medical staff as if gasoline had been tossed on a campfire. "No way," John Jetters said.

"What the hell?" Matias Maldonado said.

"Over my dead body," David Dorfman said.

A week later, Stephen learned that Leonard Kills Squirrels had called each of the staff doctors into his office and explained that new rules from Headquarters required them to submit copies of their marriage certificates to him. "I must document that no unauthorized adults are living in your quarters," he told the docs. One by one the doctors said, "I don't have one," referring to their marriage licenses.

Another week later, Stephen sat in the radio clinic room waiting for the next call from one of the village health aides. The craggy face of that bastard Kills Squirrels flashed through his mind, accompanied by a replay of his idiotic demand that the docs produce their marriage licenses. Whoever lived in his apartment was none of Kills Squirrels' business. Stephen saw no reason to justify Jackie's presence. The irony was immense—in spite of their dissolved marriage, his and Sandra's wedding pictures, along with the license itself, were still in a folder in his bottom dresser drawer.

Chapter 4

The fingerprints on Mera's living room window were a greasy leftover from her son Marcus. She knew that someday she'd remember them fondly, but today, they represented a messy chore. In some ways, she wanted another child. But, that meant a second set of greasy fingerprints, more diapers to wash, more incomprehensible crying. None of that, however, began to explain why Marcus was an only child.

As she scrubbed the smudges off the window with dish soap, she heard a knock on the door. Between the knocks, off-key notes of "Bozo Under the Sea," sung by the giggly boys in the back bedroom, floated down the hall. She thought she heard Marcus's almost-three-year-old, crystalline voice among the thunderous noise from the other two niños but couldn't be sure. Jennifer's twins were able to out-sing all the children on the hospital compound put together.

The knocking continued. She thought it must be Leonard Kills Squirrels. He'd been hounding the doctors' wives about their marriage licenses. She continued to ignore the knocks.

"Jennifer, are you there?"

Mera didn't recognize the voice from the other side of the door. It was female and didn't have a native accent. Whoever it was, the woman wasn't at the right apartment.

Mera sighed, dropped the cleaning rag into the bucket of soapy water, headed to the kitchen, and pulled open the door. In the entry stood a young gussuk woman. Her hair, the color of burned toast, was as curly as an Eskimo's was straight. A child lay in her arms, and a lumpy duffle bag puddled at her feet.

"Jennifer?"

Mera shook her head. "No, you have the wrong building." The woman's sullen face, her hunched shoulders, and her sagging arms told Mera she was very tired. "Jennifer's in the first fourplex." She nodded toward her right. "The one closest to the hospital."

"Well . . . I'm Rachel, a teacher from Mekoryuk." The woman sounded frustrated. "Dr. Jetters said to go to the end unit. I guess I got the wrong end. He's Jennifer's husband, right?"

"Yes."

"Um . . . my son . . ." Rachel unwrapped the blanket from her child's head. ". . . is sick and Dr. Jetters—he's working at the Mekoryuk clinic for a couple days—said I should bring little Robert to the hospital for an x-ray. He said I could stay at his place while I'm here."

Mera stared at the pale, sleeping baby. He looked about four or five months old. So tiny. So precious. She took a deep breath. "Well, Jennifer is at the high school for her pottery class. Her twins are here playing with my son. She'll be back in several hours." Mera stepped back into the kitchen. "I'm Mera Maldonado, Dr. Maldonado's wife. Come on in."

Mera and Rachel drank tea in the living room while Rachel's baby napped on Mera and Matias's bed. Rachel stared at the shelf in the corner. "I save those little figurines that come in Red Rose tea boxes too," she said. "I must have thirty of them. Would you like to trade a hippo for a giraffe? I have duplicate hippopotamuses. Hippopotami. However you say that."

Mera pulled a ceramic giraffe from her collection and handed it to Rachel. "It's yours. I think I have another one around here somewhere."

For the next hour, Mera asked Rachel about her life in the tiny village of Mekoryuk, stranded in the Bering Sea on Nunivak Island. Mera had accompanied Matias on his clinic visits to several of the villages served by the Bethel Alaska Native Hospital but never to Mekoryuk.

"It's pretty quiet," Rachel said. "My husband and I are the teachers there. The state gives us a cozy little house—emphasis on 'little.' It's been three years now. Not sure how long we'll stay. The experience is great for building character. But I don't know how much more character we need."

"Mekoryuk is so isolated, even more so than Bethel. How do you pass the time?" Mera couldn't imagine the long winters on that desolate island. And she really couldn't imagine having a baby there.

Rachel shifted her body on the couch. "Indeed, it is isolated. Only 250 people live there, and we're the only gussuks."

The way she said it suggested that Rachel and her husband didn't socialize much with the Native people. *Same in Bethel*, Mera thought. Teachers and doctors have different ways than Arctic subsistence fishermen: we cook our food, they eat dried fish and raw berries; we have all attended college, most of them have little more than a middle school education; we hale from all over the lower forty-eight, many of them have never left the Kuskokwim River valley.

Rachel sighed. "Work and caring for the baby keeps us busy. We read a lot, and for entertainment sometimes we listen to the radio. I'm amazed that the KYUK signal from Bethel makes it all the way to Mekoryuk. I like that guy Corey Flintoff. When he announces the news, his voice sounds like warm honey." She paused to listen for sounds from Robert.

Mera poured more tea. She was surprised that she enjoyed Rachel's company, liked her easy manner, her common sense. When she first arrived, Mera had been irritated with being bothered. But now, she was pleased Rachel had knocked on the wrong door.

They talked about the long, light-filled summer days and the longer, dreary-dark winter nights. "It's funny, but I never know what the temperature is outside," Mera said.

"Me neither," Rachel said. "I think our outdoors thermometer froze. We don't care about the actual number though. From October to March, it's just damn cold."

As Mera nodded in agreement, she heard another knock at the door. Was Jennifer back from the pottery class already? Had it been two hours since she left? Or, maybe it really was Leonard this time. She took her time walking through the kitchen. When she pulled open the door, Jennifer swept in from the entry.

"Sorry I'm a bit late. Had to stop at Swanson's. I'm sewing myself a kuspuk and don't have any deep purple thread. Have the twins driven you nuts, yet?"

"They've been fine. They . . ."

Suddenly, a stampede of little boys darkened the hallway. "Mommy," yelled Jeff as he leaped against Jennifer's side. Brian skidded to a stop and patted his mother's leg. Marcus toddled behind them.

"Come meet Rachel, a teacher from Mekoryuk."

Rachel explained to Jennifer that Dr. Jetters had sent her baby to the Bethel Hospital for a chest x-ray. "We were lucky. The mail plane was late leaving Mekoryuk, so we were able to make that one and didn't have to wait for the one tomorrow. That's assuming there'll be a plane tomorrow."

"Rachel came to our apartment by mistake. She was looking for you, because your husband said she and the baby could stay at your place," Mera said. "But they're settled here, so I propose they stay with us."

They went back and forth with that idea—Mera wanted them, Jennifer wanted them, Rachel didn't care and didn't want to bother anybody. "Look, no one should disturb Robert to haul him to the Jetters's at the far end of the boardwalk," Mera finally said. "My grandmother used to say, 'Siempre deja que un bebé dormido mienta.' Ahh . . . 'Always let a sleeping baby lie.'"

Rachel agreed to stay with the Maldonados. Mera told her to make herself at home.

"I assume you have a ladies' room," Rachel said.

"Down the hall. At the end, past the room where the little boys are playing."

When Rachel returned from the bathroom, she asked "Do you know anything about those two guys who died in fish camp at Nunapitchuk?" She joined Mera on the couch. "We heard about that from one of the teacher's aides. She was related to them, somehow."

"I heard about it too but don't know anything more than that," Mera said. "My babysitter, who was a cousin of the two men, is pretty upset by the whole thing. I didn't think she worried about anything, but she secretly thinks that whatever got them might get her."

"It's so strange. Around here people fall out of boats or break through the ice; they run out of snomobile gas and freeze to death; or they have heart attacks, but two kind-of-young guys dying at fish camp doesn't fit any of those scenarios for dying."

"Yes, my husband also thought it was odd," Jennifer said. "Do you think they might have been murdered?"

Mera shrugged. "I don't know. People don't murder each other around here much. They weren't shot, I understand."

"That's what I heard too. One might have been stabbed, I guess." Rachel sipped the last of her tea. "Maybe they drank themselves to death. That happens."

"And," Jennifer said, "my husband says the villagers in Nunapitchuk are wondering who will be next, but no one called the authorities. There doesn't seem to be an investigation at all."

Rachel looked at Mera with a shrug, and Mera shrugged back. "Right, Jennifer. They prefer to handle it themselves. No one wants the state troopers nosing in their business," Rachel said.

After Marcus had finally drifted off to sleep, after Rachel and her baby had moved to the back bedroom to sleep, and after Matias, saying, "Busy clinic today. I'm bushed," had turned in for the night, Mera curled up at one end of the couch with a copy of *Blackberry Winter* from the hospital library. As she read about Margaret Mead's early life she couldn't help but compare it to her own.

Margaret had four siblings. Mera was her parents' lone child.

Margaret's father was a professor of finance at the University of Pennsylvania and her mother a sociologist. Mera's father was a South Texas farm laborer, and her mother a cook at her high school.

Margaret attended Barnard College in New York. Mera attended the University of Houston in Texas.

Margaret had a PhD in anthropology and was a professor. Mera received a BA in English and worked as a copy writer for *Texas Outdoors* before she and Matias moved to Alaska.

Margaret had worked as an anthropologist in the tropics. Mera now was a homemaker and part-time journalist for the *Tundra Drums* in the Arctic. Margaret obviously loved her work in anthropology, and Mera enjoyed hers. Last week she had interviewed the new social worker at the high school for an article about counseling resources for the students. Jackie, the social worker, was the woman who had moved in with Stephen and the one Leonard Kills Squirrels was trying to displace. Mera hadn't asked Jackie about any of that.

Margaret Mead had a series of lovers, male and female. Mera had Matias.

Margaret was mother to one daughter. Mera was madre to Marcus. Only Marcus. She wiped a tear from her cheek and, her mind wandered away from the book. She desperately ached for, and deeply feared having, another child. Like all of her Catholic aunts and most of her many Catholic girl cousins, she had always hoped for several babés and wanted them close together in age and temperament. She was sure they would be best friends as youngsters and life-long confidants as adults, just as Mera would have been with a brother or sister, if she had one. Her mother had only her, and Mera didn't know exactly why. Such things weren't discussed in her childhood home, but even as a young girl, from the secrets whispered among her aunts, Mera was aware that her mother had longed for more babies.

The late summer sun slowly sank toward the horizon, but its gilded light warmed her shoulders and cast a butterscotch glow on the pages of the book. The thoughts that swirled through her mind prevented her from focusing on the words of Margaret Mead. She set the book on the coffee table and picked up the mohair vest she was knitting for Matias. Her best ideas emerged while she watched the yarn and needles twirl in her hands. It was something about the way the colors of the hairy wool blended together, something about the rhythm of the stitches.

Before Marcus, she and Matias had tried for more than four years to have a child. That had been more than forty-eight endless months of taking her temperature twice a day, of scheduled sex, of crushing disappointment every time she spotted the first hint of blood on her panties. And the miscarriages. Five of them. Each more heartbreaking than the previous. She had named every one of the fetuses: Madrid, Marron, Peregrin, Teran, and Romary, and used names that could be either girl or boy because she didn't really know their sexes.

With sadness and love, she recited the names in a whisper. Madrid, because it referred to a means to cross over, a fording place, and that baby was their introduction to parenthood, albeit a very painful starter. Merron, because it meant lively, the way that child would have been. Peregrin, or pilgrim, because the baby was her visitor, if only for such a short time; Teran because, as the name suggested, the baby would have affinity for strength and connection to the earth; Romary because that child would have been charismatic, intuitive, and have a pleasing personality.

Girl or boy. It didn't matter. Each was her longed-for baby-to-be and a precious soul that needed a name.

Finally, Marcus had been born shortly before they left Texas for Alaska. For the first month of his life, she'd stare into his eyes—dark like his father's—whenever he was awake and would cry with joy and love. He was such a miracle. A cherished soul, perfect in every way. She'd stroke his tiny palm, and he'd curl his beautiful, miniature fingers around her pinky. He'd pucker his little lips around her nipple and suckle her life-giving milk. It was magic, astonishing, enchanting, and thrilling.

Did she dare try again? She couldn't face, once more, the torture of endless attempts at conception. Thoughts like that made her weep because they bulldozed a pile of mud against her Catholic family's values. Besides, it wasn't safe, or smart, to have a baby in Bethel. The hospital was primitive compared to the ones in Houston. None of the docs were real OB physicians. The place couldn't possibly be equipped for an emergency during a birth, and what if the baby were premature? Or ill? Or abnormal in any way?

And yet, Marcus was such a treasure.

She thought about how Matias had just committed to two more years at the Bethel Hospital. They had discussed that decision at length before he re-upped. He really wanted to spend more time in Alaska. Not forever, he assured her. Just two more years.

When she mentioned her worries about having a child up there, he had reminded her that Yup'ik women had been delivering their young on the tundra for eons. She hadn't liked his flippant response.

"But I'm not a Yup'ik woman," she had answered. "I'm a Hispanic woman."

"No, but you're strong."

"Maybe, but I'm scared. If I get pregnant up here, where would I deliver the baby? In this backwater hospital or out on the frozen tundra?"

"I don't see what's wrong with the Bethel Hospital. We docs have all delivered a number of babies, and George had extra OB training during his internship. Um . . . unless it's a complicated pregnancy, and then you'd go to Anchorage."

He'd explained that to her before, and the thought of it hovered like purple mist just outside her sense of reality. The Native women with risky pregnancies flew to the Anchorage Native Alaska Hospital when they were at thirty-six weeks, so they wouldn't get stuck in labor during bad weather in Bethel.

The pregnant women had to wait in Anchorage until their babies were born. Sometimes a month. Sometimes longer.

Every time she thought about it, she came to the same conclusion. Having a baby in Bethel was impossible. Would they *ever* have another child?

THE NEXT DAY, MERA RAN THE can opener over the top of the Goya pinto beans and then dumped them into a saucepan. When she placed her first food order from the warehouse in Seattle, they didn't carry any canned pinto beans. Mera scolded the order-taker about that, and the next year, the Goya beans were available.

While she stirred the beans, she watched Robert as he snuggled against Rachel's abdomen. The sight of that beautiful baby brought back all her thoughts about another pregnancy from last night. She also felt a twinge of envy. She needed another thought.

Suddenly, a pulsating blast shrieked from beyond the kitchen window. Rachel jumped and uttered a little scream. Robert also jumped in her lap and began to cry. Several drops of Red Rose fell from her teacup to the table. "What on Earth is that?" She dragged her paper towel-napkin over the spilled tea.

"Noon whistle," Mera said. "Once a day we know the correct time." She reached for the clock on the stove, adjusted its hands from 11:28 to 12:00, and laughed. "The electrical current from the hospital power plant isn't strictly 60 cycles per second, I guess, so the clocks either speed up or slow down over the day."

Rachel covered her nervous giggle with the back of her hand and then rearranged Robert on her lap. "Yeah. I'm sure the locals here, just like in Mekoryuk, pay no attention to time, anyway. When we arrange parent-teacher meetings, the moms and dads wander in anywhere from 10 minutes to over an hour late. We call it Eskimo time. Probably it's the same at the hospital."

Mera nodded. "That's what Matias says. He's gotten used to it."

Someone was knocking, again, on the kitchen door.

Mera didn't want to answer. Rachel squinted her eyes; obviously she didn't understand why Mera didn't head for the door immediately.

Mera pulled open the door, and Leonard Kill Squirrels bounded into the kitchen.

"Hello, Leonard," she said. Maybe being nice to him would help.

"The Indian Health Service has a new rule, and we must document the marriages of all commissioned officers who live with a person of the opposite sex in IHS quarters."

That's a lie, she said to herself. "The IHS never told us about that new rule."

"Straight from headquarters in Anchorage."

Mera stared at Leonard, at the belly that sagged over his beaded belt buckle; at his greasy, thick hair that was black as tar and was tied in a tail at the back of his neck; at the frown-wrinkles permanently etched into his forehead. "IHS headquarters are in Washington, D.C.," she said.

He cleared his throat. "Straight from headquarters in Anchorage."

"Well, it doesn't matter where the rule came from, because our marriage license isn't here."

"Where is it?"

If he could lie, so could she. "Lost."

Leonard turned away from her, stepped into the back entryway, and slammed the kitchen door.

"Well, that was pretty unpleasant," Rachel said.

"Indeed." Mera explained Leonard's marriage license fiasco while she stirred the beans for their lunch. "One of the doctors is living in hospital housing with a woman who is not his wife. Leonard—the hospital administrator—wants to punish them and is pestering all of us to produce our marriage licenses. No one will comply. If he follows through on his stupid, invented rule, he'll have no medical staff."

"Sounds mighty nutty to me." As she sat up straight in her chair, Rachel slashed the air with her arm and snarled, "I'd say, 'Off with his head.'" Robert was now asleep in her lap. She carried him into the back bedroom.

Marcus rolled into the kitchen aboard his wooden, three-wheeled kiddie scooter. "Hey, you arrived just in time," Mera said to her son. "Are you hungry?" She hoisted him into his highchair and planted a kiss on his forehead. It was the same tall forehead as Matias, same black hair that dangled in his eyes, the same deep-as-a-well brown eyes as his father. He was as precious as the day he was born.

"That's a pretty cute little vehicle," Rachel said of the scooter.

"Yeah, it was custom made for Marcus by his buddy, the chief engineer of the hospital." Mera picked up the scooter by one handle and pointed to the lettering burned into the back of the seat. "BUILT BY BIFF."

MATIAS JOINED THEM FOR LUNCH. As they began to eat, he said, "Good news. Robert's x-ray is normal. How's he doing?"

"Seems better, and his fever is gone," Rachel said with a quiet smile. "He's taking a nap right now."

While Rachel and Matias finished their beans and discussed Robert's illness, Mera ran a damp wash rag over Marcus's face, his gooey hands, and the tray of his highchair, and then lowered him to the floor. She stared at her husband, smiled at the manner in which he spoke to Rachel about the x-ray report. He was kind, attentive, confident. She could tell from Rachel's sallow face and the way she had thrummed her fingers on the kitchen table that morning that she had been worried about her baby. Of course she had been worried. That's what mothers do when their children are sick.

Poor Rachel. She'd had to make the trip all the way from Mekoryuk to Bethel to see the doctor, contingent on the weather and space on the mail plane, and she couldn't know when she'd be able to return. Mera couldn't imagine raising a child on Nunivak Island, probably twenty-five or thirty miles off the coast of the mainland and surrounded by the raging Bering Sea. Mekoryuk was just a small colony, the only inhabited place on the island.

On the other hand, if she *could* have another baby, Mera'd raise it anywhere. Rearing the child wasn't the hard part. For her, bearing the baby for the forty weeks it took had been nearly impossible. One in six. Only 16.6667%.

They didn't know why. Her doctors thought perhaps the miscarried babies had severe anomalies that prevented their survival. A genetic problem? A bad mix of her genes with Matias's? Maybe that meant the next pregnancy also had an 83.3333 percent chance of failing. Matias thought maybe her cervix was too lax and couldn't hold a growing fetus inside her uterus. That made it her problem alone. Maybe it was bad luck. Or misalignment of the stars. Wrong food? Bad air? Evil omens? For sure, she wouldn't take a chance trying to have a baby in Bethel.

Marcus wasn't interested in taking his nap, so Mera sang to him. "Los pollitos dicen/Pío pío pío/Cuando tienen hambre/Y cuando tienen frio/su mamá les busca maíz y trigo para comer." Baby chickens, she sang, go twit, twit, twit, when they are hungry, and when they are cold, their mama finds corn and wheat for them to eat. Over and over, she sang the same words. He lay in his crib, kicking the rails until his legs finally settled on the mattress, his eyes closed, and he was asleep.

Mera poured two cups of fresh tea and waved Rachel into the living room.

"Now I have to figure out when to go back to Mekoryuk," Rachel said. "Can we get in touch with someone about the mail plane?"

"Sure." Mera wasn't eager for her to leave. She looked out the window behind the couch, at the waving wires that ran from a utility pole to their apartment, at the twisting, tossing seats on the hospital playground's swings. "It's pretty windy today. Terrible flying weather. Maybe tomorrow."

Rachel nodded and sipped at her tea.

"You must have been living on Nunivak Island when Robert was born," Mera said. That comment probably seemed to come out of nowhere to Rachel. Mera had waited since yesterday to ask.

"Yes. It was a nine-months-of-winter pregnancy and then, as tiny flowers began to dot the tundra, that beautiful child was born."

"Where? Where was he born? On the island?"

"Oh, God no." Rachel tipped her head to the west. "There. At the Bethel Hospital."

"Wasn't that scary?" No one Mera knew had delivered a baby at the hospital in the two and a half years she and Matias had been there. Her friend Deidre, though, was pregnant and refused to return to her folks' home in New York to wait for the birth. She wouldn't leave her doctor-husband, who had to work in Bethel. "David needs to be there when the baby is born," she had told Mera. "He helped get this project started, and he needs to see it through to the end."

"No," Rachel said, shaking her head. "I wasn't scared. He's the only baby I've had, so I don't really know anything different. The doctors and the nurse-midwife were terrific. The health aide in Mekoryuk examined me about four weeks before we thought I was due and said I'd better head to Bethel while travel was possible. I stayed with one of the teachers at the high school until my labor began. I took one of those jalopy taxis to the hospital and about an hour later, Robert was born. Easy-peasy."

"Where was your husband?"

"Back in Mekoryuk, teaching. We couldn't both be gone that long."

Mera took a deep breath. What a story. Compared to that, Marcus's birth at Methodist Hospital in Houston had been a breeze. It was twenty minutes from their house, and Matias was with her the whole time.

Mera heard another knock at the kitchen door. Leonard, again? Surely not this soon.

It was Jennifer. "Hey, the barge is at the mouth of the Kuskokwim River," she called in a joyous voice. "It'll be here tomorrow morning. Finally, we'll get our food."

Celebration filled the air. The anticipation was electric. The closer they came to the town dock, the more crowded the boardwalk became. Some of the locals were still at fish camp for the summer, but those remaining in town, seemingly every last one of them, headed toward the waterfront. The women giggled as they walked, the men smiled, the little girls poked their sisters, and the little boys threw clots of tundra weeds at each other.

Mera and Matias, along with Rachel, hiked the wooden boardwalk toward the wharf. Matias carried Marcus on his shoulders, and Rachel cuddled her baby in her arms. They passed the lemon-colored Bethel Bank that clung to the edge of the river with the desperation of a shipwrecked sailor. Matias said to Rachel, "We expect to see that poor bank riding the river downstream toward Kuskokwim Bay any day now." At least seven rusted-through car bodies, three pieces of muddy carpet, and a collapsed refrigerator had been jammed into the sandy cliff beneath the tilting building. He added, "That junk is Bethel's failed attempt at erosion control."

"Is your money inside?" Rachel asked.

"Heavens, no." Mera answered. "It's secure with the credit union in Houston. Near our marriage license, which is in the safety deposit box."

Rachel chuckled.

As they walked past the wind-whipped houses, sled dogs crawled out from their little houses to survey the passersby. Mera had thought the fifty-five-gallon oil barrels, with door holes cut in their sides, were cruel quarters for the dogs, but soon learned from the locals that they were perfect shelters: dry, wind-proof, sturdy, and cheap. The dogs' chains, anchored to metal posts near each barrel, clanged as the animals stretched and shook the kinks from their muscles. They looked like wolves—some might have been part wolf—and Mera was afraid of them. When she watched them tear into a slab of salmon, in her mind's eye she saw them rip off a child's arm. They howled at seemingly nothing. They were strong as oxen and tough as caribou gristle. Their ebony eyes watched her in icy, seemingly hate-filled stares.

They finally reached the edge of the crowd that had gathered at the wharf. Mera studied a native woman, who stood alone, as she gazed across the river at Three Step Mountain in the distance. The woman—maybe forty years old, although Eskimo women seemed ageless—remained still for several minutes as the rest of the crowd swayed like waves in a storm. The woman's face in profile, with its smooth rounded nose, sculpted brow, and haunting eyes, was framed by strands of blowing black hair. *What was she thinking?* Mera wondered. The mountain's peaks and foothills, blurred by the haze, hugged the far horizon. Those triple tiers of rock and ice had reigned for eons over the events at its feet. And it would continue to reign for eons into the future. The mountain had watched as many generations of the woman's people were born, lived—fishing, hunting, berry picking, drying salmon, dancing, loving—and then died. Maybe the woman was contemplating all of that.

A shout rang out—"There it is"—and every face turned in unison downriver. A tugboat chugged around the bend, followed by a massive barge at the end of its cable. An armada of kayaks studded the water. The boys in those little boats flipped their paddles, splashing each other and laughing as they traded Yup'ik insults. Closer to town, a floatplane took off from the river, sputtering its way northeast, its pontoons dangling beneath its belly like oversized boots. It sounded like a giant wasp as it buzzed up into the clouds. *Must be headed for Aniak or Tuluksak,* Mera figured. In the summer, the river teemed with traffic; it was the heartbeat of Bethel.

Mera spotted Jennifer and the twins at the dock. Jeff was jumping over puddles and Brian, his mouth wide open, stared at the approaching barge. Jennifer seemed far calmer today than she'd been since her arrival. The poor woman had spent her first six weeks in Bethel worrying—about the coming winter, about the coming darkness, about their food order from Seattle. Mera couldn't remember if she had worried that much when she and Matias first came. Everything was new, then, and worry might have been folded into the whole adjustment. The biting cold and the endless nights would be upon them soon, but at least Jennifer could stop fretting about the food.

Behind them, Stephen stood with his feet apart and his eyes shielded from the sun by his hand as he watched the tugs maneuver the barge alongside the wharf. His dog, Soldier, sat at his feet. Mera liked Stephen and wanted life to be easier for him. He was still figuring out what to do with himself without his ex-wife and had extended his Public Health Service duty for several more years. She wished, however, he'd be more careful with his laundry. Last week she came home from a trip to Swanson's to find her loaves of bread dough, which had been rising in the back entryway on the top of their shared clothes drier, collapsed. Beneath them, the drier lurched and rattled as if it were alive while Stephen's tennis shoes tumbled inside.

"How on Earth do they keep from falling off?" Rachel asked as she stared at the trailers and shipping containers stacked five high on the barge. "Nothing that enormous ever comes to Mekoryuk."

"The longshoremen are geniuses, I guess," Mera answered. She too was amazed that those loads didn't slide into the water as the barge wound around the bends in the river. It had come all the way from Seattle. While the waters of the inland passage were relatively calm, the open Pacific was wild and restless.

"In a way, it's beautiful," Rachel said. "The ends of those containers—those yellow, orange, and red squares—all lined up like that remind me of a Mondrian painting. And, look at the car on top."

Perched like a crow at the upmost peak of the load was a black Jeep. "Must be Stephen's new vehicle," Mera said.

"Where will he drive it?" Rachel asked. "It's not like there's hundreds of miles of roads around here."

"I don't know. Maybe to Swanson's for supplies. Or, more likely on the river after freeze-up. He likes to go off into the tundra, hunting."

They stayed at the wharf for another hour and watched the port cranes unload the shipping containers, one by one. Slowly the crowd dissipated as the clusters of moms and dads and kids returned to their everyday lives. One infant was strapped to his mother's back, and his head stuck out the neck of her kuspuk; his older brother stumbled down the rutty road beside their mother and clutched the strap of the purse that swung from her arm. Those children looked comfortable and happy. So did their mother. That was what Mera longed for. As Matias had said, Eskimo women had borne babies since the dawn of time on the tundra. Rachel had too. Could she?

Chapter 5

Their house was very different from Virginia's, more different than a weasel's white fur in January and its brown coat in July. Theirs was big, even though only three people lived there: Marcus, Mrs. Maldonado, and Dr. Maldonado. Virginia Tom stepped over the puddles in the road and considered her own house. It was like most in Bethel: small, crowded, and kept warm in the winter by the oil stove.

Marcus had a whole bedroom for himself while her own nine kids slept wherever they found an empty spot, sometimes three or four to a bed, sometimes stretched out on the couch, sometimes cuddled in a corner of the floor. Dr. and Mrs. Maldonado's bed was huge; they'd barely be able to reach each other during the night. At her house, she and her husband shared a cot; she liked his warm body next to hers while she slept. She felt safe and cozy. She didn't understand what the Maldonados did with all that room, but some days she wished she had that.

Her family spent much of the summer at fish camp on a slough near Nunapitchuk. They had a lot of work to do there: gather and dry salmon and pick berries to store in seal oil for the rest of the year. Home at fish camp was a tent.

As she walked toward the hospital compound, Virginia kicked at the loose planks on the boardwalk. She clutched a greasy paper bag in her hand, and the tops of her muck boots rubbed against the backs of her knees. That didn't happen to other people. It was because she was short, very short, and the boots belonged to her oldest son.

She passed Raymond Andrecheck's house. His dogs crawled out of their oil drum houses and began to bark at the sky. She slid the paper bag into the pocket of her kuspuk. "Stay back," she yelled. The dogs pulled at their chains as they leaned toward her. They continued to bark. "Back," she yelled again. They wanted the dried salmon in her bag.

She knew it was normal for the dogs to jump toward her. They weren't mean. They wanted food, but still they frightened her. Their eyes sparkled like ice in the sunshine, their teeth glistened like salmon bones, and their bushy tails whipped the air behind them.

She waved at Raymond when he stepped out of his house. He began to toss a dried salmon slab at each dog. They jumped as if they had springs for legs and barked with excitement like wild animals.

Raymond had to catch a lot of fish for both his family and his dogs. His fish camp was across the slough from her family's. She wondered if he knew anything about Luther and Morris, her dead cousins. She didn't dare ask him. It was bad luck. Somebody else might die, and she didn't want to be blamed for that.

She'd always liked Morris. He was a gentle man who used to play games. He usually won the stick-pull and the cutting-a-dog-out-of-paper-while-blindfolded contests in Nunapitchuk each winter. He could really make those scissors go, and he even got the ears right. She was very sad when Morris died. Luther, though, was trouble. He had crooked teeth and also liked games. He usually won the who-can-get-out-of-a snowsuit-fastest contest.

A couple weeks ago, her son Quentin had taken her in their boat to the funeral in Nunapitchuk. They joined the crowd at Aunt

Lucy's house for the wake. Virginia didn't know the words to the songs her relatives were singing and didn't understand what the priest was saying, but she nodded when the rest of the people nodded. Her Uncle Abe, who was also Luther and Morris's Uncle Abe, rocked back and forth on a chair at the end of Aunt Lucy's bed. Abe was the guy who found the dead boys. He held his head down and twisted a knit hat in his hands.

When they marched with the group into the Orthodox Church, a cousin handed Virginia and Quentin lit candles. They faced the two pine boxes in front of the altar, with Morris's picture balanced on the top of one and Luther's on the other. Virginia shifted from one foot to the other and wished she could sit in a pew, like she did in Our Mother of All Saints in Bethel. The Orthodox church had no seats.

She scanned the faces of the people around her; many were her relatives. Did any of them know what happened to Morris and Luther? Or, would any of them die of whatever killed the Uttereyuk brothers? Her questions seemed to waft around the room like a ghost and join similar questions from everyone there. It was like a spirit cloud of blended inquiry.

The priest, wearing a robe that seemed stitched with gold, walked to the coffins, raised his arms above his head and his eyes to the ceiling, and called, "Our blessed brothers, Luther and Morris, have fallen asleep in the Lord." He waved the little metal smoke box as he moved, and the crowded church started to smell like burning Labrador tea bark and serviceberries. Luther and Morris would be underground on cemetery hill as soon as the village elders could melt enough permafrost to dig holes for their caskets. What had killed them would be buried there with them so only the angels would know.

Virginia thought the Uttereyuk brothers had been poisoned, and she had some ideas about who did it. Maybe Edmund Nopoka. He was a strange, cranky fellow who drank too much. Sometimes when he wandered through town with his jacket inside out and his pee-stained trousers half falling off, he muttered to the clouds overhead. Sometimes he showed up in Nunapitchuk hunting for more liquor. She'd heard that Nopoka had picked a fight with Luther over a bottle of rum; he'd accused her cousin of stealing it. Virginia's kids were afraid of Nopoka, said he cursed at them and called them names like "son of a whore" or "half-breed." It wasn't the kids' fault that she was Yup'ik and their dad was Athabascan from way upriver near Aniak. "Ee," she muttered to herself. Edmund was a good guess for the poisoner.

As soon as she had passed Raymond's house and yelping dogs, she pulled the paper bag out from the pocket of her kuspuk. The fish inside smelled so good. She hoped the oil that had seeped through the bag hadn't stained her kuspuk. She liked that cloth with its blue and yellow flowers. She stared at her waist. No smudge.

There were others too who could poison Luther and Morris. Her cousin Milton Mike, for one. He too drank too much and had been thrown out of Nunapitchuk for a couple months because he was too drunk too often. Luther had accused Milton of breaking his oar, and Milton was crazy mad for being blamed.

Or maybe it was Jesse Kameroff. He'd gotten Seraphine Palanak pregnant a while back, and Luther had been sweet on her. Luther thought Jesse had ruined his girlfriend. Virginia wasn't sure Jesse was still around though. Someone said he'd gone up to Pitkas Point because he wanted nothing to do with Seraphine and her baby.

Virginia's cousin Melvin wondered if it might be Dr. Steinberg. Virginia didn't think so, because he seemed pleasant enough when she saw him from her post in the hospital gift shop. But he was different from the other doctors. Folks had seen him wandering the tundra all alone near Oscarville or Napaskiak or paddling that squatty boat of his up the creek at Tuluksak with his coal-black dog on board. She didn't know if he ever went near Nunapitchuk, but he might have.

She stepped over a missing slat in the boardwalk. Some days, when she worried about her sons, her daughters, and her aging mother, she wondered if Nicholas had poisoned the men. He was the fourth oldest of her kids, and he wasn't quite right. She'd been sick when she was expecting him sixteen long years ago and wondered if that had something to do with the way he turned out. His brain was like a house-on-fire. He did badly in school and got into fights with the other boys. And he was sassier than most. What if Nicholas was the one? Maybe he and Luther got into a fight. But he wouldn't hurt Morris. She couldn't stand the thought of Nicholas sneaking around, doing whatever it was that killed those Uttereyuk fellows.

There had been a long gap between Nicholas and the next of her babies. Three or four years. She'd hated those endless years at that TB sanitorium way down in Dillingham, and every night she'd thought about home and cried. She had wanted to go back to Nunapitchuk. Not to the hospital in Anchorage, nor the one in Bethel, but back to her little house in Nunapitchuk and the four kids. Especially she wanted to return to little Nicholas because a child that young needed his mother. Then, when she finally got out of the san and they moved to Bethel, the babies started coming again. Nine in all. It ended eight years ago with little Mitchell.

She was happy the babies ended. There were too many of them, too many mouths to feed, bodies to dress, clothes to wash, demands to meet, and fights to settle.

She kicked a clod of tundra sod off the boardwalk and tried to remember what Nicholas was doing around the time her cousins died. She thought he'd gone to school but didn't know for sure. He played hooky a lot. Sometimes he snuck into the motorboat and sped over to Nunapitchuk. It took him less than an hour each way, because he drove that boat like a crazy guy. He was home for dinner though those nights; she remembered because he'd tried to pry a piece of dried salmon away from his next older brother.

Off to her right, she could now see the row of fourplexes on the hospital compound. The one on the far end, like the tail of a goose, was Marcus's house. She walked faster. Marcus would be glad to see her.

And she would be happy to see him. She loved taking care of Marcus while his mother did her work at the *Tundra Drums*. The Maldonado's house was quiet as a winter night, not the constant racket at her place, and Marcus was the only one, so different from her many whining, begging kids. Mrs. Maldonado kept their huge house spotlessly neat, while her own tiny house was full of heaped-up laundry, both dirty and clean; plastic pails of assorted snow-go and boat motor parts; an old smelt bucket full of rags; fishing nets that needed mending; bolts of cotton for making kuspuks; and beds everywhere. Muck boots spilled out of the wooden box just inside the door and smoke from the oil stove leaked into the wooden walls where her ulus hung. Her favorite ulu was the one her father made from an old handsaw. That ulu's blade had the perfect curve, and the driftwood handle fit her hand just right; she could really make that ulu go when she was cutting salmon for drying. The prettiest thing in her house, though, was the picture of Jesus that hung on the wall beside the window; she kept her rosary looped over the frame.

When she reached the end of the road, she saw that Dr. Steinberg's dog was in his pen beside the corner of the fourplex. His tail wagged like a willow in a windstorm, and he began his light-hearted yip. "Easy boy," Virginia said. He was a gentle creature and didn't scare her like the sled dogs did. And he didn't seem inter-ested in her paper bag. Dr. Steinberg fed him store-bought dog-gie food, rather than slabs of dried salmon. She climbed the stairs, stepped into the back entryway, and knocked. Mrs. Maldonado opened the door and let her in.

"Hi," Marcus yelled as he raced to Virginia's side.

"I brought lunch." Virginia dropped her paper bag on the kitchen table. "Are you hungry?"

"Yeah," he said and cautiously eyed Virginia's oily sack.

"Have you ever eaten dried salmon?" Virginia asked.

Marcus gave her a blank stare. "Um, I don't believe we have," Mrs. Maldonado said.

"It's best with smushed berries, but I don't have any of them right now." Virginia pulled a plate from the cupboard and set the greasy fish on it. At her house they just passed the dried fish around, but Mrs. Maldonado liked food on dishes.

"Ah . . . how do you eat it?" Mrs. Maldonado asked.

"Just pull off a hunk, stick it in your mouth, chew, and swallow." Virginia grinned. "Be careful of the bones. Pull 'em out before you eat it." She ripped off a small piece of raw fish flesh, plucked out a needle-like rib, and handed it to Marcus.

He glanced at his mother. "It's okay," she said. "Eat it like Mrs. Tom eats hers."

Mrs. Maldonado pulled a piece from the dried slab, picked out two bones, and put it in her mouth. Virginia watched her chew it. She wanted Mrs. Maldonado to like it. She probably would. Mrs. Maldonado had gotten used to Eskimo ways quick, it seemed. Today, she looked nice in her cotton dress and pretty sweater. Virginia didn't own any dresses. All she ever wore was pants and a kuspuk with a t-shirt underneath.

"How is it?" Virginia asked.

"Fishy," Mrs. Maldonado giggled. She then stooped and picked up the soggy fish piece Marcus had spit out. "It's probably a little too strange for him."

"Ee. Gussuk kids like gussuk food, and Eskimo kids like dried fish," Virginia said.

"Where will you go today?" Mrs. Maldonado asked.

"I have to pick up some candle stubs at the Moravian church." Her husband used them on the seams of his kayak; the wax stuck real good to the sealskin. "Then I need to go to the funeral at the Catholic Church. Michael Nick died, you know. He was my mother's second cousin."

"I'm sorry to hear that."

"Ee, his liver went bad, and he dwindled away."

"How will you handle Marcus at the funeral?" Mrs. Maldonado's mouth sagged, and her brow wrinkled.

"Oh, he'll be fine. He went to Matthew Mike's funeral with me last spring, after Matthew drove his snow-go through the ice on the river. It was too soft. He should of knowed better."

Mrs. Maldonado closed her eyes and shook her head. Virginia thought she had told her about that funeral after Matthew went in, but maybe not.

When Mrs. Maldonado headed off to work, Virginia and Marcus, hand in hand, walked to the Moravian church. They found Rev. Munson in the back of the sanctuary, straightening the hymnals in the racks behind each pew. When they had services in that church, Virginia could hear the singing if she wandered past, even in the winter. The voices sounded like angels, beautiful angels.

Rev. Munson had a whole box of candle stubs for her. She thanked him, and then she and Marcus headed toward the Catholic church. Marcus skipped as they walked on the muddy road. He was a happy boy. Virginia liked happy children. Most of hers were happy. Except for Nicholas, he was gloomy.

Inside the church, the ladies of the Catholic Social Services Society were packing up the leftovers from the rummage sale. Virginia sorted through a stack of clothes and found a shirt that would fit her youngest son. Mitchell was a chubby boy, and he liked blue, so she handed the lady a dime and stuffed the sky-colored t-shirt into the pocket of her kuspuk. She pulled a floral printed scarf from the same pocket and tied it around her head.

She led Marcus into the sanctuary and marched him up to Michael Nick's casket. A bouquet of tundra grasses sat on top of its wooden lid, and, off to the side, pictures of him were pasted to a poster board. She didn't know Michael real well because they grew up in different villages, but his wife was a nice lady and probably pasted up the photos. Virginia crossed herself and then found an open space in one of the pews. Marcus laid his head on her lap and drifted off to sleep as soon as Father Brogan began the Mass.

On the way back to Marcus's house after the funeral, Virginia watched Milton Jimmie as he staggered down the middle of the road toward her. His eyes wandered to the left and to the right, but he didn't stare directly at her. *Where'd he get the booze, now?* she wondered. Probably stole it from someone's house. She stepped into weeds at the edge of the road and pulled Marcus in front of her. Milton was a bad man. He certainly could've killed the people at fish camp. He was afraid of her after she told everybody in town he'd kicked one of Raymond Andrecheck's barking puppies. Milton lurched past her without saying a word.

When she turned the corner, she spotted a group of boys outside Swanson's. Nicholas was among them. She called to her son. He turned his back to her, probably pretending he hadn't heard her. She called louder. Several of his friends spun him around and shoved him toward her.

"Why ain't you in school?" she called.

"They let us out early today."

She was sure that was a lie. She didn't like her children to tell tales. She expected the truth from them.

He walked over to her in his slow, slouchy way with his hands in the pockets of his jeans and his head hanging low.

"Out early, huh?" she asked, staring up at his face which towered above her.

"Ee, Ma."

One of the other boys appeared at his side. "He's right, Mrs. Tom," the boy said. "The teachers have a meeting or something."

Nicholas nodded and kept his head down.

"Okay," Virginia said. "Go home then, and watch Mitchell until I get there."

Nicholas nodded again and stooped down in front of Marcus. "Hey, buddy." He tickled the boy's neck. Marcus giggled as he wiggled his shoulders. Then Nicholas stood up and trudged down the street toward their house.

She called after him. "Nicholas, don't take the boat to Nunapitchuk alone. Only go there if your father goes with you." She didn't want him near trouble, and Nunapitchuk had seen its share of trouble.

While Virginia continued walking back toward the hospital compound and thinking about Nicholas, she shook her head. He was the most difficult of her children, and yet he wasn't an evil person, just sneakier than she'd like.

She looked down at Marcus, who trotted beside her. He would grow up very different than Nicholas had. Her son had been a pretty baby and very easy; the easiest of the four she had had then. He didn't cry much and would lay for hours on a pillow and stare around the room. He seemed to like the way his older brothers and sister would tie flowers in his hair and blow into his ears. She looked at Marcus again, at the way he skipped on the road, the way he sang to himself. She had been gone when Nicholas was that age. She'd missed that whole part of his growing up.

Her sisters in Nunapitchuk had passed baby Nicholas around the village for the three or four years—she couldn't remember exactly how long it had been—she was gone. Her husband tried to keep the family together, but it was really hard for him. He had fish to catch, fish to dry, berries to pick, nets to mend, repairs to do—all his chores plus hers.

Marcus was a smart little fellow. Nicholas, not so much. Marcus would eventually go back to the lower forty-eight with his parents when his father's time at the hospital was over, while Nicholas would stay in Bethel. What would he do when he grew up? Gather food like his dad? Work odd jobs? He was strong and big like her husband. Maybe he could get on either the water truck or the honey bucket wagon crew. Basically he was good. Not the kind of kid who would poison people, she hoped.

They had almost reached the Maldonado's apartment. Virginia sighed. She'd never lived in a house that big or that nice.

CHAPTER 6

Mera was washing the lunch dishes when she heard someone knocking on the entryway door. She held a drinking glass up to the sunlight that streamed through the kitchen window, spotted a greasy smudge, and dunked the glass back under the suds. She longed for the days in Houston when whoever was at the door could call with their messages, but there was no public telephone service in Bethel.

The knocking persisted. Someone called, "Deidre's in labor."

Just as Mera dried her hands, the door swung open and Jennifer, followed by her twins, tumbled in. Mera pointed down the hallway. "Marcus is in the back bedroom, guys. Go help him build a Lego ladder." She then ushered Jennifer to the living room.

This would be Deidre's first child, and so far everything had gone well. Mera had visited Deidre often over the past months and had noted the progress of her pregnancy with interest. Keen interest. While they chatted, Mera had knitted a banana-yellow blanket for the baby and taught Deidre how to crochet purple edges on large squares of flannel. "Nice pattern," Mera said when she first saw the pink and blue elephants that danced, as playful as puppies, across the yards of soft, fuzzy fabric. Together, Mera and Deidre had painted the second bedroom in the Dorfmans' trailer—they chose a color that looked like sunny mint—and assembled the crib Deidre had ordered from Sears. The box had arrived by air freight and cost the Dorfmans a fortune, but Mera agreed that a nice bed for their baby was worth it.

She thought, however, Deidre was crazy to have her first child there in backwater Alaska. So much could go wrong, especially with a first pregnancy, and the only medical back-up was a plane-ride away in Anchorage. She'd quizzed Matias about obstetric complications, and he'd reluctantly answered only after insistent goading on her part. Placenta previa. Abruptio placentae. Eclampsia. Nuchal cord. Transverse lie. Strange words; she'd memorized each of them. The thought of endless bleeding from placental abnormalities, high blood pressure seizures from eclampsia, or a baby strangled by its cord or stuck sideways in the birth canal made Mera dizzy. But Deidre ignored all that and was wildly enthusiastic about having the baby at the Bethel Hospital. Further, David, her doctor husband, was all for the idea.

"He trusts his fellow physicians to do a good job with us," Deidre had said. "George—he's my doctor—has delivered a fair number of Eskimo women."

"Eskimos deliver themselves, I hear," Mera had said. "They don't need the doctors around."

Now, Mera brought a cup of tea to Jennifer.

"I just talked with John," Jennifer said. "He says David is trying to get plane reservations to New York."

Mera nodded. The plan was for David, Deidre, and the baby to fly to New York for the circumcision, which would be conducted at Deidre's parents' synagogue. Then she stopped nodding. "But they don't know yet if the baby is a boy."

"Right. I guess David figures that by the time he has to actually pay for the plane reservations, they'll know. If the baby is a girl, he cancels the transaction."

Mera didn't have any Jewish friends who'd had baby boys, so Deidre had explained the circumcision ritual to her. She said that even though they weren't orthodox, or even observant practitioners of Judaism, certain ceremonies were a must, and a bris was one. "It's a sacred sign of the eternal Covenant between God and Abraham and his descendants," Deidre'd said as if she were teaching a Sunday school class. "It must be performed on the eighth day of life and is expected of every Jewish male."

Like a baptism, Mera thought. *Sort of.* Marcus had been baptized, even though she and Matias were lapsed Catholics. Their relatives would have considered them irresponsible parents if they hadn't gone through with it. So when Marcus was three months old, on a beastly hot summer-in-Houston morning, he was baptized in the park beside Lady of the Lakes Catholic Church, with the proud grandparents, aunts and uncles, and a swarm of cousins milling around. The gnarly branches of the ancient live oak trees above their heads seemed to claw at the sky like witch fingers. When the priest drizzled water on Marcus's head, the little guy let out an indignant shriek, and Matias laughed. Afterward a four-man Mariachi band, hired by Mera's father, played lively Mexican madrigals while everyone ate tacos and beans. Mera and Matias hadn't darkened the door of a church since.

Mera wasn't sure about circumcision. It sounded brutal and bloody. With Marcus's baptism, there was no cutting, no bleeding, no wound. He had emerged from his christening ceremony with a wet head, but otherwise everything was intact.

"I guess there might some health advantages to circumcision," Mera had said to Deidre, trying to be diplomatic about it.

"For us, it's a spiritual procedure, not a medical one. A physician usually isn't involved."

An operation without a doctor? Mera would never go for that. "Who does it, then? If your baby's a boy, who will perform his circumcision?"

"My parents will find an experienced mohel. They're a dime a dozen in New York City."

Jennifer had just announced that she was leaving when the hospital phone in Mera and Matias's bedroom rang. Mera answered and heard her husband's voice explain the situation with Deidre and the baby. She clutched the phone and lowered herself to their bed. Poor Deidre. Poor, poor Deidre.

Mera returned to the living room, flopped down on the couch, and rubbed her eyes. "Bad news," she said. She could hear the wobble in her own voice.

"Oh God," Jennifer turned the color of plaster. "What?"

"That was Matias. The Dorfman child has been born. Apparently, the baby came out very fast, and Deidre ended up with . . ." What had Matias said? "Oh, a fourth-degree tear."

"What's that?" Jennifer's voice was wispy as a shadow.

"I'm not exactly sure but Matias said something about the cut they make in the mother ripping open when the baby came out." Mera took a deep breath. "He wasn't at all happy about it, said it would be tough on Deidre."

"Girl or boy?"

"Boy. A healthy one."

"Gosh. What'll they do about the bris? That's awfully important to them. Will she be able to travel all the way to New York?"

Mera shook her head. "Don't know. This is really awful." She had come to believe what everyone had said. Her husband, Deidre, David, and John. They all agreed that Deidre should have no trouble delivering the baby. That the doctors at the Bethel Hospital could handle it without difficulty. How could it go so wrong at the very end?

DEIDRE'S SON WAS THREE DAYS OLD, and both mother and baby were still in the hospital. The docs wouldn't allow visitors. When she retrieved the mail from the hospital's post office, she wandered to Deidre's room. "Let the poor woman rest," read the handwritten sign Scotch-taped to the closed door.

"What's going on?" Mera asked Matias.

"That extended tear is pretty uncomfortable. She's not in the mood for visitors, and every person on the hospital compound wants to see the little guy. And her. We have to protect her from all the well-wishers."

Sounded strange to Mera. Having a baby was supposed to be a blissful occasion. Even though Matias didn't want to go into details—he probably knew they would scare her into insanity about having a baby in the Bethel Hospital—Mera knew it was bad. And, indeed, she was very scared.

Deidre's baby was five days old, and mother and child remained in the hospital, still without visitors. Mera stood in Jennifer's kitchen—an identical twin of her own apartment, because they were both on the southwest side of their fourplexes. The sun had fallen below the horizon leaving an orange and purple glow in the darkening sky, and snowflakes pelted the window. The electrical wires into the house whistled in the wind, and the yard light that shined high above the hospital's parking lot swayed with each gust as if it was inebriated.

Mera held her good sewing shears in front of Jennifer's face, ready to trim her bangs. More familiar with cutting black curly hair, Mera was willing to give Jennifer's pencil-straight locks a try. The color, the tan of an acorn, was pretty in the dim light from the kitchen ceiling light. "How much off?" she asked.

"Enough so it doesn't scratch my eyeballs anymore," Jennifer answered.

Mera snipped while Jennifer kept her eyelids closed and her head still as a stone. A third of the way across her forehead, she heard a door slam from the back entryway.

"That's Leonard," Jennifer muttered, "returning to his apartment. Of all the people at the hospital, it has to be him across the hall from us."

Mera kept cutting. "Wonder if he's found anyone's marriage

license yet?" Snip. Snip. "Personally, I prefer sharing the entry to our apartment with Stephen rather than Leonard."

Jennifer smiled and then asked, "What's the deal, anyway, with Stephen and Jackie?"

"I'm not sure." Mera said. "She's young and on an adventure here in Alaska." Mera stood back and gazed at Jennifer's bangs. Not short enough. She looked at the half-scowl on Jennifer's face. She seemed sadder today than usual.

"Yeah, I suppose. She's certainly not locked into the jail of marriage and kids."

Whoa, Mera thought. *Jennifer thinks she's imprisoned.* But rather than saying anything, she turned Jennifer's face slightly to the right and kept snipping.

When Jennifer started talking about her graduate work back in California, her voice turned hard as a brick. "I really hated to leave before my thesis was done. I'd worked hard to get into the program, and the research was going well. Leaving felt like giving up."

"Why'd you leave?" Mera tried to sound supportive. She'd never heard Jennifer speak like that.

"To come here with John. So our family could be together." Jennifer opened her eyes briefly, and Mera saw the glistening tears. Jennifer snapped them shut again.

"Oh, dear." Mera kept snipping. She'd been fine with leaving her job at *Texas Outdoors* when she and Matias came to Bethel. "Can't you go back when your time here is over?"

Jennifer seemed to ignore Mera's question. "Sometimes, I think I made a very big mistake." Jennifer's voice now cracked and carried a note of deep regret. "Instead of marrying John, I should have followed my own path rather than settling for the life everyone else expected of me."

Boy, Mera thought. That was a big one, wishing to not be married after you were. So many years wasted, so much of a lifetime squandered. It would be like taking the left fork in the road and ending up drowning in quicksand.

Mera thought of her own marriage. She and Matias didn't always agree, but she didn't feel marrying him had been a mistake, just something she had to manage. She didn't see herself as a prisoner at all. Rather, in dealing with him, she stuck up for herself, for her ideas and her concerns, and for equal partnership.

Mera continued to snip Jennifer's bangs. She moved the scissors left, then right, then left, back and forth as she was having trouble getting them even. The more she thought about it, the more confident she became that marrying Matias had been a very good choice for her. She treasured Matias's humor. His escapades sometimes went over the top, but they were always interesting. She trusted him. He was kind. She could see them growing old together and becoming like her parents who had lots of secret signals between them, honed to perfection over the years. They had no hidden longings for past, or imaginary, lovers that she knew of and had built decades of precious memories together.

When the haircut was finished, Jennifer wandered into her bathroom. "How is it?" Mera called.

"Fine." Her voice sounded uncertain to Mera. The cut would have to do though because the bangs were now too short.

Jennifer joined Mera in the living room. "Has John said much about Deidre and the baby to you?" Mera asked, glad to leave the subject of marriage. She reached down to pet Ginger, who lay on the floor at her feet.

"No, not a word from John. He's very hush-hush. Something must be terribly wrong."

"Matias won't say anything either, except that she's in a lot of pain. I really wish we could visit."

"Me too. I hope the 'no visitors' sign was her idea." Jennifer reached into the shelf beside her head and pulled out a bowl. "I made this in my pottery class."

"Where'd you find those tiny plants?" Mera stared at the green-brown growth in the bowl.

"Dug 'em from a patch of the tundra alongside a hot water pipe where the snow has melted. It's for Deidre. Maybe I'll have John take it to her." She set the bowl back on the shelf and held up the teapot. "Refill?"

"No, thanks." Mera ran her hand over Ginger's silky, shiny-as-a-new-penny coat again. "She is really a nice dog." She raked her fingers through her own curly hair. "How about the Dorfmans' trip to New York? How can Deidre possibly make that long flight if she isn't even out of the hospital yet?"

"Good question," Jennifer said.

With that, Mera called down the hallway for Marcus. He didn't want to leave. She promised him a cookie once they got home.

"No."

She dangled his snowsuit in front of his face. "We're going."

"No, I don't wanna."

When she began to stuff his leg into the snowsuit, he started kicking. When she set the knit hat on his head, he pulled it off and threw it across the room. He screamed, "I wanna play here."

Mera squatted in front of his and grabbed his arms. "Marcus, stop it. We're going home to make dinner for Daddy. Jeff and Brian are done playing for now."

Marcus looked up at Jennifer. She nodded her head slowly.

Mera tied his scarf under his chin and slipped his hands into two pairs of mittens strung together with yarn that was threaded through the sleeves of the snowsuit. Finally, she tugged on his boots. As she put on her own parka, scarf, gloves, and hat, she thought, "How could I ever handle two like this?" Then, she opened Jennifer's kitchen door to the back entryway and said, "Here we go, out into the winter." As they headed down the outside steps and trudged along the snowy boardwalk back to their apartment at the other end of the fourplexes, the moon appeared from behind a cloud. Its silvery light bounced off the snow like a dancing dime and illuminated their way.

AFTER MARCUS WAS ASLEEP FOR THE night, Mera grabbed Matias's hand and led him to the couch. "Sit," she commanded. "We have to talk. Tell me exactly what happened to Deidre."

He scratched his head. "Are you sure you want to know?"

"Yes." Her imagination might, after all, be worse than the reality.

"Well, that baby is a big, strapping boy, and when he decided to be born, he erupted from her like a rocket. George wisely did an episiotomy to open her vaginal outlet and ease the baby's exit, but that kid just shot out and tore the episiotomy open through her perineal muscles and down into her rectum."

Mera leaned her spinning head against the back of the couch and closed her eyes. It sounded so terrible; even worse than she had thought. A ripped-up rectum? "What'd they do, then?"

"George sewed up the tear, so it should be fine. But she's awfully sore, and it'll take a couple weeks for the thing to heal."

Mera tried to visualize the pictures she'd seen of a woman's crotch at the time when her baby was about to be born—the widened opening with the baby's hair visible inside; the bulge of the surrounding tissues; the neat, thin surgical slit through the ring of the opening. The added image of torn flesh, blood, and ragged edges made her head spin even more. "How can she poop with a wrecked rectum?"

"Mineral oil. Lots of it. Until she leaks."

Mera shook her head. Her bottom hurt just thinking of Deidre's injury.

"By the way, we're invited to the bris at their place on Sunday." Matias scratched his arm.

"What?" Mera sat straight up. "Here, in Bethel?"

"That's right. If the baby can't come to the synagogue, the synagogue comes to the baby, I guess. David contacted the Air Force rabbi at Elmendorf, who contacted a rabbi in Seattle who is certified to perform circumcisions. They've got it all figured out. Eleven in the morning, on Sunday."

THE SUN HAD BARELY CLEARED THE horizon when Mera and Matias began the walk to David and Deidre's trailer. The boardwalk was slippery; the trampled, snowy path had turned to ice in the bright sunlight the day before, so Mera held on to the sleeve of Matias's parka.

"Is Deidre home?" she asked.

"She was supposed to be discharged last night. My guess is wild wolves wouldn't keep her away from the doings."

They crossed the hospital parking lot and continued toward the trailers. Mera had arranged for Virginia to watch Marcus; Virginia planned to take him to the hospital gift shop when her 11:30 shift began. Although the shop's shelves groaned with adult supplies—boxes of sanitary napkins, aspirin and Maalox bottles, hairbrushes, and toothpaste—along with lidded baskets and trays woven from seagrass by the Yup'ik women, Marcus loved to play with the empty boxes and wrapping paper. He'd be happier there than with the crowd in the Dorfmans' trailer.

It was only 10:30 or so—Mera hadn't reset the stove clock since noon yesterday, so she wasn't sure of the time when they left home—but people had already started to gather at David and Deidre's place. Matias and Mera kicked their boots off and added them to the stack already piled up in a cardboard box on the outdoor landing. Then, they went inside and tossed their parkas on the heap that overflowed one of the easy chairs. Mera spotted Rachel—she'd come all the way from Mekoryuk—and gave her a big hug.

"How are you? The school allowed you to be away?"

"It's a good thing this shindig is on Sunday so both Richard and I could come."

"Where's your son?" Mera asked.

"Robert's with one of the village ladies."

"Have you seen Deidre?"

"She's in bed with the baby." Rachel tipped her head toward the rear of the trailer. "And pretty miserable."

Stephen joined them. He wore a nice shirt and pressed pants

with strands of Soldier's dog hair clinging to the creases. Mera had never seen him so dressed up. "Hi Stephen," she said. "Have you met Rachel, the teacher from Mekoryuk? Stephen's one of the docs at the hospital."

"I believe your husband is one of the minyan," Stephen said.

"Right." Rachel flashed a warm smile.

Mera glanced around the crowded room. All five doctors as well as both dentists and one of the pharmacists were there, along with their spouses. Her glance stopped at the cluster of men wearing skullcaps who stood around a white-bearded man in a black and white-striped robe beside the Dorfmans' tiny dining room table. "Who are those guys?" Mera asked.

"The old fellow is Rabbi Kaufmann from Seattle," Stephen answered. "He's the mohel and master of ceremonies."

"All the way from Seattle?"

"Yeah, he arrived on an Air Force plane early this morning and brought boxes and boxes of food prepared by the women of his congregation. The other fellow—the one in the white robe—is Rabbi Bloch, the chaplain from Elmendorf. The others are the rest of the minyan. Are you familiar with that term?"

Minion? Mera had heard a word like that back in Texas. She thought for a moment then remembered. It meant a weakling, a follower. That couldn't be the same word, here. "No," she said.

"Like all Jewish prayer and ritual services, the bris must be attended by ten Jewish men as witnesses. They are the minyan. It's like a quorum, the minimum number of Hebrew men to make the procedure valid." Stephen chuckled. "It's incredible that David was able to round up ten Jewish guys in this corner of Alaska. They kind of crawled out of their caves when they heard a baby was involved." He pointed to the man furthest to the left. "That handsome fellow there is Richard, Rachel's husband."

Rachel giggled.

"And next to him is Adam Fisher, a teacher at Bethel High, and his son Jason—he's eighteen, so he qualifies. Next is Edgar, the shopkeeper in Aniak. He hasn't seen his yarmulke in years, so David loaned him one."

Stephen paused and fished around his pants pockets. "Speaking of which, I'd better put mine on." He set the blue and white striped cap on his shaggy-haired head. "Then there's Noah, one of the crazy bush pilots, and over there on the end is Jonathan, an air traffic control guy from the airport. Add me and David and the rabbis, and you have ten. Amazing."

Rabbi Kauffman banged a pen on a wine glass and called, "Someone get the father. It's time to begin. Who's the sandek?" Stephen leaned toward Mera and explained the sandek as the person who holds the baby during the circumcision.

"Richard," called Rachel, who raised her hand toward her husband and then headed for Deidre's bedroom. Richard squeezed through the crowd and sat down in a chair beside the dining room table.

Rabbi Kaufmann briefly explained the ceremony—pretty much what Deidre had told Mera earlier—to the heavily gentile group. Soon, Rachel returned from the bedroom carrying a bed-pillow, its slipcover dotted with faded yellow roses. On top was the baby, a dewy, precious newborn wrapped in one of the elephant-printed flannel blankets Deidre had edged with crochet stitches. Rachel handed the pillow with the squirming baby to her husband, and he lay it on his knees in front of the mohel.

The rabbi from Anchorage passed out half-sheets of paper. "Here's the recitations," he said with a slender smile and glistening eyes.

Mera leaned toward Matias. "Isn't this something?" He nodded. "I think I'll take notes for a story about it in the *Tundra Drums*." Matias nodded again. She fished an old envelope from her kuspuk's pouch and pulled Matias's pen from his shirt pocket.

In a deep, solemn, echo-ey voice that reminded Mera of God, the Seattle rabbi boomed, "Blessed art Thou, O Lord our God, King of the universe, who hast sanctified us with Thy commandments, and hast given us the command concerning circumcision." His words bounced off the walls of the trailer and nearly raised its ceiling.

The mohel then unwrapped the baby and reached for something from his bag. David held his script in front of his face and read in a clear, confident voice, "Blessed art Thou, O Lord our God, King of the universe, who hast sanctified us with Thy commandments, and hast commanded us to make our sons enter the covenant of Abraham our father." He then grinned.

The rabbi from Anchorage signaled to the crowd that it was their turn to speak. Led by the minyan, everyone read, "Even as this child has entered into the covenant, so may he enter into the Torah, the nuptial canopy, and into good deeds."

In spite of standing on her toes, Mera couldn't see what the mohel was doing to the child, who seemed buried in a heap of flannel blanket and baby clothes. Her inability to witness the actual procedure was okay. Deidre had described it, step by step: the way the mohel retracts the skin over the tip of the baby's penis, pulls it through a clamp, cuts it off with a scalpel. That was enough information for her. She studied the faces around her. None were horrified, all were serene; the room was peaceful as a lullaby. She didn't hear a sound from Deidre's baby.

The mohel chattered as he worked. In a now gentle, soft voice he spoke of the blessing of babies, the wise leadership of Abraham, and the commitment of Deidre and David to the proper religious upbringing for their child. His face was calm, intent on the task at hand.

Then he stood up straight, raised a glass of what looked like red wine, and announced that the baby's name would be Daniel. He passed the wine glass to David and yelled in his once again thunderous voice, "It's time for a party."

Mera watched as David carried the baby to the back of the trailer. She then helped Rachel unpack the boxes from Anchorage and arrange the food on hospital cafeteria trays. There were bagels and lox, hard-boiled eggs, raisin and almond coffee cakes, deep-fried balls of something spicy, and what looked, and smelled, like fish sticks. And, several bottles of Manischewitz wine. All from Jewish women in Seattle who had never met David nor Deidre. Unbelievable. Mera wondered if the Catholics would be so thoughtful and generous. Maybe. Maybe not.

Then the dancing began. Led by songs from the minyan, the music swirled through the trailer, rising in eddies and falling in dips.

Mera watched the others bounce and kick their feet forward and sing. Poor Deidre had to miss the party. Mera edged through the crowd toward the hallway to the bathroom and slid into Deidre's bedroom.

"Hi," Deidre said. Her thin voice was barely a whisper, her skin the color of ashes.

"It was a lovely ceremony," Mera said. She didn't know what else to way. The room was stuffy and smelled of body fluids. She couldn't identify them. Probably they were a mix: breast milk, baby poop, vaginal discharge, and healing wound.

"Daniel is a super-trooper," Deidre smiled down at the baby now asleep in her arms.

"So is his mother. Are you okay?"

Deidre nodded. "I'm fine. Just a tad sore in the nether reaches. Isn't he adorable? Worth every agonizing moment." She shifted her hips on the mattress a little bit, and a grimace creased her face.

Mera leaned over the bed and kissed Deidre's cheek. Her skin was soft as silk, even though she was the toughest woman Mera knew. "You need to keep sleeping."

When Mera returned to the living room, Rachel grabbed her hand. "Come dance. It's the hora." Mera stepped into the circle between Stephen and Richard and started to kick the air. She tried to join the chorus as best as she could. "Hava Nagila" were the only words she recognized, although she didn't know what they meant. Matias was on the other side of the circle, bouncing and jerking and singing like an excited kid. She too was excited, although the word to best capture the whole experience for her was joyous. Joy for the healthy new baby, joy for David's success in pulling off the bris in Bethel, joy for Deidre with her blessed, beloved child despite her awful ordeal.

Snow had fallen all night, leaving a blanket of white as far as Mera could see out the kitchen window. The sky was still dark as tar, but the moon cast an eerie glow across the windswept tundra. She stood at the stove, stirring oatmeal for breakfast.

Matias tightened the knot of his tie and then smoothed the wrinkles from his white, clinical coat as he wandered into the kitchen. "I still can't forget that terrific bris," he said. "Deidre came to the clinic for a two-week post-partum check-up yesterday, and George says she's coming along pretty well."

Coming along pretty well, he'd said. What did that mean? Mera slid a bowl of cereal onto the table in front of her husband. "I have something important to tell you."

He shoved a spoonful of food into his mouth. "Shoot," he muttered.

"I'm pretty sure I'm pregnant."

He stopped chewing, set the spoon on the table, and stared up at her. "Really?"

"Yes, really. I've missed two periods."

"Honey, that's wonderful. Really wonderful." He leaped to his feet, wrapped his arms around her shoulders, and kissed her. "Are you okay with that?" he whispered into her hair.

She settled against his body, felt the warmth of his presence and the strength of his being. Was she okay with the pregnancy? Yes, she was okay and nervous and excited and confused. She had to assume the baby was healthy. What she didn't know was how long the pregnancy would last. Except for Marcus, the others had ended by four months. When she thought of the finale of this pregnancy and all those uncertainties—where would the baby be born? Anchorage? Texas? Bethel?—she shoved the questions aside. Those were decisions for another time. "Yes. I'm okay." She set a glass of Tang on the table at his elbow. "Maybe a little scared, but we'll get through it just fine."

<h1 style="text-align:center">CHAPTER 7</h1>

THE JETTERSES HUDDLED ON THE FROZEN Kuskokwim River near Bethel's town dock with their backs to the wind while the pilot loaded boxes and suitcases into the ski plane. He juggled each item, seeming to gauge their weights, before selecting the correct spot for each in the hold. A ragged blast of frigid air whistled out of the north. Snow flurries twinkled in the sun as they danced in the wind.

"Where's my bear?" asked Jeff.

"In the big bag. He's going to ride in there during the flight," said Jennifer.

They would fly downriver toward the coast, to the mouth of the Kuskokwim where it dumped into the Bering Sea. John would run a clinic in Kongiganak, checking on all the pregnant women and any villagers the health aides wanted him to see, and two days later, they'd go further along the coast to Kwigillingok for another clinic.

"Where's Ginger?" Brian asked, looking out over the ice-covered river.

"She's staying with Marcus and his mommy and daddy, remember? They'll take good care of her," Jennifer said.

Jennifer was leery of this trip, but John had insisted she and the boys join him. "We all need to experience the villages. They're the heart-blood of Alaska. Hopefully, the boys will remember this adventure forever."

The twins were barely four. How much of anything during these two years would they remember? She wasn't keen on riding in a tiny bush plane. They would be the only Gussuks there. What would the native people think of them and the kids? "Where will we stay, assuming we make it there alive?" she had asked.

John had shaken his head. "You are such a scaredy cat. The health aides have arranged for us to sleep at the clinic in Kongiganak and in the school at Kwigillingok. We'll take sleeping bags. It'll be fine. It'll be really fun, if you let it."

"How about meals? How will we get from village to village? Where will the plane land?"

He sighed. "The health aides have it all figured out, and the planes land on the river in the winter. You know that."

She didn't like being called a scaredy cat, and, yes, she knew bush planes landed on the frozen river in the winter, but she thought those villages might use land-based air strips, in spite of the ice and snow. He shouldn't expect her to know all those details. So many unknowns. So many worries. Yet, it was hard to justify living in Bethel for two years without traveling to a village from time to time. Finally, she had agreed to go along.

The pilot—Noah, one of the minyan at Daniel Dorfman's bris—slammed the door of the cargo hatch and called, "All aboard." Jennifer was glad she knew him. Bush pilots had a reputation for being reckless dare devils—she had heard stories of their games of chicken to see who would pilot the last plane off the melting river before break-up or be the first on the new ice after freeze-up—but she thought she could trust a guy who had shown up for a bris. He helped her into the co-pilot seat and hoisted Brian onto her lap. Then he pointed John and Jeff to the jump-seat behind him.

"I wanna sit in front," Jeff whined.

"I need to balance the load . . ." Noah's voice was apologetic.

"You're closer to your bear back here," John said to Jeff. "You can sit in front on the way home."

Noah started the engine. Once it settled into a rhythmic hum, he leaped out of the cockpit onto the ice, raced to the front of the plane, gave the propeller a hard two-handed spin, and jumped back into his seat. "Ready?" he called. Jennifer could barely hear him over the roar.

"Yeah!" yelled Jeff.

The plane bounced across the ice on its skis for several hundred feet and then slowly began to climb. Jennifer watched out the window as the ground fell further and further away. She saw Swanson's store over near the town dock and then spotted the hospital compound at the river's bend. She saw the line of fourplexes and their unit on the end. Beyond was the Bethel airport, with its runway slicing across the snowy tundra like a charcoal ribbon.

Suddenly, the window beside her flipped open. She gasped. She gripped Brian. Her heart raced.

"Shit," said Noah. He thrust his right arm across her and Brian, grabbed the window handle, and yanked it shut. "Your job will be to keep that damn thing from blowing open. Hold it tight," he shouted over the engine's growl.

She held Brian against her chest with her left hand, clutched the window's handle with her right, and wondered why she had thought attending a bris would rid a bush pilot of risk-taking. What would the rest of the ride bring? She couldn't remember why she let John talk her into this trip.

The view, though, was spectacular. The Kuskokwim snaked its way through the snow-covered tundra, leaving layers of oxbows—they looked like shaky parentheses—that documented its decade-to-decade course changes. The permafrost had heaved, the river had moved over and over. She saw a web of frozen creeks branch off the main river. Jagged ponds polka-dotted the snowy ground. She watched the river split, run along either side of an island, and rejoin again. It seemed alive, that river, even in the dead of winter.

A short way ahead, the sun reflected off a pile of something in the snow. It was silvery. Maybe metal. Then she saw the propeller and part of a wing. "Is that a plane?" she asked.

"Used to be." Noah said. "Now it's a wreck."

"How did it crash? Was anyone hurt?"

He said he couldn't remember who had been in that plane. "Sometimes they survive. Sometimes not." He went on to explain that plane crashes weren't all that uncommon. "Conditions can change in a heartbeat out here, you know."

Her stomach twisted. John said something that she couldn't hear. "Louder," she called over her shoulder.

"I asked if your arm is tired from hanging onto that window."

"Not yet."

Jennifer gazed at the horizon, at the place where the sky touched the ground, where the winding river disappeared into the white of the earth's edge. The plane was still aloft, still flying evenly above the ground. If they went down, their whole family would be gone. She tried to think of other things. The Dorfman bris. Her pottery class. Their dog Ginger.

The plane bucked, the engine coughed, and finally Noah shouted, "There it is," as he pointed out the front window.

"There's what?" Jennifer asked. All she saw was white. Everywhere.

"Kongiganak." The plane turned slightly toward the right.

"Where?" Still, all she saw was white.

"Straight ahead. That little black dot."

Sure enough, straight ahead was a tiny dark spot in the ocean of white. Soon, she could see the outlines of the buildings scattered in the snow ahead.

Noah swung the plane away from the river and headed toward a low-slung shack at the edge of the village. He said, "I'll buzz the clinic so the health aide knows we're here." Then he swung the plane back toward the frozen water and nosed it downward. They were nearly on the river when he yelled, "Little bump."

WHOOMP. The plane jolted as if it had met a brick wall, and Jeff giggled. Brian's body stiffened. "It's okay, honey," Jennifer said. "We're on the ground again." She let go of the window handle.

By the time they had unloaded the plane, a snowmobile pulling a large wooden sled had roared to a stop beside them. The driver introduced himself and explained, with a wave of his arm over their belongings stacked on the ice, that he would take them and their stuff to the clinic. "Maggie's expecting you," he said. Then he added, "That's Maggie Evon, the health aide."

The pilot, the snowmobile driver, and John loaded their gear onto the sled while Jennifer and the boys watched. Her fingertips were cold, and her cheeks burned from the crystals of snow that blew with the wind against her face. They felt like icy needles. She wrapped her scarf around her head, leaving a slit for her eyes. Upon the driver's command she climbed onto the sled.

The snowmobile dragged the sled over the snowy tundra, and then it ran beside the icy boardwalk through the village. They passed houses built of unpainted wood scattered among smaller shacks nestled into snow drifts. Lamp posts tilted helter-skelter between the buildings, and loops of electric wires overhead twisted in the wind. A flag flapped from a pole beside a hut, intermittently hiding a faded sign that said, "Kongiganak, AK 99545."

In the distance, silhouetted against the cloudy sky, stood a large building, painted white with three onion domes on the roof. *Must be a church*, Jennifer thought. Russian Orthodox. As far as she could tell, Kongiganak looked like a miniature Bethel.

Maggie stood on the narrow porch of the clinic, a broad grin on her face, and waved. Jennifer admired her kuspuk and the little yellow and white flowers scattered over its bright green fabric. *So springy on this drab winter day*, she thought. Maybe that was their way of coping: images of flowers despite the snow, pretty colors amid the forever white.

Maggie gave the Jetterses a tour of the one-room clinic, and then she and John reviewed the clinic records and stocked the supplies he had brought from Bethel—boxes of gauze, tongue depressors, alcohol wipes, insulin needles and syringes, and meds from the hospital pharmacy. Jennifer and the twins sat on the floor in the corner and read the well-used children's books from the shelves beside the door. First, she read Brian's choice, *The Animal Family*, and then Jeff's, *Fox in Socks*.

The door opened, the cold wind blew into the clinic, and a young woman leading a little girl hustled inside. Maggie motioned the woman to the desk. While she filled out the papers, the child gazed at the twins. Her mother nudged her with a gesture that said, *"Don't stare."*

Maggie helped the child onto the examining table. She listened to her chest and poked at her belly. She spoke soft Yup'ik words as she shined a light into the girl's right ear. After examining the left, she called, "Dr. Jetters . . ." to John. The girl sat like a granite statue while John took a look at the inside of the ear and felt the girl's neck. "Otitis media," he said.

Maggie handed the mother a bottle of ampicillin and spoke, again in Yup'ik, while the mother nodded. As they talked, the daughter pulled away and edged over to the twins. She reached out her hand and touched Jeff's golden hair. He laughed. Then she leaned close to Brian's face, stared into his sky-blue irises, and said to her mother, "What's wrong with his eyes?"

The mother raced to the girl's side, wrapped her fingers around her arm, and pulled her toward the door. "Sorry. So sorry," she said over her shoulder.

Jennifer smiled. "That's okay." Both twins were laughing now.

AT THE END OF THE AFTERNOON, Maggie flipped the sign in the

clinic window so it read "CLOSED" on the outside. "I'll bring you something to eat," she said on her way out the door.

Half an hour later she returned with pilot bread and dried salmon. Brian and Jeff ate the crackery bread and left most of the fish. Then Maggie announced, "I have an Eskimo treat for you: Agudak."

"A . . . gu . . . dak," John muttered. "That's a new one."

"It's delicious," Maggie said. "We call it Eskimo ice cream."

"Ice cream," the twins called in unison, their voices rising to the clinic room's rafters.

She pulled the lid from a plastic container, showed them the white, creamy mass with red-orange dots, dished it into coffee cups, and passed the mugs, along with spoons, to the Jetterses.

Brian shoved a bit of it into his mouth and looked confused.

Jeff gobbled half the cupful and furled his brow. "Tastes funny," he said.

Jennifer took a tentative bite. Greasy and sweet. Very sweet. Very greasy. She nearly gagged as she swallowed the small bit.

"Interesting. What is it?" John asked.

Maggie grinned. "Crisco with sugar and salmonberries."

"Yum," said John and turned to face his sons. "Fellows, Eskimo ice cream isn't exactly like our ice cream, but it's good."

Jennifer stared at her husband, the man who was always so positive. He was also the guy who had talked her into leaving her graduate program to come to this God-forsaken place. He readily accepted the Eskimo ways that she found difficult. He didn't understand her very justified worry. Who was he, anyway?

"Different, but good," John continued. "Just like lots of things here in Alaska."

"Like pilot bread," said Jeff.

"Like muck boots," said Brian.

Like the satellite phones. Like the off-kilter clocks, the leaky faucet in the bathtub, the bitter cold, the steady diet of canned food, the . . . Jennifer could have continued for twenty minutes.

Different, yes. Good? She sighed as she passed the rest of her agudak to John, who polished it off instantly. He liked it. He really did. He liked almost everything about being in Alaska. Some days she wished she could be more accepting of the Yup'ik customs. But she was glad she'd brought along Fig Newtons and a bag of gorp for the boys.

While Maggie packed up the remains of the meal, she said, "Dr. Jetters, do you know anything about those guys that died at fish camp in Nunapitchuk last summer? Some folks say they were poisoned."

"I've also heard that but don't know anything about it."

"Some people are afraid," she said.

"What do they fear?" he asked.

"That it'll happen again. That someone will poison them, I guess." She shook her head. "I just wonder. Luther was a bad man. He was in trouble a lot. Maybe someone was mad at Luther. But Morris was a good man. Too bad he had to die too."

THAT NIGHT, JOHN AND THE TWINS unrolled their sleeping bags on the clinic room's indoor-outdoor carpeting. "It's like camping," he told the boys. "Indoors camping, and instead of peeing in the woods, you can pee in the honey bucket." He pointed to an enamel pail with a loose-fitting lid hidden behind a partial wall.

Another Alaskan difference, Jennifer thought. The honey bucket.

"WE CAN'T TAKE THE SNOW MACHINE over to Kwigillingok," the driver said the next morning. "Something's wrong with the starter." He stood beside his high-backed wooden sled which was now attached to eight wiggling, pawing, snorting dogs.

Jennifer grabbed John's arm. "We're going to ride in that rig?"

"I guess so. Sounds interesting." He wrapped his arm around her shoulders and gave her a hug.

"Sounds awful." She turned to the driver and asked, "How long?"

"An hour or so."

Clouds covered the sun, and the wind blew new snow in swirls across the old snow. Jennifer said to John, "I'm putting more clothes on the boys." She pulled her sons back into the clinic, opened their suitcase, and dressed them each in pajamas, an undershirt, two flannel shirts, two pairs of OshKosh B'Gosh overalls, and all the socks they had brought along. She could barely zip their snowsuits shut.

"I'm too stiff," Jeff complained as he tried to bend his elbow.

"That's okay, honey. It's going to be cold during the sled ride."

The dogs were harnessed in pairs, and they fidgeted against the ropes. The black patches in their otherwise white fur looked like chunks of coal in a snowdrift. Jeff reached his arm toward one of the lead dogs. Jennifer yanked it back. "No, Jeff." She heard the shrill in her voice, saw the fear on her son's face. "Remember, sled dogs aren't for petting. They're for pulling the sled." Those animals looked majestic, beautiful, and strong, and they definitely shouldn't be messed with. The image of a mangled son raced through her head. "Stay right next to me," she said.

The driver steadied the dogs while John and Jennifer climbed onto the sled. They huddled side by side against its back, each with a son wedged between their legs and everyone covered with a muskrat fur blanket. Their suitcases and boxes of supplies for the Kwigillingok clinic were strapped to the sled behind them and at their feet. The driver stepped onto the sled's rear runners. "Let's go," he yelled, and the sled jerked forward.

Jennifer squinted to the left then to the right. Yet another endless expanse of white surrounded her. She saw no trail other than older ski-ruts, no signs, no way to know if they were going in the right direction. Her view straight ahead was of the rear ends of the last pair of dogs in the team, their hairy tails waving like wind-blown flags and their paws kicking up the snow. They ran in unison and their chests pulled against their harnesses with the strength of Samson.

She was cold. Very cold. The knit scarf that covered most of her face was stiff with breath-frost. Her toes felt like ice cubes. Would they ever get there?

"Are you okay?" John said from beside her.

"Ah . . . yes." The right side of her body was at the very edge of the open sled. No arm rests, no side boards. She leaned to her left, toward the center, toward her husband. "How's Brian?"

"He's fine."

Jeff lay between her legs. Was he still alive? She wiggled her thighs. He squirmed. He must be sleeping. She leaned her head against the back of the sled, closed her eyes, heard Jeff cough, and let herself be carried toward the setting sun by the dog team.

When she opened her eyes to the dim light of afternoon, she saw buildings over the tops of the dogs. The driver called, "Easy," and the sled slowed. Then he called, "Whoa," and the sled slid to a stop. She unfolded herself and carried Jeff toward the clinic build-ing. "We're here, honey," she said to her son.

A cluster of Yup'ik children had gathered on the clinic porch. They shoved each other, giggled, and hid their mouths behind their mittens. Their straight black hair framed their pie-plate faces and dangled in their sparkling, almond-shaped, tar-black eyes. The health aide stepped outside and shooed away the kids. "Back to school," she said to them. "Get over there."

THE SUNLIGHT FROM BELOW THE HORIZON glowed in the sky when they walked over to the school. The teachers, a married gussuk couple originally from Massachusetts, greeted them. "Make your-selves comfortable here, and then come to our house next door for dinner," they said.

Jennifer surveyed the room. Desks were scattered in clusters of large, medium, or small, with an old upright piano angled in one corner. Colorful pictures of wild animals crowded the bulletin board. A poster showing the solar system was pinned to the wall beside the window. Cursive letters ran above the blackboard and onto adjacent walls like a border strip of wallpaper. It reminded her of her own elementary classroom back in California. That was a generation ago.

Her eyes stopped at the blackboard. TODAY'S NEWS was written in large orange letters. Beneath, in lemon-colored chalk, it read:

The doctor came today.

He brought his wife and two sons.

The boys are twins but don't look alike.

They have yellow hair and blue eyes.

She caught her breath. The big news at the Kwigillingok school was their visit, and the twins seemed to be a big hit. She hadn't expected that at all. She thought the natives would barely tolerate the presence of the gussuks on their land. Their ways of living were so very different.

The reporters must have been the gaggle of kids at the clinic when they arrived. "Look, guys," she said to the twins, and her voice started to crack. She paused then spoke again. "Let me read the school news for today." She dabbed her eyes with her sleeve and buried a sniffle in her elbow. Then, she read them the news.

That night, after a meal of Dinty Moore Beef Stew, pilot bread, and berry pie with the teachers, Jennifer lay on the school's hard floor in her sleeping bag and thought, again, about Today's News. Light from the swaying yard lamp outside the window pulsed on the blackboard. The words seemed to dance. Their visit was notable, was interesting to the Yup'ik kids. She thought of the way the little girl in the clinic in Kongigonak had touched Jeff's hair and asked about Brian's eyes. Yellow hair. Blue eyes. *Different, but good.* Those were John's words. And, they were true.

Her mind meandered: the plane ride, the sled ride, the agudak, the toilets, Today's News. It was like wandering down a dirty, dark alley and suddenly finding an unexpected patch of light off to the side that led to a beautiful garden. They were important here, worthy of headlines.

Chapter 8

Leonard Kills Squirrels tramped up the icy steps of his fourplex, kicking each riser with the toe of first one boot and then the other. Inside the entryway, his eyes drifted up to his right. It was a reflex, one he wanted to delete. He wished he could smear his neck with Wite-out and, poof, his head would never automatically tilt upward when he approached his apartment door.

He sighed. It was still there, the cluster of little holes in the Sheetrock where the ceiling met the two walls at the corner.

It wasn't his fault. Something must have been wrong with the gun. He'd set it down as he always had, butt down, muzzle up. But that afternoon, months ago, milliseconds after the stock struck the floor . . . GA-BOOM! And a scatter pattern formed on the ceiling. One of these days he'd put in a service order to spackle over the holes, but then he'd have to explain to Biff from maintenance what happened.

Neither of the Jetterses had mentioned the holes in the ceiling to him. Maybe they hadn't noticed. It was on his side of the entryway, after all. He sighed again. Everybody made mistakes.

As he reached for the doorknob to his apartment, he glanced to his left. Then he stopped and took a longer look. Two pairs of little overalls were clipped by safety pins to the chicken wire that surrounded the furnace. Jennifer Jetters would have done that. Probably she didn't want to put them in the drier because the buckles made such a holy racket during the spin cycle. Fabric near the furnace must be a fire hazard. He'd have to check the handbook. Surely, Safety had a rule about that.

The door swung into his kitchen, and the beads on the dream catcher, which he had nailed to the wooden door, rattled. He liked that sound. It reminded him of his grandmother. When he was a little boy back on the Rosebud, she used to tell him Lakota tales, including the one about the spider who wove the first dream catcher. As he wove, the spider explained the forces, both good and bad, that came with each time of life. Spider said the good forces—ideas and visions and goals—would be caught in the web for his use, and the bad ones would disappear through the holes. When his grandmother spoke for the spider, she used a high-pitched, whispery voice that made little Leonard giggle.

He particularly liked the feathers that swung from the bottom of the dreamcatcher's willow ring. Those feathers, from the tail of an eagle, swept away the bad forces that had fallen through the web. He had been very proud when his grandmother gave it to him. She wanted good luck to always come his way.

Inside his apartment, he hung his parka on the back of a kitchen chair. The thought of the little overalls and his neighbor Jennifer brought back the thought of Stephen Steinberg and that woman who lived with him. The two women looked alike: long, straight, brown hair and bodies as skinny as an oar.

Steinberg. Those doctors were so high-minded, and Steinberg was the worst. They acted as if they ruled the world. Indian Health Service doctors were all like that, even those back on the Rosebud where his grandmother lived. He felt the wave of rage rise inside him. He needed to put it down before it ate him up. He opened the cupboard door and reached for supper.

No matter what, he was right about the problem. Co-habitation without marriage was a sin, and he couldn't allow sinful behavior on hospital property. Asking for proof of Stephen's marriage was the best thing to do. In fact, Leonard had been pretty pleased with himself for thinking that up. But, the doctors had ganged up on him, and they had all refused to produce their licenses of marriage. Even his appeals to the wives (if they were really wives) hadn't worked. Now what?

By the time he had warmed up two cans of turkey noodle soup for supper, his mind had moved from Steinberg to sin to the days of his youth. The Rosebud was a rough reservation: achingly poor, alcohol-soaked, government-warped, barren as only the South Dakota prairie could be. As far back as he could remember, he'd lived with his grandmother. Ina Yellow Thunder was her name, one of a long line of dignified Yellow Thunders. She dragged him to Mass every Sunday and gave him a rosary for his seventh birthday; what he had really wanted was a bike, but he didn't dare tell her that.

His grandmother used to repeat to him her oft-told stories about his great, great, great grandfather, Sitting Bull, while she patted fry bread dough between her palms. He liked being related to such a strong, important man, but when he told his schoolmates about it, they didn't believe him. Several of the boys boxed his ears and told him to shut up. He never mentioned that to his grandma.

Later, when the priest gave him Teddy Night Pipe's old bike, he saw Father Edwards in a new light. He no longer resisted going to Mass with his grandmother. He listened closely to the homily and took the priest's words to heart. He attended confession every week and admitted to hating the boys who boxed his ears. He promised his grandmother, Father Edwards, and himself that he'd be a good servant to God.

He set the pot of warm soup on the kitchen table and sat on the chair with his parka. At the other end of the table was his current jigsaw puzzle. This one was hard—a 1000-piece kind—and one of his favorites. The picture, a field of daisies, reminded him of the wide-open prairie of the Rosebud. He'd loved puzzles ever since he'd gotten his first one when he was in third grade. It was in the box of toys sent by the Lutheran charities. Even though it had come from the Lutherans, he still liked that first puzzle, with its picture of a parrot and a palm tree. Now, he was almost half finished with the daisy one and would work on it after supper.

He dipped the stirring spoon into his soup. A descendant of Sitting Bull should be able to force Steinberg and his slutty girlfriend out of IHS property. That, after all, was the job of the service unit director: enforce the rules and keep the place moral. He was strongly committed to his job.

But what was IHS's commitment to him? He blew on the spoonful of soup to cool it. What had they done for Leonard Kills Squirrels? Demoted him, that's what. He'd been a good service unit director back at the Turtle Lake reservation, but then he had been "reassigned" to Bethel. Freezing cold, desolate, dark, dinky Bethel. Turtle Lake wasn't paradise, but at least he could drive over the border to Boissevain, Manitoba, for a change of scenery. Nowhere to go from Bethel.

Two dogs were fighting beneath his kitchen window. Damn noisy animals. He didn't recognize them. Not the Jetters's, not Steinberg's. Why couldn't people keep their pets chained up? The hospital needed a fence to keep out the curs from town that sometimes wandered into the compound and dug through the garbage cans. The IHS had a rule about unattended pets, but Biff and the boys had better things to do than chase away stray dogs. He couldn't figure out a way to enforce a dog rule, other than lacing a raw round steak with gopher bait and leaving in on the road. Gopher bait would do it. It had worked on the Rosebud Reservation, it could work here. He'd have to think about that.

His soup was now cool enough to eat without blowing on it. He shoveled a spoonful into his mouth. He heard Jennifer and her boys rattling in the entryway. They must have just come home from somewhere. She too had refused to show him her marriage license and then was smarty-mouthed about it. There must be a way.

He chewed a piece of tough turkey then a carrot coin. He took a drink from his water glass and set it on the circle in the table-top. He repositioned the glass until its bottom fit perfectly over the mark in the maple, a left-over from a sweaty Coke can. He wrestled the beaded slide on his bolo tie. A new idea rolled around in his head. He finished his soup and dropped the saucepan into the sink. He walked across the entryway and banged on the Jetters's door.

Jennifer opend it. "Yes?" Her voice was cold as an ice cube.

"I see you wear a wedding ring." He pointed to her left hand. "That must be evidence that you and John are married. Right?"

"Wrong." She splayed her fingers, looked at the gold band, and gave it a spin. "That ring was my grandmother's. She gave it to me when I graduated from college."

Back in his apartment, Leonard slammed the soapy sponge against the sides of the soup-stained saucepan. Those white-guy doctors and their wives were royal pains in the butt. He was just trying to do his job.

Chapter 9

DEIDRE WANTED A BIRTHDAY PARTY. FOR herself. Alaska was sinking into the dark and frigid winter, and she missed the light and the warmth of her friends back in New York. The walls of their trailer had become too familiar. She was about to turn thirty, was a new mother, and needed a celebration.

Over dinner, David told her about one of his patients, a technician from the White Alice station. "That guy cut his thumb wide open on a dirty old hunk of equipment," he said as he shoveled boiled salmon into his mouth. "He was a pretty tough fellow." He swallowed another bite of fish. "He watched the whole time as I sutured him up."

"What's a White Alice station?" Deidre asked.

"I wondered the same thing. The guy said it's an AC&W site." David took a gulp of his water.

Deidre glared at her husband. This was his one irritating habit—dragging stories out too long. "Okay. So what is that?"

"The guy with the cut thumb told me they call it the Agonizingly Cold and Windy site, but it really means Aircraft Control and Warning."

Deidre shook her head. She didn't know what any of that meant. "Just answer my questions, please."

Her husband gave her a funny look, one that said she needed to try harder. "Well, it's a communications network that relays radio signals from station to station to guide military planes over this God-forsaken land," David explained. "It's out past the airport, in the direction of Nunapitchuk."

"Nunapitchuk. That's where those Eskimo men were found dead at fish camp, isn't it?" she asked.

"That's right."

"Do you think one of those workmen killed them?"

"I don't know, but I'd say that's pretty darn unlikely. Why would they do that? Besides, Nunapitchuk is a long hike—a very long hike—over the tundra from the White Alice." He took a deep breath and continued. "Anyway, I needed to distract my patient while I sutured, so I encouraged him to keep talking. He did a lot of complaining: hardest duty assignment anywhere, bad food in the dining hall, lumpy beds in the berthing quarters, radar antennae that constantly needed repair in the worst possible weather."

Deidre sighed and finished her portion of supper, Chef Boyardee spaghetti.

DEIDRE CONTINUED TO LONG FOR A birthday party—the thirtieth was a landmark event, after all—with good meat, real rolls, fresh vegetables, and flaming candles on top of a cake. Her mother had always made a big deal of birthdays. "It's a special day for a special person," she used to tell her daughter, and then serve her favorite supper: brisket, sweet noodle kugel, potato latkes, and apple cake. Bethel had, of course, no cafes, no restaurants, no bars, no ballrooms, *nowhere* for a celebration. She couldn't get David's words, *the White Alice dining hall,* out of her head but couldn't figure out what to do with them either.

Nevertheless, she spent her days dreaming about a party. She'd wear her dressiest dress, find a new little outfit for baby Daniel, and make a fancy ribbon for her unruly hair. She'd invite her Alaska friends: the Maldonados, the Jetterses, Stephen Steinberg, and George the OB. The more she thought about it, the more expansive her plans became—real invitations, tall tapers, sparkly party hats.

Finally, she decided to make it into a party for everyone who had a birthday in 1971.

"That's the entire hospital staff," David said. "In fact, it's everyone living in Bethel, and in Alaska."

"Well," she said. "Let's limit it to our friends. We can all celebrate a year of birthdays together."

It came to her in a dream. A party for every one of her hometown friends held in the ROTC training building at her college, guarded by soldiers and three huge cannons.

"I know where we can have the party," she told David over breakfast.

"What party?"

He was so thick some times. "The birthday party."

"Where?"

"That dining hall at the White Agatha, or Adelle, or Alma, or whatever it was called."

"Uh . . . the White Alice station? I don't know if that's possible."

"It might be. Worth a try."

David made a few inquiries. His patient with the stitched-up thumb put him in contact with the evening manager. Later that night, David described the unpleasant conversation in detail to Deidre. "He said, 'Let me get this straight. You want to throw a party in our dining room? Are you crazy? This is a secure, federal surveillance facility, not the Kuskokwim Regional Dance Hall.'"

"I told the manager I'd like to speak with his supervisor." David smiled. "I said 'please.'"

Deidre nodded. "Please is good."

The operations director had heard him out. "Then he said to me, 'The answer is simple. No.'"

David grew increasingly animated as he replayed it for Deidre. "I told him, 'We're tax-payers, you know. And as doctors at the Native Alaska Hospital and officers in the Public Health Service, we're, technically, federal employees.' I really let him have it. But he was unmoved, stiff as the proverbial old oak board. He said 'I don't care if you're the angel Gabriel and his cherubic buddies, the answer is no.'"

The White Alice station was out of the question. Deidre began to consider alternatives. Their trailer? Way too small. The hospital dining area? Too small, smelled of medicine, and was under the control of Leonard Kills Squirrels. She certainly didn't want him at her party. Finally, she flashed David a frown and said, "There must be a way."

"Well, I can't think of one."

A WEEK LATER, AGAIN OVER DINNER, DAVID mentioned that the White Alice technician had returned to the clinic for a recheck of his repaired thumb and for a doctor's signature on his return-to-work form. "This time, the commander of the White Alice accompanied him."

David explained how he'd unwrapped the dressings and examined the wound. "It looked pretty good," he said. "No bleeding, no evidence of infection, edges nicely approximated. I opened a suture removal kit, and as I snipped free one of the stitches, I told the commander we'd been unable to get permission to host your birthday party at the White Alice dining hall."

Deidre settled into her chair, ready for another of David's endless stories.

"The commander pursed his lips when he told me, 'That's a very unconventional request.'" David said, "I snipped free another stitch and told him I understood that, but it'd mean a lot to me and my wife and the entire hospital medical staff.

"Then I snipped the last stitch. I bent the technician's thumb in all directions and said, 'In order to permit you to return to work, I need to understand what, exactly, you do with your hands in the conduct of your duties.'

"The technician explained his work with the equipment while the commander listened," David continued. "When the commander handed me the return-to-work form, I laid it on the table and held my pen above it. That pen hovered over the paper like a sneering vulture, but the ink didn't touch it."

Deidre leaned forward, eager to hear what came next. "And . . .?"

"The commander seemed kind of twitchy. Finally, he said, 'Dr. Dorfman, I just remembered a provision in our policies that would allow a gathering of other federal employees and their spouses at our installation.'

"I told him, 'Great' and then explained what a rough delivery you'd had when Daniel was born, lowered my pen to the document, and signed my name."

Deidre clapped. She had such a clever husband.

"He'll rent the dining hall to us for one night. The fee is $1.00," David said, "and he'll have the cook prepare a meal, for $5.00 a head." Then he added, "He'll even sneak in a couple bottles of wine."

"Wine? How will he swing that?" Deidre asked. "Bethel is dry."

"The White Alice is way beyond the city limits," David said.

"Does Bethel *have* city limits?" Deidre asked. There certainly were no fences or signs to indicate what was town and what was open tundra.

"Maybe not. But as a federal facility, the White Alice is probably exempt from village laws. Whatever. We'll have wine."

If she had an excitement meter, it would have registered VERY HIGH. *Such a luxury*, she thought. Dinner out. With wine. With her friends.

SHE BEGAN TO PLAN THE PARTY in earnest. She needed invitations. With gusto, she dressed Daniel in a lipstick-red sleeper, slid him into Marcus's old baby-snowsuit that Mera had loaned her, and wrapped him in his elephant-print flannel blanket. They headed to the gift shop at the hospital to see if they carried anything she could use as party invitations.

When Deidre walked into the gift shop, Virginia Tom was leaning on the counter and smiling.

"Do you have any invitation cards? For a birthday party?"

"Invitation cards?" Virginia's face looked blank. "What's that?"

"Cards with a picture of a birthday cake or a wrapped present or something like that on the front. Inside it says 'you are invited to a party.' There are spaces to fill in the time and place." *Surely, everyone knows what party invitation cards are,* Deidre thought.

Virginia slowly shook her head, and her smile turned into a frown. "I guess we don't have those," she said.

As she started to leave the shop, Deidre spotted an unusual object hanging on the wall beside the door. It looked like a giant scoop made from the skin of a tree. "What's that thing?" she asked.

"A baby basket."

"A . . . baby . . . basket," Deidre repeated. "I've never seen anything like that."

Virginia unhooked it from the wall and handed it to Deidre. "You use it to carry your baby."

It was interesting. Quirky. Beautiful in a rugged, natural way. Deidre turned it over, ran her hand over its papery surface.

"Dorothy Alexander, up in Shageluk, made it," Virginia said. "They use birch bark for baskets way upriver where she lives." She thought a moment, then continued. "Dorothy is a good basket maker. She's a Athabaskan lady. See how she sewed the bark? Her stitches are perfectly even." She rubbed her pointer finger over the thin strips of willow that anchored the birch bark to the frame of willow branches.

"How much is it?"

"Seventy dollars. It's a very good baby basket."

Deidre didn't know if that was a fair price or not. But the more she looked at it, the more she liked it. Daniel needed one. "I'll buy it," she said.

Virginia took the basket from Deidre and stroked its birch bark lovingly. "Do you know how to put your baby in it?"

Deidre shook her head. She'd never seen one, let alone one used by a baby. Virginia then stretched out her arms. "Give him here," she said. She laid Daniel on the counter and removed him from the snowsuit. She set his legs on either side of the beaded, rawhide panel, pushed his bottom into the birch bark scoop, and placed his arms above the leather straps. "He'll be real cozy in there," Virginia said.

Deidre still needed invitations. When she returned home, she found a package of ivory paper in their desk. She cut several sheets in half, folded each half in half, and drew a slobbery-looking birthday cake on the front. She put blobs of bright colors on the frosting and drew candles—many flaming candles—on top. Inside, she wrote the details of the party in fancy script. The next day, she talked the mail room lady into slipping an invitation into each of the clinical staff's boxes.

DANIEL, DRESSED IN A BLACK AND white sleeper with a little red bow tie—a gift from his paternal grandmother—was ready for the party. Deidre tied him into his birch bark basket and set him on the kitchen table. She liked the smell of the smoky rawhide fastenings; they were as buttery as chamois. A Jewish baby in an Athabascan basket, she thought and then cooed to her son. "Daniel, you are definitely a man of the world."

A gray cloud passed over the sun beyond the kitchen window. A similar gray cloud passed over her mind. He wouldn't fit in the baby basket forever, maybe for only several more months. She could already see that he was growing like kudzu. And he'd keep growing. She treasured his babyhood more than she could have imagined. She had considered leaving him with Virginia Tom during the birthday party—Mrs. Tom was watching Marcus Maldonado and the Jetters twins—but, in the end, she just couldn't do it. She didn't want to abandon him for a minute, let alone several hours and certainly not during her big party.

STEPHEN AGREED TO DRIVE THE DORFMANS and the Jetterses out to the White Alice station for the party. John, Jennifer, and David, with a cardboard box on his lap, squeezed into the back of the Jeep while Deidre and Daniel, nestled in his birch bark basket covered with a wool shawl, sat beside Stephen. He drove out toward the airport and then took an icy side trail that Deidre hadn't noticed before. The ride was bumpy. Very bumpy.

"You and Daniel okay?" David called from the back seat.

"Yeah, we're fine," Deidre called back. Her bottom, still sore from the repaired fourth-degree tear after Daniel's birth, throbbed with each bounce of the Jeep, but it'd be over soon.

After about twenty minutes, the trail took a sharp turn to the right, and after ten more minutes, Deidre saw several huge, strange structures looming above the tundra far ahead. They looked like gigantic outdoor movie screens facing different directions. "What's that?" she asked.

John said, "Beats me."

Stephen said, "I think it's part of the White Alice station."

David said, "They must be the radio relay antennae that the guy with the cut-up thumb talked about."

When Stephen pulled to a stop in front of a Quonset hut covered with rusty corrugated metal, he announced, "Here we are at Chez White Alice. Allow me to help you out." He opened the door beside Deidre and held Daniel while she climbed slowly out of the Jeep. He then pushed the front seat forward and held the box from David's lap while he crawled out.

Inside the Quonset hut, Deidre balanced Daniel and his baby basket on the seat of one of the folding chairs and told David to set the carton on another of the chairs. She pulled a dozen candles from the box, sank one into each of the paper cups-filled-with-sand she had brought along, and arranged them on the tables. Then over each water glass she placed a cone-hat she had made from peach-colored poster board decorated with blue glitter. She'd tried to write Happy Birthday with the glitter on the cone hats, but they had turned into sparkly, azure blobs. She decided that the abstract splotches looked nice, kind of like a Clyfford Still painting.

The commander appeared with a cigarette lighter and lit the candles. Deidre smiled at him. She'd completely forgotten to bring matches. She eyed her table decorations. They were beautiful, even better than she'd expected.

She glanced around the room. John and Jennifer, who was dressed in a slinky, black satin dress, were sipping their wine while they talked with Matias and Mera, who wore a pretty, beaded woolen caftan that covered her expanding, gravid mid-section. Deidre had never seen either of those women dressed in anything other than pants and kuspuks or baggy shirts. The men all wore corduroy jackets or sweaters, and she, herself, wore a long cotton gown, which was really a lounging robe. She'd wanted to wear her dressiest dress, but couldn't get it zippered around her still bulging baby-belly. In her hair she wore the fancy black bow she'd made by ripping up an old silk slip.

She was pleased that everyone had dressed up, at least a little bit. She wanted this to be a festive night. She spotted Stephen waving his arms as he chatted with George the OB. The two dentists and two pharmacists with spouses soon arrived too.

Despite the industrial concrete floor and the steel girders overhead, Deidre thought the dining hall was lovely. David handed her a glass of white wine. She'd had no alcohol since before she learned she was pregnant with Daniel. She took a sip. It had a flinty tang and a gentle buzz; it tasted very good. Then she pulled her donut-cushion from the carton and set it on her chair. Her bottom was almost healed. This was an insurance policy so she could enjoy the evening.

When the cook signaled it was time to eat, Deidre led the way to the steam table and heaped stewed chicken, boiled peas, scalloped potatoes, and grated-carrots-in-green-Jell-O salad on her plate. A large, metal mixing bowl overflowed with dinner rolls, not pilot bread, not stale Holsum, but warm yeasty buttered-on-top rolls. David was behind her in line and said, "This's like hot lunch in junior high. I don't know why that guy with the cut thumb complained so much about the food here."

"Shush," she giggled. "It's wonderful. Best birthday party ever."

As she finished eating, Daniel began to fuss. He must be hungry. She carried him to the corner of the dining hall, sat in one of the extra folding chairs, and began to nurse her baby. After several minutes, he quit suckling and began to wail. She burped him, then rocked him back and forth. He started to wail again. She stood up and swayed side to side. He still hollered.

Usually Daniel was placid but curious. He took after his father in that way. She didn't know what was bothering him now. She brushed the top of his head with a kiss. He continued to cry.

From the corner of her eye, she thought she saw fire. Daniel's body jerked as she whipped around. The commander carried a tray with a sheet cake, chocolate frosting, and a whole box of spiral-striped birthday candles aflame on top. He set it at the end of the steam table. Stephen rose to his feet, lifted his wine glass, and began singing "Happy birthday to us . . ." over Daniel's cries. Deidre leaned over and kissed him again on his soft, warm forehead. *Best birthday, indeed,* she thought. *But what's wrong with this child?*

Mera was singing the end of the Happy Birthday song as she moved to Deirdre's side. "Let me take him," Mera said. "He's probably overwhelmed. You blow out your candles and eat a piece of cake while I deal with Daniel. Save me a piece, please."

Mera and the baby disappeared into the front entry of the dining hall and closed the door. Deidre couldn't hear him anymore and headed to the dessert table. Had Mera figured out how to settle him, or did the heavy wooden door block the noise?

It didn't matter. The baby was quiet and safe. Deidre took a deep breath and blew into the inferno on top of the cake. About a third of the candles flickered and went dark. The rest continued to blaze to the cheers of her friends.

IT WASN'T LATE WHEN STEPHEN DROVE them back to the hospital compound from the party at the White Alice, but Deidre was tired. It was from all the excitement she guessed. John and Jennifer invited them to their place for one last glass of wine, and David immediately accepted. Deidre looked at him, trying to signal her fatigue. His eyes sparkled; he wasn't finished partying. She sighed. David was having a very good time and didn't want it to end.

Stephen declined the invitation. "I'm heading to Aniak tomorrow and need to get up early to check on the plane." Deidre guessed the trip to Aniak was an excuse and that the real reason had something to do with Jackie; the beautiful but secretive social worker still lived at his apartment on mysterious terms that Deidre didn't understand. She hadn't dared ask him about Jackie. He'd talk about it if, and when, he was ready.

David held sleeping Daniel in his birch bark baby basket while Deidre climbed out of the Jeep. As her feet hit the ground, she saw a yellow, dancing glow from beyond the edge of the Jetters's fourplex. A moment later, Virginia Tom, waving a flashlight, rounded the corner.

Jennifer crawled out of the backseat of the Jeep and called, "What's up, Mrs. Tom?"

While wide-eyed Virginia shrugged, Brian and Jeff, dressed in their snowsuits, waddled around the end of the fourplex. Marcus followed immediately behind them. They stopped at the bottom of the steps, beneath three decaying jack-o-lanterns that sagged on the rail of the landing.

"Mommy," Jeff called. "Ginger ran away."

Jennifer gasped.

"How the hell did she get out of the house?" John called.

"She's a runner," Jennifer explained to Deidre and David. "That's why we don't let her out on her own. She's only off a leash when John takes her hunting."

During the next ten minutes, John and Jennifer tried to get the story of Ginger's escape. From the reports of horrified Virginia and the three little boys, they patched together the most likely account of what had happened. One of the kids, maybe Jeff, had come up with the idea that Ginger needed to go for a walk. They'd forgotten to snap the leash onto her collar, and when they opened the door, Ginger had bolted out into the night.

"When did she leave?" John asked.

"A while ago," Virginia said. Her mouth drooped and her eyes were dull.

Virginia isn't good with time, Deidre thought. The Yup'ik generally weren't.

"Which direction did she head?" John asked. He didn't seem mad, just exasperated.

Virginia shrugged. "I'm sorry."

When Jennifer held out the payment for babysitting, Virginia reluctantly opened her palm and twisted her face with a question.

"Take it, Mrs. Tom," Jennifer said. "It isn't your fault Ginger escaped."

As Virginia trudged out the door, Mera walked in. She looked from face to face. "What happened?" she asked. John explained. "So, Marcus was in on that?" Mera asked.

"Very likely he was a follower," Jennifer said. "But we're not assigning blame here. It was a misfortune."

Mera led her son out the door and promised to send Matias to help search for the dog.

Deidre stayed in Jennifer's apartment with Daniel and the twins while the rest of the adults wandered the hospital compound, calling for Ginger. She helped the boys into their pajamas. "I miss my Ginger," Jeff said. "I want to stay up 'til she comes home."

"Me too," Brian said, stifling a sob.

"Ginger wants you to get some sleep," Deidre said. After several rounds of discussion, the twins finally crawled onto their beds.

Deidre could hear the calls in the distance from all directions. Over and over. "Ginger." "G I N G E R." She leaned her head against the back of the couch and closed her eyes.

When she woke up, everyone was back from the search. No dog. Jennifer sank down on the couch beside her.

"You know, there's nothing to stop that animal between here and the North Pole. Or the Bering Sea or the base of the Aleutian Peninsula," Jennifer said. "In fact, Ginger could walk across the frozen river and go all the way east to Hudson Bay."

Deidre nodded. It was a sobering truth. The thought of Ginger, ragged with cold and hunger, stumbling across the desolate tundra turned her stomach.

"She's such a good dog. Just last night she lay right here . . ." Jennifer pointed to the floor at her feet. ". . . and I watched her breathing while she slept. Up and down. Up and down. Her chest moved so gently. Quietly. , almost like a baby. Each breath sounded like . . . ah . . ." She paused. "Like water running over a smooth rock. And then she'd sigh, a great big, solemn canine sigh as if to say, 'Life is so tedious.'"

Deidre reached for Jennifer's shoulder and gave it a pat. "How old is she?" she asked.

"Ah . . . six or seven. We got her as a tiny puppy from the dog pound. She was very patient with the boys, and they were devoted to her. Every kid needs a pet, and Ginger was perfect for my twins." Jennifer wiped her eyes. "Sometimes Ginger got the hiccups, and the boys thought that was so funny. Her body would jerk and jerk again, over and over."

Deidre patted Jennifer's shoulder once more. Her weeping friend had spoken of the dog in the past tense. She'd already written Ginger off. Easy to do when the night was so cold and the tundra so vast.

Jennifer stood up. "You and David can go home and get some sleep. Thanks for helping with the search." She paused and then added, "And thanks for the wonderful party."

The next day, Sunday, the Dorfmans, the Jetterses, and the Maldonados again spread out over the hospital compound and called for Ginger. They asked everyone they met if they'd seen a penny-colored, overly friendly, golden retriever. They wandered past the maintenance buildings, around the entire hospital perimeter, between the trailers where the Dorfmans lived. Nothing.

By the third day, Deidre knew the dog was gone, permanently. Maybe someone had stolen her; maybe she'd died like those guys from Nunapitchuk that her husband had told her about. He thought they might have been poisoned. Maybe she'd gotten into stuff that poisoned people, like Drano, but there would be no Drano at fish camp because there were no drains. Maybe rubbing alcohol. Or Pine-Sol. The thought of Ginger lying dead on the frozen tundra scratched at Deidre. Even if that hadn't happened, it was cold out there, and the dog would have nothing to eat.

DEIDRE SAT AT THE JETTERS'S KITCHEN table and watched Jennifer wash Ginger's food and water bowls and set them on the highest shelf in the cupboard. Jennifer, indeed, had given up on finding Ginger alive. *Was her resignation premature?* Deidre wondered. Poor Jennifer. She was having trouble adapting to Alaska and worried so much about her flagging career as a microbiologist. And now a lost pet?

The twins still asked about their dog constantly. How long should they keep up hope? Deidre didn't know. Outside, snowflakes flew sideways and the empty swings in the playground danced in the wind as if they were convulsing. Poor Ginger. Freezing to death must be a terrible way to go, even for a dog.

CHAPTER 10

As Stephen stepped out of the mail plane onto the iced-over Yukon River at Aniak, he zipped the front of his hunting jacket and donned his gloves. He shielded his eyes against the sun with his hand and surveyed the unpainted wooden houses tucked into an oxbow of the river. "Do you know where the school is?" he asked the pilot. "I'm supposed to meet a guy there. His name is Lincoln Egoak."

"Don't know him." The pilot unloaded Stephen's gear from the back of the plane. "Does he work at the school?"

"I don't think so. He's going to show me how to hunt caribou."

The pilot bobbed his head, and a soft grin of approval mixed with understanding and a tinge of envy erupted on his face. "School's up that road to the left."

Stephen thanked him, hooked his pack over his shoulder, picked up his snowshoes and rifle, and started up the hill. He'd never met Lincoln Egoak, but one of the nurses' aides at the hospital said he was among the best hunters in the area. "They eat more caribou at his house than any other family in Alaska," she'd said. Lincoln was also her uncle, so she had arranged for him to take Stephen on a hunting expedition.

Stephen had never been to Aniak, but it felt very familiar, the same as every other native village he'd visited. As he walked past oil tanks, some atilt on spindly iron legs and beside weathered wooden houses wedged into snowbanks, he watched the ribbons of smoke as they drifted southward from each chimney. He stepped warily on the buckled boardwalk that snaked through the settlement. The out-buildings were topped with slanted roofs, presumably, he figured, to allow snow to slide off more easily. Snowmobiles, some broken, some seemingly intact, were parked helter-skelter. Sheds of every shape and size, all gnarly, dotted the terrain. He'd seen those elements of native villages many times before and admired their honesty.

Halfway up the hill, the United States flag waved from the top of what must have been the school. Out front, a sled was tied behind a snowmobile, and a man stood on the porch. Stephen waved. The man waved back. It was likely Lincoln; he must have heard the mail plane land.

They loaded Stephen's gear onto the sled, and Lincoln reviewed the plan. Once they arrived at a likely grazing area, they'd pick up a caribou trail in the snow and follow it to the animals. He went over gun safety and checked to be sure Stephen had a warm sleeping bag, a foam mat, and the right ammunition. "I've got food and the tent," Lincoln said. They would be out overnight. "My cousin says there's a small herd over by Windy Lake. We'll try for that one."

Stephen rode, seated, on the sled, with his back against the gear, his legs out straight ahead of him. The snowmobile was loud, and its gassy exhaust hit Stephen squarely in the face. He wasn't used to the noise and the stink. He preferred the quiet and the clean-scented air of ptarmigan hunting, but on this trip, they would cover too much territory to go by foot. The wind blew his hair into his eyes; he stuffed it under his cap. The sky was now overcast, the sun a mere orange glow behind the clouds. Acre upon acre of snow-covered tundra sped by.

They drove into the taiga and wound between the spruce trees. Snow-laden branches slapped against Stephen's head; he grabbed his cap with his gloved hand. He glanced upward. The trees there were so close together that they blocked out much of the sun. Lincoln steered the snowmobile with all the confidence of a master hunter. He obviously knew where he was going in spite of the total absence of landmarks. Mid-day was turning into afternoon.

They sped deeper into the spruce forest and scared a pair of indignant red squirrels that chattered their reaction to the interruption. He heard the raspy voice of a raven and spotted the jet-black bird swaying like an acrobat at the very top of an evergreen. The air was clear as glass, and Stephen could feel the beauty of the place down to his fingertips.

The engine began to cough. Stephen tried to look at it but Lincoln, seated astride the machine, blocked his view. Then, it began to sputter. The snowmobile started to buck. It slowed to a crawl and then stopped with a jerk, sending the sled into its rear end with a WHOMP. Stephen leaped to the frozen ground. "What happened?"

Lincoln turned toward him. "Motor trouble."

"Oh, God," Stephen said under his breath. They were in the middle of absolutely nowhere, at least six hours from where they had started. They had seen no evidence of people anywhere along the way.

Lincoln knelt beside the machine's left ski, loosened several screws from the engine's cover, and set them, one by one, in the snow beside him. They dropped beneath the surface. He lifted off the cover and set it beside the buried screws.

Stephen watched as Lincoln worked. How would he ever find those screws again? Even if he did, how would he tell which went where? What if he couldn't get the snowmobile going again? The cold would keep their flesh from rotting during the winter, but the local wolves would have a feast. No one would find them until their bones emerged from the melting snow next spring. Only dumb luck would send a passing hunter across their corpses.

A pang of panic shot through his belly. Who would notify his parents of his disappearance and likely death? Jackie—sweet, innocent, social-worker-do-gooder Jackie—didn't know anything about his family and certainly would have no idea how to contact them. No one in Bethel would know how to reach his ex-wife. When Sandra left, she just blew out of town like a raging storm, without ever looking back. Slowly, methodically, Lincoln continued to unscrew engine parts and set the screws and pieces of hot metal in the snow. Stephen wondered if they would starve first or freeze first.

Finally, Lincoln pulled a short rubber hose out of the engine compartment and blew through its hole. He blew again, held it up to his right eye, and stuck it back down in the compartment. "Plugged fuel line," he said. He reached down into one of the snow holes for a screw, then reached for a half-buried part and hooked it back to the engine. Over and over, he reached into the snow for screws and parts and reinserted them.

Lincoln rose to his feet. "All done."

"God damn," Stephen said. "That's amazing."

"Let's go," Lincoln said as he climbed aboard the snowmobile. The engine roared to life, and they were off.

Shortly, they emerged from the spruce trees and drove through a stand of alders whose now leafless branches reached toward the sky like a flock of skeletal hands. Lincoln slowed the engine, stood up on the snowmobile, turned toward Stephen and shouted, "There's Skag Lake." He pointed toward a large patch of blue-white near the horizon.

Nearer the lake, he slowed the snowmobile to a crawl and stared at the ground. After about ten minutes, he said, "Caribou trail." Indeed, a trampled path in the snow led across the open tundra and disappeared into the alders in the distance. Lincoln idled the engine and stepped down to the ground. He leaned over and then stood up with something in his hand. "Caribou shit," he said, thrusting his open palm toward Stephen. "Less than a day old."

Stephen stared at Lincoln's glove. The seven or eight dark brown pellets looked like acorns resting in a leather nest.

For the rest of the afternoon they followed the trail, into the taiga and out again. Up low hills, down shallow valleys. When it was too dark to see, they made camp in the shelter of a spruce forest. Stephen stared at the outlines of the trees against the deeply purple sky. Their tall, majestic spires stretched upward like rockets aimed at the heavens.

Stephen unfolded his foam mat and sleeping bag on the floor of the tent while Lincoln lit a candle with his BIC cigarette lighter and set it in a battered coffee can. "Heat for the night," he said. He snapped open a Tupperware container and showed Stephen the slab of pink flesh inside. "Gussuks like this better," he said. "Cooked salmon."

"What'll you eat?"

"Sheefish." Lincoln pulled a frozen, raw fish from his pack. He leaned out the door of the tent and laid the fish in the snow, hacked it with his ax—the same ax he had used on the permafrost to anchor the tent—and, returning inside the tent, held up a slice.

"Is there enough for me to try?" Stephen appreciated his guide's attempt to cater to gussuk taste, but he wanted to try the native food. Lincoln passed him a sheefish steak.

Stephen stared at his slice of fish and wondered what he should do with the guts that clung to the frozen flesh. He watched as Lincoln's fingers shoveled sheefish entrails into his mouth. Stephen did the same. The warmth of his tongue melted the delicate frozen innards into a slushy mass. He expected it to taste fishy and to feel slimy. It didn't. It tasted like the walleye he'd caught in the Delaware River back in Philly. He liked it, and when Lincoln offered a second steak, he accepted.

"My niece Cindy. Is she a good nurse?" Lincoln asked.

Cindy was the nurses' aide who'd arranged the hunting trip. "Oh, yes. She's terrific. The patients really appreciate everything she does for them."

"Good. We're proud of her."

Lincoln continued to ask questions. How did Stephen like Alaska? Was doctoring at the hospital hard work? Stephen replied that he had grown to love Alaska, with its wide-open spaces, the magic of the wild, the challenges of the unknown, and its generous people. Yes, some days doctoring was hard, but it was always important. And meaningful.

Stephen also asked questions. Where did Lincoln grow up? The answer was Aniak. Did he think they'd find the caribou herd? The answer was "sure." Finally Stephen said, "This may seem like a strange thing to mention, but why would two guys die together at fish camp?" It just didn't make sense. Stephen thought things like life and death should fit into a logical pattern.

Lincoln shook his head. "Dunno. Some people think Luther murdered his brother and then killed himself." He pushed another piece of sheefish into his mouth and, with downcast eyes, began to rearrange the meal gear on the tent's floor.

Stephen wanted more information than that, but Lincoln clearly didn't want to talk about it. To the docs in Bethel, those unexplained deaths were bothersome, but the native people seemed to accept them as due course. Maybe the Eskimos considered those fatalities to be a tiny arc in the circle of nature and as belonging to the natives alone. They likely had their own ways to explain the sudden loss of life at fish camp and weren't interested in letting the judgmental gussuks in on that.

Stephen changed the subject and then learned that Lincoln had recently been elected mayor of Aniak and that he'd never been out of Alaska. "I went down to Juneau once, to meet with the legislature, but never beyond. Maybe someday."

Stephen looked into the wrinkled face of his Yup'ik companion with his wise, Asian eyes and settled mouth. Although they differed in many ways, they had several things in common: both carried big responsibilities, and each had valuable skills. Lincoln could fix a broken snowmobile in the depths of backwoods Alaska, and he, Stephen, could fix broken bodies. And they both liked to hunt.

Soon, all that was left of the sheefish was the skin. Lincoln flicked a spark on his BIC and dangled a scaly coil of fish peel over the flame. "Best part of the meal," he said as the skin caught fire. When it was completely charred—like a burned pork rind—he handed it to Stephen.

It felt greasy and tasted fishy, yet was unexpectedly good. The oily meat and skin of the sheefish had filled him up and would keep him warm—that's what the Native Alaskans said of all their food.

Something cut the quiet of the dark. Stephen cocked his head to hear better. Distant calls of wolves, shrill and insistent, echoed over the hills. *Even night sounds in Alaska are beautiful*, Stephen thought.

They took off their boots and heavy outerwear and, still wearing the rest of their clothes, crawled into their sleeping bags. Soon Lincoln was snoring, and Stephen was gazing at the flickering shadows cast by the candle on the tent's muddy green ceiling. He settled into the joy of coming on this trip, into his appreciation of Cindy for arranging it, and into his immense gratitude to Lincoln for guiding him on the hunt and for saving his life in light of the snow machine's engine failure.

The wolves began howling again. His mind drifted to Sandra, to her inability to tolerate living in Bethel, or to live with him, any longer. For the last year or so, he only thought of her when he was at peace with whatever was going on around him. Her departure had opened huge possibilities for him. And, he realized he had actually begun to act on those possibilities—Soldier the dog, the boat, the hunting guns—before she flew back to Philadelphia. They were definitely part of the reasons for her leaving. That and the night of the intruder.

Stephen had been at the hospital waiting for the x-ray of a guy's injured leg when, at two in the morning, she called on the hospital phone, hysterically screaming something about a strange man walking down the hallway in their apartment. "He's calling for Joe," she shrieked.

"He's probably lost," Stephen said. "I bet he's looking for our Joe." Joe was one of the pharmacists who lived in the next fourplex.

"He's still here, Stephen," she screamed. "Get him out of here."

"I'm at the goddamn hospital, Sandra." He heard the door slam. "He's gone now, right?"

"Yes." Sandra was sobbing so hard he could hardly hear her.

When he returned home, she was still beside herself. "I can't stand living in a place with no locks, where any old drunk can walk into my house in the middle of the night, where I could be attacked, where . . ." He tried to settle her down, told her it was an honest mistake, that all the fourplexes were identical. She would have none of it.

Stephen hadn't intended to chase his wife away, but living in Alaska had changed him and not to her liking. The next day, she started throwing stuff around the kitchen and then left. He wished it could have turned out differently, but that was utterly impossible.

AFTER A BREAKFAST OF MORE FROZEN sheefish, they packed up their sleeping gear and took down the tent. The sun hadn't cleared the horizon yet, but the sky glowed as if it were painted with tangerine juice. Lincoln climbed on the snowmobile and said, "We'll follow the caribou trail again." They roared through the taiga and over the tundra beside the path of trampled snow. Lincoln stopped several times to examine the caribou scat. "Still pretty fresh," he said.

Once again they exited a spruce grove, and straight ahead on the open tundra, they saw the caribou, at least a dozen of them. They all had antlers, and Stephen couldn't tell if they were male or female. Meat from males tended to be tough and, since this was near the end of the breeding season, might taste rutty. Females might be pregnant and that would bother him. But . . . He'd take whatever he got. Several of the animals were pawing at the snow. Somehow, they sensed the lichens and tundra grasses—food—below.

Lincoln stood up on the snowmobile and tested the air for wind direction with his bare hand. Stephen studied the movements of the aspen branches, the way the breeze moved them in sometimes sweeping, sometimes dipping curves. Lincoln started the engine and slowly positioned the sled and snowmobile downwind from the herd.

He then cut the engine and motioned for Stephen to climb off the sled. They strapped on their snowshoes, grabbed their guns, and headed toward the caribou. The only sound was the whistle of the wind past their caps and the crunch of the snow beneath their feet.

When they were in range, Lincoln leaned toward Stephen and whispered in his ear, "Aim for the lungs. Don't blast the meat."

Stephen raised his gun to his shoulder, lined up the sights on a medium-sized animal who stood at the edge of the herd. It was a magnificent, clove-colored beast, thick-bellied with a rack that reached wide like two outstretched boney arms tipped with thick, stiffened fingers. The animal bent its neck and began to browse under the snow.

Stephen fired. At the sound of the shot, the herd bolted and disappeared into the trees, all except his target. That majestic caribou crumpled to its knees and then fell on its side. It made no sound, no cry for help, no scream of pain. Bright red blood from the chest wound splattered on the snowy white ground. Stephen lowered his firearm. The once stately animal was now a heap of unmoving mammalian matter. He could think of it as a tragedy. Or, as a victory. All those hours of practice shooting at empty bleach jugs with Vernon George behind his house at Kwethluk had paid off.

Lincoln slapped him on the shoulder. "Good shot." They snowshoed over to the now dead caribou.

Lincoln pulled his knife from his pack. "We'll take the meat off the bones and leave the skeleton here. No need to haul useless weight back to Aniak." In one clean motion, he slit the carcass from the base of its neck, down its chest and belly to its pelvis.

Stephen spotted the animal's mammary glands; this caribou was a female. With deft slashes of the knife, Lincoln removed the skin from the body and spread it, hair side down, on the snow. He hacked out the tongue, liver, and heart and laid them on the skin. Stephen peered into the animal's pelvic cavity and spied the uterus. It didn't look enlarged, and if she was pregnant, the fetus was only an embryo. A sacrificed embryo—an amorphous collection of cells—was less bothersome to him than a fetal calf killed late in pregnancy.

Lincoln showed Stephen how to scrape the tendons away from the bones with his curved blade and then handed him the knife. In some ways it was like the anatomy lab in medical school. Both carcasses represented dead beings. Both had reached the tail end of the cycle of life. Philosophically, though, it was very different—butchering a newly killed caribou for food wasn't the same as dissecting an already deceased human for educational purposes.

The pile of scraped bones in the snow grew taller and taller as did the heap of meat on the caribou's skin. When they finished, Lincoln tied the skin into a bundle with a piece of rope, and together, they hoisted it onto the back of the sled. "Let's head home," Lincoln said.

HE WAS ALONE FOR DINNER; JACKIE had a meeting at the school. After his meal of canned peas, scalloped potatoes from a box, and caribou roast—the meat was lean but tender and delicate and tasted like mild venison—Stephen took Soldier out for a walk. They headed toward the open tundra on the road along the fourplexes. Lights in all the units were on; everyone had settled for the evening. When he passed Jennifer and John's unit, he thought of the heartbreak inside. He'd heard about it after his return from Aniak; Ginger'd been missing for four days now. Too cold for an indoors dog to last outdoors.

They walked toward town, Stephen on the boardwalk and Soldier zigzagging across the snow-laden tundra. The clouds had drifted east, leaving a full moon whose silver light sparkled off the hoary white terrain. After a week of roaring wind, the air was now calm. He loved winter in Alaska.

Lincoln had insisted that Stephen take home a third of the caribou meat. He had cut it up and packaged it in freezer wrap, and it now rested among the packages of frozen salmon and ptarmigan in the storeroom's freezer. He'd taken two frozen caribou roasts to Cindy in the clinic. "This is your finders' fee," he said. "Thanks so much for organizing the hunt. Lincoln is a great guide and prince of a fellow." Cindy didn't make much money. She appreciated the food.

When he reached Raymond Andrecheck's house, Stephen stared into the shadows. Rather than asleep in their oil barrel houses, most of the dogs were outside, pulling on their chains. Someone was lurking among the animals, stooping then standing, over and over, moving from barrel to barrel. "Raymond?" he called. It was too dark to make out the man's face.

No answer. "Raymond, is that you?" he called again. The man stumbled forward into the beam from the yard light. His parka was ragged around the hem, and his footwear didn't match: on his left foot he wore a rubber Wellington and on the right what looked like a fur-lined woman's snow boot. A cowboy hat was perched on his head.

He finally recognized Edmund Nopoka. Stephen had discharged him from the hospital five mornings ago. The man had been brought to the Emergency Room too drunk to walk and had spent the night on the ward sleeping it off. Now Edmund, again, was staggering. "Hi Doc," he slurred.

"What are you doing out here with Raymond's dogs?"

"Looking for . . . my . . . house key."

Stephen was sure Edmund didn't own a house key; no one else in Bethel did. He wasn't even sure he had a house. If he had to guess, he'd think Edmund lived in one of those abandoned shipping containers down by the river.

"Good luck with that," Stephen said and walked on. Poor Edmund.

At Swanson's, he tied Soldier to one of the newel posts, climbed the stairs, and went inside. He needed a jar of mustard—he'd decided caribou sandwiches would benefit from Dijon mustard; the boring, bright yellow kind, which Sandra had ordered, just wouldn't do.

One last jar of Dijon stood all alone on the shelf. He bought it, along with the last loaf of dark rye bread. A decent caribou sandwich needed good bread rather than that crackery pilot bread.

When they returned to the fourplexes, Soldier bolted ahead of him and, growling, started to dig under one of the units between his and Leonard Kills Squirrels's. "Here, Soldier," Stephen called.

The dog ignored him. Soldier kept growling and digging.

"What are you after?" Stephen headed toward his dog. He stopped. In the quiet of the calm night, he heard something. He held his breath and listened harder. He heard it again. Kind of a whimper. "What the hell . . ."

He walked around the fourplex and on the other side saw a gap in the corrugated steel skirting. He yanked it open and leaned in. Soldier pushed him aside and, barking, ran into the crawl space. The whimpering grew louder.

Stephen walked to his apartment, fetched a flashlight from the junk drawer in his kitchen, and returned to the gap in the skirting. Soldier was still inside, barking in an urgent, high-pitched howl. Stephen stepped through the gap and waved the light up five feet to the flooring joists of the apartment above and then over five feet toward his dog's sound. Soldier stood, trembling, over something on the bare dirt. Stephen drew closer. Finally, he could see that it was a pile of hair—copper colored and streaked with mud. Even closer, he saw four legs, a head, and a tail. "Oh, my God," he said out loud. He took off his glove and felt Ginger's fur. Chilly.

He opened her mouth. It was warmer. He felt her belly—she was breathing. "Good boy, Soldier."

He scooped Ginger into his arms, ducked back out through the gap in the skirting, marched up the steps to Jennifer and John's entryway, and kicked at the bottom of their kitchen door.

It opened. Jennifer looked into the entryway, screamed, and started crying. "She's alive," Stephen said. "Cold, but alive. We need some warm towels."

While Jennifer ran the hot water in the bathtub, John and Stephen crouched over Ginger, who lay sprawled on her side on the living room floor. "Jeff and Brian," John yelled. "Get up."

The twins wandered into the living room and, spotting the dog, started shrieking.

Neither John nor Stephen knew much about veterinary medicine, but they knew how to resuscitate a hypothermic human. They wrapped the dog in the damp, warm towels and dripped tepid beef broth into her mouth with Jennifer's turkey baster. They figured Ginger had taken refuge in the crawl space because it was warm—or at least warmer than outside—from the pipes that ran under the apartments' floors.

Soon the twins, one dressed in a Superman pajama top and Mickey Mouse pajama bottoms and the other in Superman bottoms and a Mickey Mouse top, stretched themselves along either side of Ginger, keeping her warm with their flannel-clad bodies. They jabbered in a language known only to them and sang "Sing a song of six-pence" to their dog.

An hour later, he and Soldier headed home. A sense of peace floated like a film of fine silk over him. Finding the Jetters's dog had squared the equation. One animal dead, another animal alive. It was the mathematical wonder of Mother Nature and her uncanny laws.

CHAPTER 11

"This is Dr. John Jetters at IHS Hospital Bethel signing in. Over."

While he waited for the first radio clinic call, John studied the map that covered the wall behind him. It detailed the entire Bethel Service Unit. Once again, he marveled at the vastness of the land. Thousands of square miles. He started to count the villages but soon quit. There must have been sixty of them, little clusters of people scattered over that enormous landmass of tundra, taiga, rivers, and creeks, and occasionally, mountains. Six inches under it all was rock-hard permafrost.

He stared at the CONTACTS sheet with its curled edges, at the radio license in its dusty frame, at the cartoon about a doctor and a boa constrictor on a tiny desert island. Stephen had Scotch-taped it to the electrical outlet that had inexplicably been set midway between the floor and the ceiling. The scenery in that windowless room never changed, except one of the bulbs in the overhead light had burned out, so the place was gloomier than usual.

He hoped this afternoon's radio clinic would be quick and

uneventful. These thoughts—this impatience—was new. Usually he was excited about his medical practice in Bethel. Maybe the shortening days and lengthening nights were getting to him. He'd thought winter in Alaska wouldn't bother him, even though his old life of endless sunny days in California hadn't prepared him for it. He missed the fruit from the lemon and orange trees in his backyard, the smell of the gardenias. So different. So far away. So long ago.

To his surprise, Jennifer seemed to tolerate the dark and cold better than he did. Of course, she didn't have to sit in that dreary radio clinic box for hours at a time. Rather, she ran after the twins and the dog all day, either through the rooms in their apartment with windows to the outside or through the outside itself. He gazed at his watch and then at the wall-clock. As always, the time on the clock was incorrect. As always, it didn't matter.

On days like this, he wondered what he had been thinking to accept the assignment in Bethel. He'd been so idealistic—actually, he'd been impossibly naïve—about the reality of it all. He'd looked forward to hunting with Ginger and, indeed, they'd had some good ptarmigan hunts in the fall. Same with fishing; their freezer was loaded with salmon he'd caught in the Kuskokwim. But there was less hunting or fishing during the winter. At least, less for him. Somehow sitting in balmy California, he hadn't been able to envision the tedium of Alaskan winters.

But then it all came back, like a slap in the head. The alternative. He could be working in a field hospital in Vietnam. The irony was stunning—dodging bullets in the hot, muggy jungles of the Mekong Delta versus the sensory deprivation of this dismal room on the cold, dark tundra of the Kuskokwim River valley or resuscitating blown-up young American soldiers versus managing mono and muscle spasms in Native Alaskans.

In her last letter, his mother had enclosed an article from the *Santa Rosa Press Democrat* about Jerry Rafferty, the kid who lived across the alley from the Jetterses when John was growing up. He and Jerry were wrestling teammates. Nice guy. The article reported that an army landing craft had capsized in bad weather in the East Sea. All eleven on board died. It listed the casualties: Jerald Rafferty of Santa Rosa was one of them. John tapped the ball point pen on the metal desk and then laid it down again. That was such a goddamn tragedy, the waste of such a good life. Bethel had been the right choice for him, and now he'd have to make the best of it.

The radio began to sputter. He picked up the pen to document the call just as the voice cut through the static. "Dr. Jetters, this is Tammy Alexie from Nunapitchuk. Over."

"What do you have, Tammy? Over."

"Abe Achee, yet again. This time his belly itches. He says it's been going on for one day. No fever, no diarrhea, no nausea or vomiting. He didn't eat anything funny. Over."

In spite of all the dark stuff of Alaska, John still enjoyed the staccato, rocking-like-a-swing sound of the Yup'ik accent. In some ways it was monotonic, but he found it strangely refreshing. Well, not exactly refreshing, but certainly interesting. Soft spoken and soothing. "Did you examine his abdomen? Over."

"Ee. It's soft and not tender. The skin looks good, except where he's been scratching. Over."

"See any critters? Over."

"No bugs. Over."

"What does he think might be causing this? Over."

"He says it may be his new long johns. Over."

John sighed. "Have him wash the long johns and check back with you in a couple days. Let us know if anything new appears. Over."

"I'm fine with that. Over."

He sat up straight in the desk chair. This aide was from Nunapitchuk. "Say, isn't he the guy whose wife died a while back, and he's been a regular in your clinic ever since? Over."

"Ee. That's him. Over."

"And, wasn't he the one who found his two dead nephews at fish camp? Over."

"Ee. Over."

"Okay." *Tough time for the old guy*, John thought. "We have a plan. Over and off."

He pushed back the chair and set his feet on the desk. He cradled his coffee cup, took a sip of the lukewarm Nescafé, and listened to the crackle from the radio. It sounded musical, with pops of sound in tones that sometimes moved up the scale, sometimes down. He preferred to think of it as a somewhat grating song than as static from atmospheric storms that disrupted the radio waves.

He shook his head as he thought more about Mr. Achee, about the poor man's desperation after his wife died; the long, lonely evenings; the empty space in his bed; the aching memories of togetherness that could no longer be. He'd never met the man but had cared for plenty just like him.

Achee was among the legions of the worried-well seeking solace in the medical system. He was in the special category of widowed worried-well, trying to cope with a loss of massive proportions. He thought of Tammy the health aide and her patience with him. He recalled his grieving grandfather after his grandmother died and realized that, back then, he hadn't understood how miserable his grandfather must have been. John tapped his pen on the desk again. He should have been a better grandson.

He thought of Jennifer and what he'd do if she died. It was such a jarring thought. He wished he had a window so he could see the sky. But he didn't, and those thoughts of Jennifer dying sawed at his mind. If that happened, what would he do? Could he stand to go on living? It would be the little things that would paralyze him. He didn't know how she got the blood out of his shirt sleeve cuffs or how to poach a salmon. Who'd settle him down when he ranted about Leonard Kills Squirrels? Who'd talk with him late into the night?

The twins without a mother. His thoughts went blank there. Losing her was unimaginable. He closed his eyes and tried to steady his breathing.

Static rattled the air, and John sat up straight to answer the call, but none of the health aides were there. It was just random radio static.

Tammy had done such a good job with Mr. Achee. Finding his nephews dead was another blow. Family was important to the people of Alaska. He guessed they were important to people everywhere, but somehow it was different here. His own relatives were scattered from California to South Carolina, from Wisconsin to Texas. Alaskan relatives usually were geographically much, much closer. And they depended on each other intensely, for food, for transportation, for company on those long winter nights.

A voice interrupted the radio's sputter. "Dr. Jetters, this is Denise Kaganak from Aniak. Over."

"Go ahead, Denise. Over." John sighed. Several hours yet to go in this room.

"This is kind of strange, Dr. Jetters. Lincoln Egoak is here with tummy pain. No vomiting or diarrhea. When I examined him, his belly is fine. The funny part is he says he's seeing two of everything . . . says he sees two of me. He's a little hard to understand because his words are mushy. Here . . . listen to him." The radio broadcast paused, the static sputtered. Then she returned. Her voice sounded farther away than before. "Lincoln, tell Dr. Jetters what I look like."

A voice, coarse and scratchy, said, "I schee twa har."

Denise returned. "His daughter says she gave him an aspirin, and he choked on it and spit the water and the pill all over his shirt. Over."

John closed his eyes. That was weird, indeed. "Does he have any fever? How about his vitals? Over."

"No fever. His blood pressure and heart rate are good. His breathing is funny though. He's kind of gulping for air. Over."

John's eyes flipped open. Was the guy having a stroke? "How old is Mr. Egoak? Does he have any heart disease? Over."

"Um . . . he's about fifty-five. He's been healthy. He thinks his funny breathing is from getting too close to a fire made from tainted driftwood. Over."

That didn't make any sense. John had never heard of tainted drift-wood smoke causing respiratory trouble. And how would that explain the diplopia and slurred speech? The fellow was probably having a stroke. "Denise, we need to get him to Bethel. How long does it take to fly from Aniak to here, and what's the weather there? Over."

"It's usually an hour to Bethel by plane. The clouds are hanging low though. Over."

"I'll phone for a plane and get back to you. Over and off."

John ran his finger down the CONTACT sheet and called the airplane service. While he waited for someone to answer, he did the calculations in his head. Two o'clock now. One hour plus to Aniak and one hour plus back, with load time in between. Mr. Egoak wouldn't arrive until 4:30 to 5:00 pm. at best, probably later. The Wein Air Alaska jet would take off from Bethel about 5:00 p.m.—assuming it could take off at all. If Egoak needed to go to Anchorage, he'd miss today's flight.

A voice on the other end of the line said, "'Allo." It sounded as if it echoed up from the bottom of a well.

John explained the situation to the coordinator at the airplane service.

"Aniak, huh. I'll have to check with the weather people. Call you back as soon as I get clearance."

John took several more radio clinic calls. Draining ears. Runny nose. Funny feeling in an ankle.

Then, the airplane guy called back. "Weather's pretty bad. Can't fly now. I'll keep checking and let you know when it might be a go."

John radioed Denise in Aniak and told her to alert Mr. Egoak and his family that he'd fly to Bethel as soon as the weather improved. Hopefully, sometime later today. "How's he doing? Over."

"Not much change. I got him to take a few sips of water, but it was slow. Over."

John answered several more radio clinic calls. Nothing exciting: a sore throat, a rash, an infected pimple. He worried about Mr. Egoak. If this was a stroke, there wasn't much they could do for him, but he'd rather do nothing in Bethel than leave the man out in the village. The health aides were very good, but they weren't trained to make an accurate assessment of a patient with a complex or confusing medical problem.

John radioed Denise at 4:00 p.m. No change in Mr. Egoak's symptoms. That was reassuring, but how long would it last? He called again at 6:00 p.m. Denise reported that Mr. Egoak dropped the water glass when she tried to get him to drink. John worried the guy would get dehydrated.

"Has he urinated? If so, what did it look like? Over." John asked.

"Ee. It was the color of honey. Over."

"Light honey or dark honey? Over."

"Medium. Over."

The health aides weren't trained to start IVs or to give intravenous fluids either, and they didn't have IV needles, tubing, or bottles of ¼ normal saline in their clinics anyway.

Before he left work in the early evening, he signed out to Stephen who was on call that night. He explained the information from the health aide in Aniak.

"I'm worried the guy may have had a stroke and that the health aide won't be able to get enough liquids in him by mouth."

"Not much we can do about a stroke," Stephen said.

"Yeah. But I'd rather we had the chance to actually examine him, and he likely needs IV fluids."

Shortly after midnight, Stephen called John, who lay in bed tossing and turning amid dream fragments of people with blown off legs, or plague, or massive strokes.

"He's here . . . the guy from Aniak," Stephen said. "The awful thing is he's the guy who took me caribou hunting recently."

John shook the sleep from his eyes. "Are you okay taking care of him? Want me to come in?"

"No, I'm fine. He's stable and resting comfortably," Stephen said. "Whatever this is, I hope he comes out of it in one piece."

John patted Jennifer, asleep beside him, on the butt. It was a gentle pat. She was there and breathing. For sure, Stephen would take good care of Mr. Egoak. Now hopefully, he could drift off.

The next morning, Stephen reported that Mr. Egoak's breathing was somewhat labored, even with an oxygen mask strapped over his mouth and nose. "He's a really great guy," Stephen said. "His niece is Cindy the nurses' aide here. She's the one who arranged for our caribou hunting trip."

Stephen and John both examined Mr. Egoak. The man's eyelids sagged over his eyeballs, and he complained that John had two heads. When they asked him a question, he lifted the left lid with his fingers, trying to see them. His words seemed to bubble through a mouthful of oatmeal. He had trouble lifting his feet to walk.

John and Stephen discussed the case with Matias, who asked a few questions, scratched his head, and said, "You know, something is goofy here. Strokes are usually limited to one region of the brain, and if I remember my neuroanatomy correctly, the visual and vocal symptoms may fit with that I think, but how about that leg weakness? That's controlled by a different part of the brain. Something else might be going on."

Matias was right. Maybe the guy had something in addition to a simple stroke, or maybe he hadn't had a stroke after all. Could it be a brain tumor? Encephalitis? John called the Native Alaska Hospital in Anchorage and spoke with one of the neurologists. They agreed Mr. Egoak should be flown to Anchorage on the next flight. "Is his respiratory status likely to deteriorate before he gets here?" the neurologist asked. "Should you intubate him before leaving Bethel?"

John hesitated. Egoak hadn't gone south overnight, and he was fully awake. He'd have to be heavily sedated for an intubation, and then they'd have to keep him sedated so he wouldn't yank out the tube while airborne. That in itself would be dangerous. "I think we shouldn't do that. We don't have anesthesia support. The guy's very alert. We'll send him on oxygen and have a nurse accompany him with an Ambu bag and an oral airway in her lap."

"Can you get two seats on a plane today?" the neurologist asked.

"Only one flight a day out of Bethel. Leaves at 5:00 p.m. or so. The weather seems pretty good. Getting a couple of seats going out of Bethel usually isn't a problem. It's coming *into* Bethel that can be tricky because many of the plane's seats are removed to make room for freight, mostly cartons of booze. If we have to, we'll ask Wein Air to bump a couple of passengers."

Over the next two days, Mr. Egoak seeped into John's awareness at unexpected times. When he read an article on hypertension and strokes in the *Journal of the American Medical Association*, he reassured himself that Egoak's blood pressure had been normal. He wondered how the guy was doing when he took another radio clinic call from Aniak, when he summoned a plane to bring in a patient from Chefornak, when Jennifer served salmon steaks for dinner. Stephan had called him a really nice guy. That was often the case: the nicest guys got the sickest.

CHAPTER 12

"We need a Christmas tree," Mera said.

"Sure we do," Matias laughed. "About as much as we need a golden chariot."

"I'm serious. We have to maintain our cultural traditions for Marcus. I want him to have a full-bodied Christmas, complete with a tree."

"I'm serious too. Where do you propose we get one?" Matias put on his doubtful look, the one with puckered lips and side-glancing eyes. "Swanson's certainly doesn't carry something like that, and there isn't a tree of any kind around Bethel."

"We'll go downriver to where the evergreen trees grow and cut one down."

"That's twenty-five to thirty miles from here. How are we going to get there?" His voice had a hesitant, impatient edge to it.

"We're going to borrow Stephen's Jeep and drive on the frozen river," Mera said. "I'll pay him with a plate of wedding cookies."

OFF IN THE DISTANCE ACROSS THE river, the silhouette of Three

Step Mountain looked like a fuzzy, lumpy haystack against the hazy sky. The sun, hovering bright as a fireball above the opposite horizon, would set soon. Mera hoped they'd find a tree before day turned into night.

She and Matias, with Marcus on her lap, bounced over the icy road-on-the-river in Stephen's Jeep. She had packed a thermos of hot coffee, a jug of water, and the rest of the churro cake she made last Sunday, along with rope to tie the tree to the roof of car, two sets of snowshoes, and a saw Matias had borrowed from Biff in maintenance. Previous traffic had created a two-track on the ice, but the ride was rough. Moguls dotted the path, sometimes in pairs, occasionally in triplets. Mera worried about her unborn baby and hoped the layers of muscle and fat between her insides and the outside world would cushion the bumps. She braced her feet against the floor, clutched Marcus to her chest, and sang his favorite song about the little flower. "Flor pequeña, flor pequeña . . ." Her voice bounced against the inside of the Jeep. She really wanted that tree.

Matias slowed the Jeep. He leaned forward and squinted as he surveyed the terrain. "I think it was near here that Stephen and I saw the stands of evergreens," he mumbled. He sped up, only to slow down a short while later. On the fourth slow-down, he said, "There. See them?"

Sure enough. A short walk from the river a cluster of fir trees huddled together like a small flock against a storm. Matias stopped the Jeep at the river's edge. They strapped the snowshoes to their boots, Matias tied Marcus into the child carrier and slung it onto his shoulders, and they trudged off across the frozen tundra.

Mera liked the squeak of each step, the only sound out there except for the whisper of the wind. She liked the pattern the raw-hide laces on her showshoes made on the flakey crust of the snow. It reminded her of cobwebs. The sky was so clear she thought she could see out into the far reaches of the universe. She took a deep breath. The air smelled fresh, clean, and pure. Mostly she could no longer smell the mossy, earthy, sagey, hard-to-describe scent of the tundra, now buried beneath the snow.

Soon it would be dark, the tail end of another stretch of brief sunlight in the prolonged dark of winter in Alaska. It was mid-December, close to the hibernal solstice. Soon the periods of light would grow longer, by six minutes every twenty-four hours, as they always did. To Mera the shortening or lengthening of days felt like a rat racing on a treadmill. One hour difference in light, or dark, every ten days. For her, that was the eeriest part of living in Bethel.

As they approached the copse of evergreens, she saw that each tree was boney. None were richly needled like those that grew all over the Piney Woods of East Texas.

"Which one?" Matias asked. "And how are we going to make it stand up in our living room?"

"We're going to set it in a pail of dirt from under the fourplex." She wandered between the trees, examining each one. "Let's see . . ."

The tallest spruce was lopsided with an S-shaped trunk. The second and third tallest were bare on the side that grew against the other trees. The fourth tallest was up to her shoulders and stood a bit away from the others. Its trunk had divided into two trunks about a third of the way up from the ground. "This one," she said.

"It's a mutant," Matias said. "Look at that weird trunk. It's like Siamese twins."

"It's interesting." Yes, the tree was unusual. Yes, it had a defect. She was accustomed to defects. Mistakes in her knitting, errors while cooking. Her precious lost babies likely had them. Dr. Mulvaney had told her most miscarriages resulted from genetic or metabolic or structural abnormalities in the fetus. That's why they couldn't survive. This tree though *had* survived and dared to grow somewhat beyond the rest of the copse. It managed to thrive even on the edge of the ideal place. And it had a personality, a nice one, a unique one. "That's my favorite."

"Okay," Matias said with a note of surrender. He unhooked Marcus from the child carrier and let him wander among the trees. Marcus was a lightweight whose boots didn't break through the icy top of the snow. Mera silently thanked the ancients for inventing snowshoes because she would have sunk to her crotch without them.

Matias knelt and sawed the base of the trunk at an angle so the tree fell away from the copse. Then he tied the rope to the lower branches, loaded Marcus into the child carrier, handed one end of the rope to Mera, and wrapped the other end around his glove. "Let's go," he said, and they started back to the Jeep, dragging the tree behind them.

It was heavier than she expected. She considered tying the rope around her waist, but didn't want it anywhere close to her unborn baby. So, she continued to pull the rope as best as she could with her arms.

About halfway back to the car, she glanced over her shoulder. Suddenly a stab of regret hit her in the gut. They shouldn't have cut it down. Those trees worked very hard to survive out there, and she now thought it should have been allowed to stay. Trees were rare on the tundra, and they had selfishly sawed one down. That interesting, strong, curious tree should have been allowed to live. But, it was too late. She didn't dare tell Matias of her throbbing misgiving but watched in silence as he tied it to the Jeep. She hoped she'd be able to enjoy the Christmas tree at least a little bit.

Fifteen minutes into the ride home, Matias had to stop the Jeep to reposition the tree. The southwestern horizon was a halo of orange surrounded by the night sky. She and Marcus stepped out onto the ice. "Pretty Christmas tree," Marcus said. He made it sound human. That made her feel even worse about cutting it down.

As the afternoon darkened into later afternoon, the trip home became more treacherous. They couldn't see the bumps and dips of the ice road and could barely make out the two-tracks as they inched toward Bethel. Stars began to appear in the sky above. She unwrapped the churro cake. "Want a bite?" she asked Matias.

"Okay." He gripped the steering wheel and stared straight ahead.

"I want some," Marcus called.

She broke off several pieces and fed them to her husband and son. "How are we on gas?" she asked.

"Fine."

"A third-full fine or drops on the bottom of the tank fine?"

"Three-quarters of a tank fine. I filled it up before we started."

Good, she thought. Matias was pretty responsible, but she needed to be sure.

The movement of the Jeep made her sleepy, and Mera closed her eyes. Sometime later, maybe minutes, maybe many minutes, she woke with a jerk. The car had hit something. It instantly stopped moving forward.

Matias jumped out onto the ice.

"What's wrong?" she called.

He didn't answer. "Matias, what's going on?"

He stuck his head back into the car and sighed. "One of the tires fell into an open patch in the ice. Must be an ice-fishing hole."

"Can we get it out?"

"Not sure."

He returned to the driver's seat, restarted the engine, put the gear shift in first, and stepped on the gas. The car rocked forward and then fell backward. He tried again. Same thing. He tried to back out. The wheel spun against the edge of the hole but wouldn't climb out of it.

He took his hands off the steering wheel and sighed again. "The hole's too big to drive out."

Mera peered out into the darkness. "What do we do now?"

Matias was silent.

"Matias, what do we do?"

"Not sure. Let me think."

"Would it help to take the tree off the roof?"

"No. In fact, the added weight should improve the traction. The tire is sunk too deep. The fact that the other three tires are on ice doesn't help."

Getting the tree had been her idea. Why hadn't Matias talked some sense into her? They didn't really need a Christmas tree. But she couldn't blame her husband. In his wildest imagination, he wouldn't expect the car to fall into an ice fishing hole.

As they sat in Stephen's Jeep on the frozen river, the sky grew increasingly dark and was dotted with stars. She watched the smear of the Milky Way and thought the bright North Star at the end of the Little Dipper's handle was winking at her.

"Want any more churro cake?" she finally asked.

"For God's sake, no." Matias's voice sounded like granite.

She fed a slice of the cake to Marcus and gave him a drink of water. The inside of the car was getting colder. *Was this really happening?* she wondered. They'd freeze out there. The three of them and her unborn child. It must not be true. She tried to shift her thoughts to something else, but it didn't work. The irony was ugly: she'd lost so many babies already and soon, because of her whim, she'd lose the one child that had survived to be born and the one currently growing inside her.

She closed her eyes. Moments, or maybe minutes later, she thought she heard voices. Was she hallucinating? She wasn't even that cold yet. The voices grew louder. Sounded something like "whoa." She glanced out the window and watched a sled, pulled by a team of dogs, stop beside the car. "Do you need help?" someone called.

Matias leaped out of the car and explained the situation to the three Yup'ik men on the dog sled. The four of them circled the car, examining the tires. Matias opened the door and said, "We have a plan. You and Marcus can stay in here for a bit longer while we gather willow sticks from the edge of the river."

Soon the four men returned with armloads of branches, which they stuffed in back of the three free tires. Matias opened the door again. "You and Marcus need to get out now."

While they waited on the ice, one of the Eskimo men crawled into the driver's seat and revved the car's engine. *Good idea*, Mera thought. They know how to drive on ice and in the winter.

Matias and the other two men hunched over the front fender of the Jeep and pushed. The car made a lurching sound, and as it jerked backward, the trapped tire clambered out of the hole. Mera started laughing. So did Matias as he wrapped his arm around her shoulders.

"Saved," he whispered.

Matias and the men shook hands, and Matias pulled his wallet from his pocket. All three men shook their heads and said, "No." They climbed aboard their sled.

Mera heard one of them call to the dogs, "Alright." The sled jumped forward and disappeared into the night.

She was about to put Marcus back into the car when she saw the green hue in the blackened sky behind her. The green moved, like shimmering waves of lime-colored air dancing through the heavens. She had seen them before, but these were particularly vibrant. "Look at the sky," she said to Marcus. "See? It's the northern lights. Aren't they beautiful?"

Her son gazed at the show, his eyes glistening with wonder.

A band of yellow-orange appeared at the top of the green, and the colors continued to dance, flickering dimmer and brighter, more intense, less intense, flaming like verdant fire above the Earth.

"We'd better get going," Matias said.

Mera nodded and climbed back in the Jeep. Part of her wanted to stay there all night, or at least until the display was over. The celestial lights were almost spiritual, a reminder of the powerful energy that controlled the happenings of the universe. Their eerie beauty always mesmerized her. Tonight, she thought they might be the heavens celebrating their escape from the fishing hole or maybe a message from the gods that taking the tree had been okay. She could watch those beams pitch and flutter forever. But another part of her wanted to get home where they'd be warm and safe.

THE TREE STOOD UPRIGHT AND NAKED in its bucket of dirt in their living room. It needed ornaments. Matias and Mera hadn't been married long enough to gather boxfuls of Christmas tree decorations, but they had a few: several childhood favorites Mera's mother had given her, two boxes of plum-colored bulbs she had bought at the after-Christmas sale at Gutierrez's Hardware in Houston, tiny hand-knit-on-toothpicks Christmas socks from her cousin, two strings of lights. All were in storage back in Texas.

Over the next several days, Mera made a Santa Claus head from an empty toilet paper roll, red construction paper, and cotton from the top of the aspirin bottle. She layered light brown paper between cut-outs in darker brown paper to make pinecones. She constructed tiny hymnals of purple construction paper and translucent onionskin, with "Silent Night" written in her version of calligraphy above the inky notes she had drawn on a treble clef staff. Now, she needed several Stars of David, two big ones for the tops of the two trunks and four or five smaller ones to hang from the boughs.

She trudged down the road from the hospital complex toward the Kuskokwim, in search of sticks to make the Stars of David. When she left the road, she crossed over the snow to get to the willows that lined the riverbank. With each step, her boots sank deep into the drifts; with each step she was up to her thighs in snow. The farther she went from the hospital compound, the harder the wind blew. It was always like that.

At the water's edge, she snapped several thin branches off the willows. She started back toward home, but, deciding she needed more sticks, she turned back to the river.

She plodded back toward the shore, trying to remember where she had put the holiday-red yarn—left over from the sweater she'd knit for Marcus—that she would use to tie the sticks into stars. Off to her right she saw the smashed cone of a blackfish trap made of willow branches, long ago discarded and forgotten by its owner. Further on, an abandoned length of fishing seine hung from the bushes, with two fish skeletons tangled in its strings and wooden bobbers anchoring it in the snow. Beside it was a pile of gray fur.

Strange, she thought. What kind of animal was that? Wrong color for a bear. Wolf? Arctic fox? Coyote? Maybe a dog. It was stone still. She looked for blood in the snow or for evidence of a fight but saw none. She considered throwing something at it to see if it moved but quickly reconsidered. What if it was just sleeping or injured and mad? It might attack her.

As soon as she returned home, she called out to Matias. He was in the playroom with Marcus.

"There's some sort of animal over by the river, probably dead, bigger than a rabbit, smaller than a big bear. Want to take a look at it?"

They bundled Marcus into his snowsuit and headed toward the river. When they reached the fishing net hanging from the bush, she pointed to the pile of fur.

He studied it. "Not breathing," he said. He lobbed a chunk of ice at the pile. It didn't move. He crept closer and kicked it with the boot on his outstretched leg. It still didn't move, but now they could see more of it.

"A wolf," Mera said. "A dead wolf." Very close to where they lived, to where they walked between the fourplexes, to where Marcus drove his plastic toy boat over the crusty snow. "What did he die from?"

"What does anything die from?" Matias gave her his impatient look. "Heart attack, stroke, or maybe cancer."

"Do wolves get cancer?"

"How should I know? Why are you asking about this?"

Mera paused. "Oh, just wondering." She pondered what made animals, in general, die out in the wild. Succumbed to old age? Maybe lost a fight?

It was a good question.

What made people die out in the wild? Frozen to death, starved to death, fell through the ice on the river, murdered. Some people wondered if those two fellows from Nunapitchuk were murdered at fish camp. Both at the same time. In June. They didn't drown, nor die in a snowmobile accident. They didn't freeze to death. How? And why?

By Christmas Eve, they had decorated the whole tree. From its lower branches, the ones Marcus could reach, paper circles, which he had made, hung by pieces of thread Scotch-taped to their backs. They were colored in Crayola burnt sienna and raw umber, his favorites that week. He had rejected Mera's suggestions of pine green and brick red. The only thing missing was sparkle; the tree had no lights and no tinsel. Nevertheless, Mera thought it was beautiful. If the tree could speak, she thought it would tell her how much it liked the decorations. It would say that the other trees in the copse where it had grown would be jealous of the ornaments. It would say it felt special.

The package from her parents in Texas sat, unopened, under the tree. She snipped the string around the outside, stripped away the brown paper grocery bag her mother had used to cover the box, and pulled out three gifts wrapped in Santa Claus printed paper, one for her, one for Matias, and one for Marcus. She smoothed the rumpled sheets of newspaper her mother had used for stuffing. One was the society page of the *Houston Chronicle*, with the late April weddings and news of the upcoming garden show. It was an old paper. Her mother must have pulled it out of the stack they saved in the garage for kindling.

She smoothed out another page from the *Chronicle*, the front page. The headlines read *Massacre at Kent State*. She held her breath as she eyed the photo showing a screaming young woman, kneeling beside the prone body of a young man. Other students mingled around the grassy ballfield in the distance. Mera began to read the article. Somehow that news hadn't reached Bethel. Not surprising. KYUK radio and the *Tundra Drums* covered only local events. They had missed so much of the world happenings while in Bethel. She continued reading.

Awful. Horrible. Those kids were so young. So were the soldiers.

It all seemed very far away, Alaska to Ohio. The peace of Alaska versus the war in the rest of the world. She didn't want to know, and yet she *did* want to know. She read the article to its end.

DEIDRE, DAVID, AND BABY DANIEL WOULD be there in several hours. They hadn't participated in a Christmas Eve dinner before and seemed excited to be invited. The bunuolos were warming in the oven; the chicken tamales were ready to go into the steamer as soon as the water boiled; the tres leche cake was cooling on the counter. Mera congratulated herself for thinking to pack bags of dried peppers and corn husks when they moved and for ordering a case each of canned hominy, evaporated milk, and sweetened condensed milk with their big food shipment. The chicken she had bought at Swanson's was scrawny but would have to do.

Someone was knocking at the kitchen door. "Come in," Mera called. She was sure it wasn't Leonard Kills Squirrels, for he had finally stopped pestering them about their marriage licenses. She assumed, however, he was incubating a new notion to move Jackie out of Stephen's apartment, but apparently he hadn't acted on it yet.

The door swung open, and Virginia Tom walked in.

"Merry Christmas," Mera said.

"Thank you. Happy Christmas to you. Is Marcus here? I have a present for him." She carried a large box wrapped in butcher paper.

"Marcus," Mera called toward the bedrooms. "Mrs. Tom is here to see you."

Marcus raced down the hall in his stocking feet and skidded to a stop beside Virginia.

"I brought you a Christmas present. Here." She set the box on the floor in front of him. "Open it."

While he tore apart the paper wrapping, Mera stepped to the counter, opened two cans of zucchini and tomatoes, and dumped the contents into a saucepan.

When she turned around, Marcus was holding a gun. Not a colorful water pistol, nor a wooden handgun, but a two-foot long, black plastic Uzi. He yelled with joy and reached up to give Virginia, who flashed a grin as wide as Oklahoma across her round face, a hug. Mera gasped in horror.

Then Marcus turned, widened his stance, bent his knees, and pointed the Uzi at his mother. Mera grabbed the barrel and screamed "NO." She twisted it out of his hands.

He shrieked, "Mine!"

She hated guns, wanted her son to have nothing to do with them. She didn't even want a toy firearm in her house. Guns were serious, not fun. She didn't want him to be comfortable with holding a weapon.

In truth, he'd used his pointer finger, a stack of Legos, and once a fresh banana as a pistol. She had no idea where he learned about such things. He hadn't seen a TV program nor a movie, ever. Maybe the twins taught that to him. She had let those ugly finger/Lego/banana-gun moments go, hoping that, like sucking his thumb and banging his head on the floor, the pretend pistols would go away.

"Gimme," he hollered. "Mine!"

She glanced at Virginia, who sat hunched at the kitchen table with a bewildered look on her face. She knew Virginia loved Marcus very much and that she meant only the best with the gift. In her world, firearms were a necessity for survival, the way the men procured their meat. And little boys imitated their fathers and grown-up men. Still . . .

Marcus clawed at Mera's jeans as he reached up for the Uzi. "Mine," he yelled again.

She squatted on the floor in front of him and held on as he tried to wrench his present from her grasp. "Wait, Marcus. Wait. Let's talk about this."

She told him that real guns hurt people, that he must never, ever point that gun, or his finger or any other gun, at a person. "If you do, I'll take it away forever." She loosened her grip, and he tore it from her fingers. "Guns are for hunting bears and elk for food and not ever for shooting people. Do you understand?"

He nodded.

"Did you thank Mrs. Tom for your present?" she asked Marcus, her heart banging against the inside of her chest.

"Thank you," he said. Virginia patted him on the head and still looked bewildered. She shuffled to the door and said goodbye.

"Goodbye," Mera said. "Merry Christmas to your family." She was sure Virginia had not given any of her many kids a gift as expensive as the one she gave Marcus. That seemed unfair to the Tom kids, but that was Virginia. She seemed to enjoy being with Marcus much more than with any of her own children.

By the time Deidre, David, and baby Daniel in his birch bark baby carrier arrived, Matias had put the Uzi in Marcus's bottom dresser drawer. "Son," he had said, "Every hunter keeps his gun in a safe place where no one will get hurt."

"Sure smells good in here," Deidre said as she and Daniel settled at the kitchen table. "Turkey?"

"Chicken tamales," Mera said, "and chicken pozole. We're having family Christmas favorites."

She then told Deidre about Marcus's present from Virginia Tom. "I may not have handled that in the best way. He was heartbroken when I grabbed it from him, and Virginia was confused and probably hurt."

Deidre slowly, knowingly, nodded, and nuzzled Daniel as he slept in her lap. "Is that what I have to look forward to?"

"Probably. Unless Daniel turns out to be a saint."

A far-away look drew over Deidre's face. "No one said being a parent was fun all the time. Or easy."

Mera smiled and moved the pan of zucchini and tomatoes off the stove's front burner.

Deidre took a deep breath. "I probably haven't told you about the decision my parents made about my little sister. Have I?"

"I don't think so."

"Becky was born when I was three years old. She had Down

Syndrome and was cute as a button. When she was about two, suddenly she went away. My parents explained that Becky was sick and would live at a place that could take care of her. I didn't understand that, because she didn't seem sick to me, and *I* had helped take care of her. I fetched toys when she tossed them out of the playpen, changed her diapers, played peek-a-boo with her, and made her giggle. Then she was gone."

Mera pulled a kitchen chair beside Deidre and sat down.

"As I grew up and asked about her, my parents tried to explain in bits and pieces. The doctors said Becky wouldn't live into adulthood because of her bad heart. They said she was such a burden on the family, she'd best be placed in a home for children like her."

Mera gasped. Deidre's sister, the one with a defect, a not-uncommon genetic abnormality, had been shuffled off to an institution, a thrown-away child. "Where is she now?" Mera asked.

"I don't know. Our parents don't want me to think about her or try to contact her. It's like she never existed." Deidre wiped a tear from her cheek. "My parents and I have had many, many terrible fights about it."

"Do you think Becky's happy?"

"I have no idea. I certainly hope so. I hope the caregivers at the institution recognize her as a person, as the sweet person I'm sure she is."

Marcus wandered into the kitchen and stood beside Deidre. "I got a new gun," he said. "Wanna see?"

Deidre glanced at Mera, the Jewish woman's face begging for guidance.

"Okay, Marcus. Deidre and Daniel can look at the gun in the drawer. Show them where it lives." She couldn't believe she was saying this. That gun was living in their house. She hoped it was okay.

The others wandered down the hallway toward Marcus's bedroom, while Mera took a deep breath and pulled the bunuolos out of the oven. Echoes from the past several days jangled through her mind, rat-ta-tat-tat like the staccato of a water hammer. The Jeep falling into the ice-fishing hole, the beauty of the northern lights, the generosity of the passing dogsledders, a dead wolf down by the river, the lovely decorations on the slain spruce tree, the Uzi. In contrast, Christmas Eve dinner was so easy. The rest of life was not.

CHAPTER 13

VIRGINIA TOM WALKED OUT OF THE Maldonados' apartment, down the ice-covered stairs, around the corner, and onto the trampled snow that covered the boardwalk. She didn't understand. She'd never seen Mrs. Maldonado yell at Marcus before, had never seen her the least bit angry. The gun was a present for Marcus. When she saw it at Swanson's she knew Marcus would love it. And he did. But Mrs. Maldonado got very mad. She acted like the gun was bad. To Virginia, guns were not good or bad. Mud boots were not good or bad. Neither was a cooking pot or a dog sled. Guns were just guns.

But Mrs. Maldonado had yelled very loud. It felt as if she, Virginia, had given Marcus a bad present. She'd never heard of a bad present. Marcus loved the gun. How could that be anything but good?

From the boardwalk, she could see the Christmas tree in the Maldonados' living room. It was so pretty. She didn't have one at her house; no room. Maybe someday she'd have a Christmas tree. Until then, she's enjoy the holiday decorations at Our Mother of

All Saints: the wreaths of woven willows; the green, red, and white candles; the long gold and black scarf-thing that Father Brogan wore around his neck on holidays; the dainty manger scene set up beside the altar. She loved to sing the hymns like "Silent Night" and "Hark, the Herald Angels Sing" and to hear the church bells that rang into the night. For now, she didn't need anything special for Christmas in her house.

As she walked, she couldn't stop thinking about Marcus's gun. Would Mrs. Maldonado let her watch Marcus anymore? She hoped so. She really liked taking care of him—liked Mrs. Maldonado; liked being at their big, nice house; liked being alone with only Marcus—and didn't want that to go away. She'd go to Mass later that night and ask for forgiveness. Only, she wasn't sure what she had done that needed forgiveness. Maybe Father Brogan could figure it out.

Ahead was Raymond Andrecheck's house. The yard light shone on his sleeping dogs, which were chained to the ground near his shed. Raymond walked out his front door, reached into his steaming pail, and started to throw wet fish slabs at the dogs. They all leaped to their feet and tugged at their chains. They were pretty hungry, she guessed.

"Good afternoon, Virginia," he called.

She waved back. When she reached his house, he invited her in. "Come, rest your feet and warm yourself," he said.

His wife moved a pile of laundry, a package of toilet paper, and a large chipped enamel basin off the sofa to clear a spot for Virginia. It felt good to be off her feet, and the fire in the oil stove quickly warmed her bones.

"Want some tea?" Mrs. Andrecheck asked.

"Ee."

When Mrs. Andrecheck poured the tea from the old steel pot, the spicy smell wafted over to Virginia. Tundra tea. It was good.

Raymond Andrecheck pulled a bucket from under the sink. "Want some stinkheads?"

"Ee." Virginia was as hungry as the dogs. She liked stinkheads, liked their tangy taste and the way her mouth tingled when she ate them. She hadn't had any for several months. Her husband didn't make them because he was Athabascan. His people didn't eat stinkheads.

"Merry Christmas," Raymond said, handing her a plate with a bit of gray mush. "Good salmon season last summer. We made lots of stinkheads."

Virginia scooped up a pinch of the mush and sucked it from her fingers. "Ee. Good." Then she ate another pinch.

When the plate was empty, she licked her fingers and said, "Mrs. Maldonado told me they found a dead wolf by the river near the hospital. She wondered why it died."

"They just do, like people."

"Ee." Virginia nodded.

She thanked him for the stinkheads and went back outside. The late afternoon was chilly, and the sky was starry. Her boots crunched on the packed snow.

She wondered about the dead wolf, and that reminded her of her dead cousins from Nunapitchuk. Her relatives all worried that whatever killed Luther and Morris would kill them, and that made her wonder about Nicholas. Sometimes, he took his father's boat to Nunapitchuk without asking. He'd say he went to visit his cousins, but sometimes they said he hadn't been there. Could he know anything about Luther and Morris dying? She'd asked him the day after she first heard about it, and he shook his head. He said he hadn't seen them since early in the spring, and they seemed okay then.

She had a hard time figuring Nicholas out. For sure, he was a sneaky boy. When she asked him a question, his eyes jumped away, and he mumbled an answer she couldn't hear. When she asked him to say it again, he ignored her.

Could Luther and Morris have gotten into poison? The poison berries from upriver on the Yukon didn't grow near Nunapitchuk. Cleaning chemicals? They wouldn't have those at fish camp; no floors to clean there. Mink poison? Most people on the Kuskokwim trapped minks; no one poisoned them.

She stomped the snow from her boots outside the door of her house and went inside. A nice fire was going in the stove. Her youngest son slouched on the couch behind a book. "Mitchell, did you start the fire?" she asked.

"No. Nicholas did." Mitchell remained tied to his book.

"Are you hungry?"

"Yeah." He peered from behind the book and sniffed the air. "Where'd you get the stinkheads? Can I have some?"

She chuckled. You couldn't hide stinkhead stink. "Mr. Andrecheck gave me some at his house."

The door opened, and Nicholas blew in with a blast of cold air. "Anything to eat around here?" He paused and then said, "Where's the stinkheads? I want some."

She explained that she'd brought home only the smell.

Nicholas sat on the couch beside his brother and started picking at Mitchell's elbow.

"Quit it," Mitchell whined.

Nicholas continued to pick.

"Quit it, dummy." Mitchell turned away from Nicholas, pulled his elbow across his belly as far as it could go, and covered it with his other hand.

That's why she liked taking care of Marcus Maldonado so much. No bickering at his house, no brothers pestering each other. She wished Nicholas wasn't like he was, getting into trouble all the time and starting fights. He was different from her other kids, mean and sneaky. She worried what would happen to him. Did Nicholas have anything to do with those deaths at fish camp? Of course not.

She pulled a dried salmon from the box under the counter and called them to eat. Nicholas bolted from the couch and grabbed two big hunks of fish flesh. He stuffed one piece in his mouth and handed the other to Mitchell.

No, she thought. It couldn't possibly be him.

CHAPTER 14

Leonard Kills Squirrels sat in his office at the hospital and tapped his fingertips on the top of his desk. The digital drumming was irregular. It echoed the rhythm of that song "She'll be coming 'round the mountain when she comes," which had been swirling through his head all day. He was waiting for Stephen Steinberg.

Steinberg was only part of the doctor problem. None of them paid attention to the rules. He'd overheard Steinberg and Maldonado joke about the bad wine at a dinner at the White Alice. How'd they manage to have dinner out there? And where'd they get the wine? The purchase of alcoholic beverages was illegal in Bethel. And that guy Jetters, he and his wife had rolled up the carpet in their living room and shoved it out the front entryway door so it moldered in the Alaskan elements on the wooden steps. He'd spoken to the office in Anchorage about their destruction of IHS property, and they essentially told him to quit worrying about the small stuff. But illegalities weren't small stuff in his book.

Finally, the door flew open and Steinberg stomped in. "You called. Need something?" he asked.

Steinberg wore his usual look of superiority. That arrogance made Leonard's bile boil, but it would be gone soon. He had figured out how to deal with that fellow.

"Well, yes. Have a seat." Leonard motioned to the folding chair across from his desk. "We need to make a few changes in the housing arrangements."

Steinberg raised his eyebrows. "Yes?"

"We need your apartment for another assignment. You'll move into one of the trailers."

"Why and which one?"

"New assignment. You'll take the turquoise and cream-colored one at the end of trailer row."

"That's bullshit. Plain old arbitrary bullshit. No one new is coming. That's revenge for the marriage license nonsense."

"Well, I have yet to see your marriage license . . ."

"Or those of the other docs," Steinberg interrupted.

". . . and that woman is still living there with you, against IHS rules."

"IHS rules? That's even a bigger pile of bullshit."

Leonard winced. That profanity banged against his grandmother's teachings. The one time he tried it on her, she had sudsed his mouth with Lava soap. "Plan on being out of the apartment in the next two weeks."

"That trailer's a wreck. Does it even have electricity?"

"We'll string a line to it, and we'll have Biff and the boys figure out some sort of running water."

Steinberg stormed out of the office and slammed the door behind him. Leonard pulled a can of Tab from his drawer and cracked open the top. He took a swig. Steinberg reminded him of that doctor at the Rosebud hospital, same wavy dark hair, same mystery eyes, same cocky attitude.

A dark cloud seemed to crawl into his office. Leonard had been only eight at the time, but he remembered every detail as if it happened an hour ago. His grandmother was howling like a donkey and then began to yell, "I want to see him. Let me see my son." The doctor kept saying, "That's not a good idea. It's pretty bad."

His uncle Cameron—who taught him to play basketball, who showed him how and where to hunt rabbits, who drank way too much—had been hit by a car on the highway. The doctor said his head had been run over. Leonard's grandmother was louder than ever. "Let me see him," she wailed, over and over while she tugged on the white doctor's long white doctor coat. That guy kept refusing, kept thinking he knew more about what was good for his grandmother than she did.

Someone must have called the tribal chairman.

When he arrived, the chairman told the doctor that someone had reported Cameron to be lying on the edge of the road before he was hit, and that the driver thought he'd run over a big rock. The doctor said that no mother should see her child like that. The tribal chairman listened, nodded, and then made his pronouncement: death is one piece of nature's circle and, according to their tradition, she needed to see Cameron to be convinced he had traveled to the next stop on his life journey and to allow his spirit to stay with her and to guide her.

When they opened the door to the emergency room for his grandmother to enter, Leonard had caught a quick glance of his uncle lying on the table, his massive rotund body without a scratch, his red and green flannel shirt neatly tucked into his pants, and his giant boots, the ones he hunted in, sticking out from the trouser bottoms. The place where his head should have been looked like a heap of hamburger with a thatch of black hair on top.

Leonard shuddered at the memory and felt a backwash of stomach acid rise in his throat. He swallowed hard to keep from vomiting. Steinberg was just like that know-it-all doctor. But for sure no woman would be willing to live in the dilapidated trailer. Just like his grandmother had won, he was certain he would too. Soon Steinberg's slut would be gone.

TWO DAYS LATER, LEONARD CARRIED HIS morning coffee into his office and sat down. Something was different with the piles of papers on the desk. There was a new stack. Leonard picked up the top sheet. "REQUEST FOR HOUSING REASSIGNMENT" read the header. Was that an official IHS form? He didn't recall seeing one like that before. The document stated the undersigned requested new housing, and the date for the requested change said within the next two weeks. In the blank for the detailed request was written "the turquoise and cream-colored trailer at the end of trailer row, IHS Hospital, Bethel, Alaska." It was signed "John Jetters, M.D."

He paged through the stack. Each form was identical, each included a request for that trailer. They were signed David Dorfman, M.D., Matias Maldonado, M.D., and George Gregoir, M.D. He examined the remaining documents. They were signed by the doctors, the dentists, and the pharmacists. None was signed by Steinberg.

Leonard Kills Squirrels slammed his fist on the stack of forms. How would he get that immoral woman out of that rat Steinberg's apartment?

CHAPTER 15

A MOVIE IN THE HOSPITAL WAITING ROOM wasn't Jennifer's idea of a terrific New Year's Eve celebration. The party, after all, was Leonard Kills Squirrels' doing. She found his administrative efforts, including the party, to be pathetic, a broken attempt at leadership engineered by a broken man. In his own tragic way, he was trying to generate good will among the hospital staff. She suspected, however, that the movie might be a new ploy on the part of Kills Squirrels to undermine the physicians and their families, but if so, she couldn't divine his angle. According to the flier that John had brought home announcing the event, even the kids were invited. She couldn't imagine that Kills Squirrels would cook up something to embarrass the medical staff with their children present. The flier also suggested the revelers bring "refreshments-to-share."

She bundled the twins into their snowsuits, called down the hallway to John that they were ready, and grabbed the bag with the cheese ball she had made of cream cheese, cheddar, Monterey Jack, and onion powder. The recipe called for the ball to be rolled in crushed pecans, but by the time she'd loaded the cheeses into her shopping basket at Swanson's, she decided she'd spent enough money, so she skipped the nuts.

They walked across the icy parking lot, past the three sets of swings whose plank seats swayed and twisted above the weedy tussocks that poked through the snow. With the children in the lead, they climbed the steps to the hospital door.

Inside, the waiting room chairs had been shoved against the walls, and two card tables stood in the center of the floor. Someone had draped a garland of tinsel over the Venetian blinds and had strung Christmas lights on willow branches that stood in the corner. Jennifer liked the lighted willows but thought the tinsel was tacky. She set the cheese ball and a box of Ritz crackers on one of the card tables, beside what looked like Mera's churro cake. Already that table was crowded with plates of cookies, a bowl of popped corn, and a dish of Lipton's onion soup dip surrounded by chunks of Holsum bread. On the other table stood a large bowl filled with red liquid. Virginia Tom had apparently been recruited to ladle the punch.

"Hello, Mrs. Jetters," Virginia said as she rearranged the plastic cups with a broad grin. She handed Mera Maldonado a glass of punch, and the two of them began to chat about the date that Marcus would need a babysitter again after the Christmas pause in Mera's work at the *Tundra Drums.*

Jennifer helped her sons out of their snowsuits and tossed them into the knee-deep pile of coats and jackets and parkas on the floor beside the door to the examining rooms. The twins each grabbed two cookies and began to dash in circles around Marcus.

She surveyed the place. Most of the medical staff were already there. "Where's Stephen?" she asked John.

"I doubt he'll attend a party organized by Kills Squirrels. They remain . . ." John thought for a moment. ". . . ah . . . in conflict." He had told Jennifer that he thought the doctors' revolt—they all, except for Steinberg, applied to move into the dilapidated trailer that Kills Squirrels had recently assigned to Stephen—was funny.

He called it a silly game that Kills Squirrels would lose. She had worried that maybe Kills Squirrels, out of spite, would select John's application, and they'd have to live in that wreck. John laughed at her worry. "No way," he had chuckled.

Jennifer and John both accepted cups of the crimson punch from Virginia and began chatting with her about the weather. "It's always like this in winter," she said referring to the recent cloudy days. She then asked about the pilot of a plane that had crashed last weekend near Crooked Creek.

"He's fine," John said.

Virginia smiled, revealing two gaps where teeth used to be. "How about that man from Aniak who went to Anchorage?" she asked. "How's he doing?"

John didn't answer. Jennifer knew her husband would be reluctant to reveal medical information about a patient. Everyone knew everything about everybody in the whole area, but still . . .

"I heard he was breathing funny," Virginia said.

"He's getting better," John said.

Marcus Maldonado ran by, chased by the Jetters twins. When they trapped him against the wall, he yelled, "You're a stinkhead!"

Brian yelled back, "You're a stink bomb."

Jeffrey yelled, "You're a poop bomb," at which all three boys giggled until they could barely stand up.

Jennifer sipped her punch and wondered where those kids learned such words. The party was not the place to scold them, but she needed to speak to her twins about it later.

"Wonder what made him breathe funny?" Virginia asked.

Jennifer decided to bail John out from Virginia's nosy questions about his patient. She asked, "How do they make those stinkheads, anyway?" She'd never eaten them, had not seen nor smelled them, but knew of their reputation.

"Well . . ." Virginia angled the ladle against the edge of the punch bowl so it wouldn't fall in. "The old way is to dig a hole in the ground and line it with tundra grass." She gestured with her hands as she spoke, making first scooping and then patting motions. "Then lay salmon heads on the grass at the bottom of the hole and cover them with more grass or moss. Months later, they're ready. Mostly men eat them, but I like them too."

Jennifer thought that sounded awful beyond belief. Essentially, they were rotten fish. She couldn't fathom eating spoiled meat of any kind. As she thought about the stinkheads, she sensed the microbiology muse awakening in her. She wondered what kind of microbes were in those grass-lined pits. Most likely both oxygen-loving aerobic bacteria and oxygen-hating anaerobic bacteria lived in the tundra soil. Gazillions of them in every ounce of dirt.

"The younger people don't like grass in their stinkheads, so they put them in jars or plastic bags to age," Virginia continued.

Thinking about aerobes and anaerobes again was like candy for Jennifer. She loved microbiology, loved to contemplate the actions of germs, how they grew, what they did to people. Her musings were interrupted when Leonard marched to the end of the room and shouted for everyone's attention. "We have a very special treat tonight," he called. "*The Unsinkable Molly Brown*."

Apparently, he'd rented the movie from a mail-order place in Anchorage. Jennifer hadn't seen the film, but most likely it would be okay for the kids. Even though she couldn't imagine Leonard knowing anything about children, she also couldn't see him, with his rigid-as-a-steel-rod moral compass, choosing a racy film.

"Take a seat on the floor please," he said while Biff from maintenance fiddled with a movie projector.

Jennifer wore tights under her corduroy slacks and two woolen sweaters, but she was still chilly. She lowered herself to the floor close beside John to stay warm. The twins wiggled themselves between them. Last New Year's Eve, they'd attended a party sponsored by the chief of staff of the hospital where John worked in California. It was held in the ballroom of one of the fancy downtown hotels. Their regular babysitter had watched the twins that night, back when she had babysitters, back when part of her life was independent of her sons, back when she eagerly worked on her thesis project, back when she was able to think about microbiology everyday. She'd bought a new cocktail dress for that party—black silk with giant sequins stitched on the sheer chiffon sleeves. She'd loved that dress, felt sexy and pretty wearing it. She'd even bought lacy hose and black patent, sling-back heels. Those clothes, along with her sundresses and good jewelry and her laboratory coats, were in storage in California. This New Year's Eve party in Alaska would be different. Everything about living was different in Alaska.

Finally, Biff called, "Okay, folks, we're all set." Leonard flipped the wall switch, and the overhead lights blinked off. The beam from the projector lit up the far wall, and soon showed the MGM lion roaring from inside the golden circle. Brian crawled into Jennifer's lap. "I'm scared, Mommy," he whispered.

She patted his head and stretched her arm toward Jeff, who sat still-as-a-stone with his wide eyes locked on the lion.

Suddenly a blast of brassy music thundered from the projector, and Debbie Reynolds began to dance across the wall-screen.

The movie portrayed a very different world from Jennifer's, both her life back in California or now in Alaska. The Denver mansion where Molly-from-the-mountains lived with her newly rich husband and entertained the Colorado social elite; the European royalty; Molly's lover, the prince. The high energy colors, exuberant dancing, and fairy tale atmosphere all rang shallow and melodramatic to Jennifer.

Her mind wandered. She, like Molly, had had dreams. Jennifer's dreams revolved around the world of microbes. She used to imagine herself spending hours every day, for years to come, gazing into a microscope at otherwise invisible germs and teaching eager students about the wondrous ways bacteria and viruses and fungi conduct their lives. Like every other living being, microbes sought to obtain nourishment, to find the most comfortable environment, and to reproduce, and they did all of that in such interesting ways. She liked their simplicity, as well as their complexity.

Since moving to Bethel, she read the microbiology journals that landed in their mailbox every couple of weeks, an attempt to keep up with the rapidly changing field. But she missed the stimulating, and intense, discussions she'd often had with her colleagues. Are viruses alive, they would ask. Yes, some said, because they have the ability to reproduce. No, others argued, because they can't reproduce on their own without assistance from the metabolic machinery in their hosts' cells. She wondered if those colleagues had settled on an answer yet.

She'd enrolled in a pottery class offered by the art teacher at the Bethel High School. She enjoyed the feel of the clay and the sense of accomplishment in converting a lump of earth into a beautiful object with form and function. But she ached for the world of microbiology, where conversations about biologic form and function had so much more meaning than manipulating a gray piece of gooey dirt.

She didn't know if she'd ever achieve her dream; certainly, her languishing in Bethel didn't further any progress toward fulfilling it. Would the two years in Alaska strike a death blow to her thesis? John had assured her it wouldn't, but what did he know? He had an MD degree, not a PhD. He was trained to be a clinician, not a scientist. And he was such a hopeless optimist.

From the look of the reels on the projector, the movie was nearing the end. Debbie, aka Molly Brown, stood in a lifeboat directing the rescue of fellow passengers as the Titanic sank into the sea. Jennifer was ready for the film to be over. She thought it was sappy, and Brian felt heavy as a sack of bricks while he napped in her lap. Jeff and Marcus had fallen asleep on the pile of coats.

Suddenly, the door to the hospital flew open, and Paul, one of the laboratory technicians, raced in. "Mr. Kills Squirrels?" he called, his voice desperate, his gaze shooting around the darkened room.

"Yes?" Leonard rose to his feet, and his body, lit by the beam from the projector, cast an eerie shadow on the wall, obscuring the image of Molly and the roiling ocean and the sinking ship.

"One of the trailers is on fire."

People gasped. Someone flipped on the overhead lights. Leonard looked as if he'd turned into a statue; his body was stiff, his face frozen, his eyes empty. The movie stopped. "Sorry, folks," Biff said. "Show's over."

"Take the kids home," John said to Jennifer.

"No. You take them." She folded her arms across her chest. "I need to see if it's Deidre's place." The Dorfmans had been at the party earlier, but she had seen them sneak out as soon as the movie started.

John's face twisted. He wasn't used to such assertiveness on her part. Usually she deferred to him, let him make the decisions, and she always managed the children. "I'm very worried about Deidre and the baby. I need to know if they are okay. John, she's my friend."

He nodded, with a distressed look on his face, and began stuffing the sleepy twins into their snowsuits.

Jennifer zipped up her parka and followed the crowd out of the hospital, across the parking lot, and toward the stretch of trailers behind the maintenance buildings. When she rounded the snowplow garage, she saw flames shoot from the top of the end trailer and light up the inky sky. Smoke, black as midnight, billowed upward and, driven by the wind, drifted toward the river. Something inside the trailer exploded with a loud pop. A shower of sparks spewed from the flames and scattered over the surrounding snow. Something else blew up with a big bang. Then a louder bang. The air, acrid and irritating, smelled of burnt plastic. She could feel the heat from the flames on her bare cheeks. She began to cough and stepped back a few paces.

The murmur from the crowd melded with the sizzle of the sparks. "Does anyone live there?" someone asked loud enough for her to hear. She knew it wasn't Deidre and David's place but didn't know who, if anyone, had moved into that one.

Leonard Kills Squirrels had parked himself at the edge of the throng. He stood perfectly still, gripping his hat with his hands, and his eyes were bolted to the horizon. As Jennifer watched his long hair blow across his face, she studied his chiseled profile back-lit by the flames. He was a tall, lean, deep-eyed man. But while he watched the fire, he looked lonely, diminished, and paralyzed.

Biff, with a garden hose looped over his shoulder, dashed into the trailer beside the burning one and soon dashed back out with water spouting from the nozzle. He was followed by the x-ray technician, who was snapping shut his jacket over his pajamas. Biff handed him the end of the hose. "Here, spray water on your house," he yelled.

The fire continued to swallow the end trailer and to send sparks high into the night sky. Stephen and Jackie appeared at Jennifer's side. "Do you know if anyone lives there?" she asked.

"That's the turquoise and cream-colored wreck that Kills Squirrels tried to foist on me." Stephen's face looked grim, but she thought she saw a glimmer of a smile.

"Gosh," Jennifer said. "How did it start, I wonder?" For a moment she thought Stephen might have done it, a final retaliation for Leonard's newest cockamamie scheme to get Jackie out of his apartment.

"I don't know, but besides everything else wrong with that place, I'm sure it was a firetrap." He paused, and then added. "Kills Squirrels is an apt name for that asshole. I might change it to Kills Everything in His Wake."

She spotted David Dorfman, dressed in mud boots and a fur hat, and wrapped in a blanket. She waved and yelled, "Is Deidre okay?"

He yelled back, "Yes."

As Jennifer watched the blazing trailer, Virginia Tom walked up beside her. She stomped her giant boots on the snow and gazed into the flames. The stoic look on her face suggested that Virginia had lived this misfortune before as if fire were a natural, but solemn, aspect of the earth's rhythms.

Jennifer stared ahead, cocked her head, and caught her breath. What was that? Something was moving in the shadows near the inferno. Jennifer blinked her eyes and tried to see it more clearly through the dark and the smoke. A hunched-over human figure staggered away from the flaming mass and fell to the ground. She gasped and started forward. Stephen grabbed her arm to stop her. Several men raced past her, gathered around the burning person, rolled the body in the snow that carpeted the ground, and then carried it over to the hospital. The crowd hummed with whispers. Who is that? What are they doing in that abandoned trailer? Are they badly burned? Are they dying?

Stephen turned to Jackie. "I'd better see if Matias—he's on duty tonight—needs any help. You should go on home, Jackie."

Jennifer stayed. She was mesmerized by the flames, by the way the tongues of blue and orange rose and fell and swayed from side to side, by the way they flickered and danced as if they were alive. The crackle of the embers, the silence that otherwise surrounded the hard-to-believe-it-was-really-true scene entranced her. So did the horror. And the danger.

The crowd began to thin. She heard a distant voice call "Virginia!" and, from the corner of her eye, she saw Virgina Tom race as fast as her short legs would carry her toward the hospital.

The flames began to die down. Jennifer still stayed, watching. The Dorfmans were safe. The smell was atrocious. Her husband and children were home. She was alone, there in the night. Finally, when all that was left of the trailer was its white-hot metal skeleton, she trudged through the snow back to her family.

Chapter 16

"This way." The nurse led Virginia Tom by the hand down the dim hallway. When they passed under a ceiling light, Virginia watched their shadows move under their feet. Those flickery images were spooky gray and looked like ghosts. She hadn't been in this part of the hospital since her last baby, Mitchell, was born. That was a long time ago. She was younger then and eager to give birth to the child. Now, she was older and afraid of what she'd find there. The hallway looked pretty much the same: green paint and worn linoleum.

"He's in here," the nurse said. They stopped at a doorway.

She didn't dare go in. She didn't want to see what had happened to Nicholas, but seeing him was the reason she had come.

"It's okay, Virginia. Go on in." The nurse let go of her hand and nudged her into the room. "He'll be glad to see you."

The air smelled funny. Clean like alcohol but sharper than whiskey. There was a lump under the bed covers, and it didn't move. *Was he awake?* she wondered. A tube twisted like a snake as it ran from a bottle that dangled on a pole and then disappeared under the sheet.

The up-side-down bottle was full of what looked like water. *They wouldn't drip that stuff into him if he was dead,* she thought.

She had been in the hospital waiting room all night while the doctors tended to him. The nurse had shoved two chairs together for a bed and given her a pillow and blanket. It was quiet there, and the Christmas lights on the willow branches twinkled like the stars in the nighttime sky. She'd slept a little but mostly she'd worried about him. She looked down at her wrinkled kuspuk—the same clothes she had worn to the New Year's Eve party. That seemed like a week ago rather than just last night.

Dr. Maldonado told her it was a bad burn. "25%," he'd said. She asked what that meant. He told her his legs and one arm were singed.

"Is he going to die?" she asked.

"We can never predict the future, but I expect he'll do okay," Dr. Maldonado said. "It'll be a long recovery though."

As she neared the bed, she could see that his eyes were closed. He had long lashes, like a girl. Some of the kids at school had teased him about that; he was suspended for a week once for kicking and cussing them. She'd recognize him anywhere by those lashes.

The right side of his face—the side toward her—was scratched as if he'd been in a fight with a fox. A bandage covered his ear and part of his neck. His right arm, which lay on top of the blanket, was wrapped in gauze. She couldn't see his legs.

His head moved.

"Nicholas? Are you awake?" she whispered. "It's aana." He didn't like her to talk Eskimo. "Nicholas? It's your mama."

His eyelids fluttered. They opened, and he groaned. Then, he stared at her face so hard he seemed to look straight through her.

"Nicholas, Dr. Maldonado says you're going to be okay. Can you hear me?"

"Yeah." His voice was faint as a whisper; she could barely understand what he'd said.

"Do you hurt?" Dr. Maldonado had told her they'd given him a lot of pain medicine, so he'd be pretty groggy.

"No." His voice was a tiny bit stronger.

She sat down on the folding chair at the end of his bed.

The nurse stuck her head into the room. "Virginia, we're getting ready to send him to Anchorage this afternoon."

Dr. Maldonado had told her that too. He'd said a bad burn like that needed the special doctors and nurses in the burn unit at the IHS Hospital in Anchorage. They were just waiting until the Wein Air jet would leave. He'd said one of the nurses would go with Nicholas on the plane. He said they had a special gurney they would use to strap him in tight during the flight.

She'd asked, "What's a gurney?" He said it was a stretcher on wheels.

She'd never been to the Indian Hospital in Anchorage. Her sister had and said the nurses and doctors were very nice, and the gift shop sold a lot of baskets made by Indians and Eskimos from all over Alaska. Virginia was sure they'd take good care of her son.

"Mama?" Nicholas lifted his head off the pillow. "Where's Mr. Nopoka?"

"Nopoka? Edmund Nopoka? I have no idea where that bum is. Why do you want to know?"

Nicholas was silent. He closed his eyes.

"Why are you asking?"

He said nothing.

"Nicholas, was he in that trailer with you?"

"Mama, I'm sorry."

"Sorry? For what? What were the two of you doing in there?"

He opened his eyes and looked out the window. "He asked me to bring him some smokes."

"To the trailer? Was he living there?"

"I guess so." He closed his eyes.

"Nicholas, how did that fire start?"

"I'm sorry." He turned his head toward the wall.

"How?"

"Mr. Nopoka knocked over his bottle, and it spilled on the floor.

When he reached for it, his cigarette dropped into the puddle of vodka, and the rug caught on fire. I tried to stomp it out."

"Nicholas, that man is nothing but trouble." The last time she had seen Nopoka, he had staggered into Our Mother of All Saints' during Mass and asked Father Brogan for some of the communion wine, right in the middle of the service. His hair had been an oily tangle, he wore huge Army boots, and his pants were stiff with mud. She didn't understand how he had gotten so muddy when the ground was covered with snow and ice.

"I'm sorry." Nicholas turned his head back toward her. "Where is he?"

"I don't know." She took a deep breath. Could he still be in that smoldering trailer? Maybe he too had burned.

When the nurse came to take Nicholas' temperature, Virginia asked if Edmund Nopoka was there in the hospital.

"No, not in the past couple days," the nurse said.

So, where was he? Must still be in that trailer. Virginia's hands began to shake.

Nicholas drifted off to sleep. She twisted the hem of her kuspuk. Now her son was *really* in trouble—medical trouble and maybe state trooper trouble. Whether or not he'd done something bad, Nicholas was always the first to be blamed.

She couldn't decide. Should she tell someone that Edmund Nopoka might still be in the burnt trailer? He didn't have a wife; no children that he claimed. His brother, who was also a drunk, died several years ago when he fell face down in a bog out there on the tundra and was too soused to get up. Their parents had died of old age, and the other kids had all moved to Juneau or Haines or Sitka or somewhere southeast. There was no one left in Bethel to hunt for Edmund Nopoka.

Nicholas tried to turn to his side and groaned again.

"Are you awake?" she asked softly.

No answer.

Nicholas attracted bad luck like fish attracted flies. Why was he like that? None of her other kids were such a problem. It must have happened while he stayed with her sisters when she was in the san at Dillingham. She never knew what all they did to little Nicholas while she was gone.

She glanced around her, at the walls and doorways and ceiling. In some ways it was like her first room at the san: tall windows, one bed, dreary paint. In Dillingham, the walls were light green; in Bethel, they were darker light green. In that room at the san, she had been so lonely. She cried all day and all night and wondered what was happening to her kids. In the summer, she lay on a bed on the porch with the sun shining in her eyes and begged to go home.

Once, the doctor took her to a dark, smelly room with humming equipment and let her look in a microscope. She saw what he said were the germs that made her sick with TB. "Looks like tundra moss," she said.

"You could think of it that way," he said. "Or you could think of it like salmonberry seeds that get into your lungs and grow into an infection." She tried to imagine salmonberry bushes inside her chest. She couldn't feel their stickers. When she coughed, no berries or leaves or anything like that came up.

Then the TB medicine came. Those shots. And the needles. She used to watch the nurses sharpen the needles in their work room.

Something had happened to little Nicholas while she was in that san.

Now, he was burned and in the Bethel Hospital, asking about that worthless Edmund Nopoka.

If she mentioned Mr. Nopoka in that burning trailer to anyone, they would eventually figure out that Nicholas had been smoking and drinking with him that night. That'd be big trouble for her son. Maybe they'd accuse him of setting the fire and murdering Edmund. They'd never believe Nicholas. He wasn't the kind of person that people would easily believe. He was tricky, and he didn't always tell the truth. If anyone knew about Nopoka, Nicholas would land in the prison at Goose Creek and rot there forever.

She sat up straight in her chair. Soon though, Nicholas would be in Anchorage. By the time he got back to Bethel, everyone would be worried about something else. She decided to sit there in his room until they took him to the plane.

The nurse came in to check his IV.

The janitor came in to mop the floor.

The kitchen lady came in with lunch. Nicholas turned his head to the wall when she tried to feed him. She begged him to eat, said he needed food to heal. He still refused. The tray, with boiled salmon, a square of orange Jell-O, and a pile of applesauce, sat on the table next to his bed. Virginia was hungry. She ate it all.

The nurse came in to take his temperature. After sticking the thermometer in his mouth, she left. "What were you doing in that trailer?" Virginia asked. Nicholas couldn't speak with that thing stuck in his mouth. "Nicholas, don't ask anyone about Mr. Nopoka. No one. Never say his name again." When the nurse returned and pulled out the thermometer, he took a breath as if he was going to answer his mother's question about Nopoka. She couldn't let him do that.

"Nicholas." Virginia interrupted him. "You'd better rest now." He closed his eyes.

Finally, the nurse and the orderly wheeled in the gurney. "Time to head to the airport," the nurse said. Then she gave a shot to the tubing that ran from the bottle of water into Nicholas' hand. "It's a little sleepy juice to keep him comfortable during the trip," she said.

He'd doze the whole way to Anchorage, and he'd be there a long time. He wouldn't be able to ask anyone from Bethel about Nopoka. Nicholas would be safe. Virginia opened her mouth, took a deep breath, and let her air out with a long, silent sigh.

Chapter 17

WHEN LEONARD KILLS SQUIRRELS HEARD THE knock on his office door, he didn't want to answer. It couldn't possibly be anything good. It never was. For sure someone wanted something he couldn't, or wouldn't, give them. Probably someone had a gripe, maybe about another employee, a frozen water pipe, a broken furnace, or lost mail. He no longer wanted to run the Complaint Department at the hospital.

They knocked again.

He hesitated and then called out, "Come in."

The door swung open, and Biff from maintenance stomped in wearing his heavy boots and winter parka. "Hey, Boss," he said. Biff always called him boss. "We're about to haul the burned shell of that trailer off to the dump. Is that okay? Anything else we should do with it?"

Leonard nodded. "Yeah, that's fine." Biff saluted him, turned 180 degrees, and stomped back out. *Yes*, Leonard thought. *Get rid of that thing. The sooner the better.*

Whenever Leonard passed that trailer's carcass, he remembered the fire. It was horrid, had ruined the New Year's Eve party, and they hadn't even been able to finish the movie. Every time he thought of the fire, he thought of Steinberg, and then the rest of the smarty-pants doctors. Hopefully, once the trailer was gone, all those ugly thoughts would also disappear.

At the end of the workday, as Leonard walked across the hospital parking lot toward his apartment, he heard a loud popping sound. It came from near the maintenance buildings. Sounded like gunfire. He ran for the nearest truck and crouched behind the cab. Who would have a gun? What would they be shooting at? And why? The sound kept coming. It was illegal to hunt on IHS property. At least, it should be.

Despite the continued noise, he slowly raised his head so he could see through the cab's side windows. The hospital deuce-and-a-half—surplus from the Fort Richardson supply depot in Anchorage—chugged around the corner of the maintenance building. Behind the truck, at the end of a heavy chain, lurched the burned-out trailer whose tires had blown in the fire and then melted. Broken glass fell from its windows, the roof sagged ever deeper into the hull's body, and the door flapped open and closed as it bumped along. With Biff at the wheel, the deuce-and-a-half dragged the trailer over the parking lot, its bottom plowing through the ice and gravel. The thing made a heck of a racket. Leonard cupped the palms of his mittens over his ears while the truck-plus-trailer jerked by. "Good riddance," he said to himself.

The trailer was finally gone, and he felt lighter and hungrier than usual. Back home, he pulled two cans of beef barley soup from the pantry closet and warmed them on the stove. To celebrate, he'd have a donut, the last one in the box he'd gotten at Swanson's a week ago.

He set the soup pan at the end of the table and sat down. His current jigsaw puzzle was spread over the table's other end. He had just started that one; he'd found all except three of the edge pieces and fitted them together. The picture on the box was a big bushy rose, and the pieces all seemed to be either the pink of the flower or the blue of the sky in the background. It'd be hard. He'd put this one together at least four or five times before, and every time it had been pretty tough.

With each spoonful of soup though, his thoughts grew heavier. His memories of the fire hadn't disappeared after all. Instead, they came roaring back to him like relentless lightning. The crackling of the blaze, the sour smell of burning plastic, the dirty orange flames that licked the dark, winter sky. He'd seen Steinberg and his slutty girlfriend watching the trailer burn. That thought grabbed his belly. He'd reassigned Steinberg to live in that trailer, but that didn't work. Then, the blasted thing caught fire.

And there was that kid who had stumbled out of the flames, Nicholas Tom, Virginia Tom's son. What was he doing in there? Probably trying to steal something. Leonard always knew that kid was trouble. This time his bad antics had caught up with him; the doctors said he'd be in the Anchorage Hospital for a long time.

One thing for sure: it was the Tom kid who started the fire. Biff from maintenance had offered the repair crew to help investigate the cause of the blaze. What did they know about investigating fires? Nothing is what. They were experts in connecting water pipes, rewiring electric, keeping the furnaces running, waxing the hospital floors. Nicholas Tom started the fire.

Through the rest of his soup and then through the donut, thoughts of that burning trailer raced like bottle rockets through Leonard's mind. In some ways, they were like the falling stars that had soared through the August night sky over the endless prairie of the Rosebud Reservation.

Lots of bad things had happened at the Bethel Hospital on his watch. The boiler exploded shortly after he'd arrived. The nurses complained about the new head nurse he'd hired. Then the doctors complained that the nurses were irritable and threatened to go to Headquarters if he didn't fire that head nurse. The accountant found a $1,205.25 shortfall when she tried to reconcile the books. They never did figure out what happened there.

He stirred his soup and picked up a piece of potato with his spoon. His thoughts grew darker. The long winter nights, the cold winter days, the boring tundra, those damned doctors.

Then, as he scooped a piece of meat from the soup and shoved it into his mouth, brighter memories began to flicker through his head. He smiled to himself as he recalled the pow-wows at the Rosebud, with thunder drums, hoop dancing, and hot, fresh Indian fry bread. He particularly liked the eagle dancers, who waved their feathered arms as if they were soaring high above the South Dakota grasslands. More memories raced through his mind: turkey hunting with his cousins, calling the prairie dogs, the colors of the spring wildflowers, the smell of the ponderosa pines, the way the dry evening breeze blew across the hills.

That's where he belonged, back with his people, not on this dreadful, cursed Yup'ik land.

IT WAS STILL DARK AS MIDNIGHT when Leonard typed the memo.

To: Superintendent, IHS Headquarters, Indian Health Service, Washington D.C.

From: Leonard Kills Squirrels, Hospital Administrator, IHS Hospital, Bethel. Alaska

I'm seeking information about hospital administrative positions immediately available, or soon to be available, in the Indian Health Service, Great Plains Area. I have been associated with the Indian Health Service for 18 years and, as a Hunkpapa Lakota, I am an enrolled member of the Rosebud Sioux Tribe. Attached is my formal resume.

I look forward to your reply.

Yours truly,

Leonard Kills Squirrels

Chapter 18

The noon sun flowed like a river of butterscotch through the kitchen window of the teachers' house on Nunivak Island. "Look at you," Rachel said. She patted Mera's gently protruding belly. "Remind me when the baby's due."

"In about two months. We're pretty excited." At that moment, Mera felt a kick on her left side. She treasured those soft little jolts, so abrupt, so random. They brought reality to the otherwise elusive concept of a tiny human being growing inside her. They had started out several months ago as flutters; it had felt like a butterfly was loose in her intestines. Then, the kicks grew in strength. Now, they were jabs from the inside. Those little pokes meant the baby was alive and healthy enough to swing its leg.

Mera and Matias had just arrived on Nunivak Island for Matias's visit to the clinic at Mekoryuk. Rachel's house, cozy and warm, was small, as she had described when she first met Mera in Bethel.

"Where's your son?" Rachel asked.

"At the clinic with Matias."

Of course, Marcus had come with them. Mera never left her son except when Virginia Tom came to their house to watch him while she worked at the *Tundra Drums* office. She finished taking off her parka and laid it on a chair. "Another good thing about kuspuks," she said, smoothing the hem of her tunic. "Besides being comfortable and simple to make, they fit easily over pregnant bodies."

Rachel's living room floor was a sea of toys: three wooden cars with wheels made of juice bottle tops, a hand-crocheted mouse, pine blocks, and a cardboard house made from a huge pilot bread carton with a swinging cardboard door and orange bandana curtains at both windows. Mera said, "I see Robert lives here. Where is he?"

"Trying to take a nap." Rachel leaned her head toward the bedroom. "I don't hear him anymore. Maybe he finally fell asleep."

She turned back toward Mera and placed a small object in her palm. "I haven't forgotten that I owe you a hippopotamus."

Mera looked at the tiny figurine, a gray ceramic hippo from Red Rose tea. Rachel had remembered that she'd traded it for a giraffe. "Thanks a lot," she laughed.

"How was the flight?" Rachel asked. "I'm a little surprised you ventured away from Bethel while so pregnant."

Mera cocked her head and wondered at that comment. She viewed Rachel as the fearless one, the teacher from Mekoryuk who dared to deliver Robert at the Bethel Hospital, who chose to raise him on a desolate island dangling like an iceberg in the Bering Sea. But now Rachel expressed surprise that she, Mera, while seven months pregnant, had flown in a bush plane to Nunivak Island in the dead of winter. Mera would have thought Rachel considered the trip to be nothing at all. She looked around for a place to sit. Coming to Mekoryuk had been a last-minute decision, hatched late in the night yesterday, less than twelve hours before they took off from the frozen river in Bethel. "Are you sure you want to go?" Matias had asked.

"Yes, I'm sure." She wanted to see Rachel again, wanted a change of scenery. She was tired of looking at the same walls in her apartment, tired of the same view of the tundra from her windows.

"It's a risk, albeit a small one," Matias had said. "I don't want to have to deliver our baby . . . our premature baby . . . myself out on that island at the end of the world."

She figured the risk was tiny.

Her husband continued to quiz her; she continued to want to go. All those failed pregnancies had ended by three or four months, so this one seemed secure at thirty-two weeks.

She moved a giant stuffed panda to the end of Rachel's sofa and sat in the vacated space. Now, in the light of day, and after the bumpy flight in that plane, her mind had shifted gears. The world looked different. Was it smart to risk going into premature labor on Nunivak Island? They would be in Mekoryuk for two more days. Then, they would ride the plane back, hoping they had decent weather when their visit was over. "I couldn't miss the opportunity to see you again," she said to Rachel. "I enjoyed your visit with us in Bethel, back when Robert was sick, very much."

Rachel shook her head and smiled. "That's so sweet. We're really pleased you came. Are you okay sleeping on that thing?" She pointed to the sofa. "It pulls out into a bed."

"That's fine, so much better than a sleeping bag on the floor of the clinic, which was IHS's plan." *Where would Marcus sleep?* she wondered. With them on the hide-a-bed? It would be possible—anything was possible—but crowded. Yet, she liked the idea of her entire family, Matias, Marcus, the unborn baby, and herself, snuggling together all night.

"And we made a special bed for Marcus. We thought he might enjoy that." Rachel pointed to a big cardboard box across the room. Someone had painted it to look like a cobalt-colored boat, but the words Quaker Oats showed through the blue paint. It was filled with blankets.

"He'll love that. You guys are so creative."

Rachel giggled in her musical, lilting laugh that Mera so enjoyed. The last time she'd heard it was back in October at Daniel Dorfman's bris.

The front door opened, and Marcus tottered in, followed by his father. Mera unzipped her son's snowsuit and pulled it off him. He raced toward the boat/bed and crawled in.

"Wow, what a gorgeous sweater," Rachel said. She was talking about Marcus's red wool pullover, the one with the white stars knit into it. "I remember from when I stayed at your place last fall that you're a knitter," Rachel continued. "Did you make that?"

"I did."

"Let's go next door then, to Ida's. She's the teachers' aide at the school. She has something you'll like to see."

They headed toward the faded, blood red, wooden house beside Rachel's. Off to the right were the dogs, eight of them, each lying inside its own fifty-five-gallon oil barrel, each with its snout sticking out from a hole cut in the drum's side, eying the neighborhood. Beside each barrel, an iron stake anchored a chain that ran into each hole. Mera could see the dogs' eyes, beady black dots with light gray haloes, back in the shadows of their barrels. Those wary eyes followed the women while they walked up the boardwalk. When they'd reached the path to Ida's house, the dogs emerged from their barrels and stretched their hairy legs. Their rattling chains sounded like rusty bells. "Ida's husband is proud of these fellows," Rachel said. "They're the best sled dogs on the island."

The door to the house swung open, they stepped into the warm room that smelled of fuel oil, and Rachel introduced Mera to Ida Amos. "Mera is also a knitter," Rachel said, "and she'd love to see some of your work."

"Ee." Ida grinned. Her eyes narrowed as her smile widened, deepening the gentle wrinkles on her face.

"And this is Albert, Ida's husband," Rachel said, pointing to the man seated at a table. He looked up from the wooden kayak he was carving and nodded.

Mera glanced around the room. Like all Yup'ik homes, it was stuffy, compact, and dark. Pans hung from nails in the wall over the cook stove, boxes of pilot bread and cans of engine oil as well as drinking glasses, chipped cereal bowls, a Coleman lantern, and a drip coffee pot crowded the counter. Heaps of fabric—they looked like folded kuspuks or possibly yards of unsewn printed cotton—stood on a shelf.

On the opposite wall, someone lay on the lowest bed in a triple-layered bunk built of rough wood. "That's Albert's mama," Rachel said, nodding toward the lump in the bed. "Very old," she murmured quietly so Ida couldn't hear. "They take good care of her." In a louder voice, Rachel called, "Hello, Granny Amos." A wrinkled hand emerged from under the quilt, waved, and then dove back under the bedding.

Mera spotted a pile of ashy brown spun yarn and several sets of knitting needles, some straight, some double pointed, some circular, on a table near the door. Ida unfolded one of the knitted pieces stacked near the needles. It was a neck scarf with a lacy pattern.

"This is the harpoon stitch, from Mekoryuk," Ida said in her Yup'ik voice, a quiet low-pitched murmur with clipped words and long pauses while she considered what to say.

"Harpoon stitch?" Mera asked. She wasn't familiar with that.

"Ee. It was etched into the ivory of a harpoon head. A really old one that my nephew found out at Nash Harbor, where the sand meets the sea. We figured out how to knit that pattern."

Ida rubbed her knobby fingers over the lace stitches and handed the scarf to Mera. It was much lighter than she expected, about weight of a leaf. Yarn-overs followed by knit-two-together stitches made little holes arranged to look like six-pointed stars, with panels of diamond-shaped holes surrounding them. She hadn't seen anything like it. "This is so beautiful," she said. She rubbed it against her cheek. "I've never felt wool so soft—softer than alpaca or even cashmere." It smelled faintly of pepper, laced with the tangy odor of dried weeds from the tundra.

"Ee. It doesn't shrink and isn't scratchy. It sheds water too. And it's warm." Ida looked at the floor, embarrassed by Mera's compliment. "Not strong though. No good for socks."

"The yarn is called qiviut," Rachel said.

Mera heard kiv-ee-ute. "How do you spell that? In English?"

Rachel spelled it out. "It's Yup'ik for down, as in goose down. It's the underwool from muskoxen, which run wild on this island. I'll show you where it comes from."

Mera rubbed the scarf against her cheek once more—the downy feel was irresistible—and thanked Ida for showing it to her. The story of the qiviut might make a good article for the *Tundra Drums*. She'd pitch it to the editor next time she saw him.

While she and Rachel walked away from Ida's house, the chains once again jangled as the nosy dogs crawled out of their barrels. Mera kept a respectful distance well beyond the length of each chain. She usually didn't fear dogs, but she *was* afraid of them now. They could hurt her unborn baby.

They strolled shoulder to shoulder on the boardwalk to the edge of town, past the sheds of weathered raw wood, past the small houses with smoke twisting from their chimneys, past the crates, fish traps, oil tanks, and boats bottom-up on sawhorses that littered the ground. At the end of the boardwalk, they turned and looked back from where they'd come. Down the hill, over the roofs of the houses, Mera could see the sea frozen solid.

Her breaths were fast and deep. The uphill climb had been harder than she imagined. She asked herself, again, why she had thought it was a good idea to come to Nunivak Island. And where on earth were they going now? And why? She felt another little kick in her belly. Her baby was still alive.

They turned, again, and walked an icy path that meandered through the frozen tundra ahead. Rachel stopped until Mera caught up and then grabbed her arm. "How's it going?" Rachel asked.

Mera nodded, too breathless to speak.

"We're almost there."

Panting, Mera looked up. Ahead, wooden crosses leaned every which way above the snow-covered ground; some had fallen completely over. As they neared the cemetery, she could see that the names on many of the crosses had weathered away, the letters fading into the sun-bleached wood. The wind had driven the grave markers sideways in different directions, and they reminded Mera of the pick-up sticks she played with as a child, those wooden sticks that were scattered willy-nilly on the kitchen floor waiting for her to gather them. Everything about the crosses seemed crude. Overhead the sky was dull gray, echoing the sense of death in the windswept graveyard.

The hill of the dead reminded Mera of her mother's family burial plots in Mexico. Same haunted air, same simple crosses. They looked as if they were made of lath boards, a shorter piece nailed perpendicular to a longer one. The ground, though, was different. No ice or snow in Mexico.

The crosses were different sizes. Mera wondered if the little ones marked the graves of babies. She stooped to read the names: "Elsa Da . . ., . . . MA . . . RIT . . ." Dead children? She moved to the next small cross and read the name. "Je . . . Nic . . ." She and Matias hadn't buried their dead children because they really weren't children yet when she'd passed those little bloody blobs. Rather, they'd given each a name and then let the hospital pathologists handle the precious but lifeless tissue.

It wasn't just the absence of her babies now that saddened her. It was the loss of their future possibilities. They might have become doctors or lawyers or professors, the same as these dead Yup'ik babies who might have mastered how to catch salmon or mend nets or hunt moose or knit qiviut scarves when they grew up. She wiped her eyes with the back of her glove.

"For some reason, the muskoxen like the cemetery," Rachel laughed from several feet away. "Let's see . . . I was up here the other day and saw . . ." She wandered among the crosses. "Ah, here it is," she called.

Mera joined Rachel in front of an otherwise unremarkable cross. "See? The brown stuff? That's shed qiviut," Rachel said.

A hairy patch the color of lightly creamed coffee was impaled on the splintered horizontal bar of the cross. "A muskox must have rubbed up against it last spring during molting season. Hard to believe it's still here this winter. The native people pick this fur from the ground or bushes after the molt. They then spin it into yarn."

"Is that where Ida gets hers?" Mera was eager for her thoughts to move away from the dead children. It was too sad, with achy echoes of her own dead children. "Seems like a lot of work for a little bit of the fluff, and it would take a whole lot of that fluff for a scarf."

"Actually, Ida gets most of her qiviut from the hides of the animals that her husband and relatives hunt. It's the best meat on the planet. Her cousin spins it for her." Rachel plucked the wool from the cross. "Here." she handed it to Mera. "A souvenir from Nunivak Island."

Mera pulled off her right glove and clasped the wool fluff between her fingers. It was soft as dandelion fuzz. She held it to her nose. Rather than the peppery, woodsy scent of the yarn, the raw wool smelled like a mouse. She stuffed it into her parka pocket, whispered goodbye to the buried babies, and followed Rachel back down the hill.

THE LATE MORNING SUN, A BLAZING ball of fire, dangled at the horizon. There were no clouds to reflect its rays; rather, the tangerine skyline bled upward and slowly turned to light mauve. Mera glanced at the sun quickly. The orange globe seemed to bounce on the edge of the earth. Then, squinting, she looked away. She wanted to look again, to see if the sun was really bouncing, but it was too bright.

She had stepped outside to see what was taking Rachel so long. Minutes earlier, Ida had banged on Rachel's door. She seemed upset about something. Rachel had said, "I'll be right back," over her shoulder as she pulled on her parka. Mera looked toward Ida's house. The front door was wide open.

Mera stepped back into Rachel's house and put on her outdoor clothes. "I'll be next door," she called to Matias.

The sun now hung well above the horizon, and the whole sky was sea blue. Perfect flying weather. Yesterday had been overcast and very windy. Some things changed as quickly as a gasp in Alaska: the weather; the hours of daylight; and the way the river broke up in the spring, sending torrents of ice chunks slamming together while the newly thawed water raced to the sea. Other things stayed constant: the dogs, the warm smiles of the native people, their ways of living on that difficult land. Mera was glad she had come to Mekoryuk, glad to see Rachel and where she lived, glad to learn about qiviut; she was looking forward to writing about it for the *Drums*. In her notes she'd made a drawing of the knitted pattern and written "Nash Harbor harpoon" to remind herself of its origin. All in all, the trip was worth the risk. She and her baby would make it back to Bethel without any trouble.

She walked into the open door of Ida's house. Rachel leaned over a man who lay on the sofa. "It's Albert. He's not well."

Eskimo men didn't lay on sofas. Mera knew something bad must be wrong with him. She couldn't see his face. It was hidden by Rachel. "I'll get Matias," she said.

She was breathless as she told her husband about Albert. "You better check him out. I'll stay here with Marcus." Matias shot out of Rachel's front door.

While Mera waited, she worried. Was it a heart attack? An ulcer? Was he going to die?

When Matias finally returned, he explained that Albert needed to get to the Bethel Hospital quickly. "I think we'll have room for him on the mail plane that takes us back today. Are you okay with that?"

"Of course." Why wouldn't she be? "If there's not enough room, he could go with you, and Marcus and I can come another day."

He wrapped his arms around her shoulders and kissed her on the forehead. His embrace was strong as a bull's and yet gentle; she felt very secure. "I have the best wife ever," he whispered.

It was two days before Mera and Marcus could get a mail plane back to Bethel. She and Rachel spent the late afternoons—after school was dismissed—with Ida, who sat in her chair and slowly knit a qiviut scarf. She said very little, other than offering them tea. Mera could tell from the faraway look in her dull, ebony eyes though that terror lurked behind that stoic exterior.

The morning they were to return to Bethel, Mera felt a cramp in her belly. While she finishing packing Marcus's stuff, she felt several more.

"Rachel," she finally said, "I wonder if I'm in labor." It was too early. The baby wasn't due to be born for two more months.

"The mail plane will be here in about an hour. Lay down here, and stay there until we can get you to the plane."

Mera was scared. She desperately wanted Matias there. He'd know what to do. She lay on Rachel's sofa-bed with her feet propped up on a Rice-A-Roni carton. *Please, baby*, she whispered to herself, *don't come now.*

Rachel bundled Marcus in his snowsuit and told him they were going to find the plane. He turned to Mera and saw that she wasn't coming. "No," he said.

"Marcus, honey, you have to go with Rachel while I stay here. We'll both get on the plane soon."

He screamed "No, no, no. I don't wanna go," and was still screaming and kicking while Rachel carried him out the door.

Mera began to weep. She'd lose yet another baby. Why did she want to come to Mekoryak? Why did Matias have to leave her there? Because Mr. Amos was very sick and Matias was a doctor. That thought made her weep even more.

Rachel returned with the pilot, the health aide from Mekoryak who carried a canvas litter, several young men, and a neighbor with a dog sled. Marcus raced to his mother and climbed onto the sofa beside her.

"Easy, honey," Mera said as she patted Marcus on his bottom. "Rachel will carry you while we go to the plane."

"We're going to ease you to the sled so you don't have to walk to the plane," Rachel said and rolled her into her parka.

They helped Mera scoot onto the litter and laid her on the sled. She felt a little bump when the dogs took off, but the team walked, rather than ran, over the snowy ground to the frozen river and the waiting plane.

At home that night, Mera lay on their bed with her feet propped on two cushions from the couch and Marcus at her side.

Matias brought in a bowl of Lipton chicken noodle soup, "Any more contractions?" he asked.

"Not since right after I got here," she said. "They never were regular, just every once in a while and not terribly strong, but definitely there. Matias, that baby can't come now. It's way too early."

Matias told Marcus to go to his room and put together a Lego drum. Marcus looked confused but left the bedroom. Matias examined his wife. His face was solemn, and then he smiled. "You're not in real labor, Mera. Those are Braxton-Hicks contractions, or false labor.

She started to weep again.

"How's Mr. Amos?" Mera asked a few minutes later.

"Well, it's the damnedest thing. His symptoms are similar to those of that fellow from Aniak. We sent Mr. Amos on to Anchorage. What's going on with these folks anyway? It's a long way from Mekoryuk to Aniak, so likely not contagious."

Mera shook her head, another Alaskan mystery. There were so many of them, but most importantly, her baby was safe.

CHAPTER 19

THE ENTIRE APARTMENT SMELLED OF CHOCOLATE, warm and gooey, rich, and sweet. The alluring odor swirled up from the oven, floated around the clean dishes stacked on the drying rack, and headed out into the living room. Jackie was learning to cook.

To Stephen, who walked into the kitchen, sat at the table, and watched as she finished swabbing the counter, Jackie moved around his apartment like a song, a smooth, gentle ode to an otherwise cold but sunny day. Certainly, she was more comfortable with cooking than Sandra had ever been. His ex-wife had never learned to cook. While in Bethel, she had warmed up cans of Chef Boyardee spaghetti or ravioli, Chung King chow mein, or boxes of Stouffer's frozen dinners. She seemed most suited to the kitchen the day she threw the spatula and saucepan at him; the day before she decamped to Philadelphia.

The timer on the stove buzzed. "It's done," Jackie said. She draped a towel over her hands, reached into the oven, and pulled out a square baking pan.

"Smells wonderful," he said. "Um . . . what is it?"

"A crazy cake." She waved the pan toward him so he could see the dark brown substance inside. "Dr. Jetters taught me how to make it."

"What's crazy about it?" He admired her spunk and the way she followed her curiosity, wherever it led. She liked to try new things and was learning to knit from Mera. In the evenings, Stephen marveled at the way Jackie slouched over a pair of knitting needles, her hair draped like a veil over her face, as she painstakingly wrapped the yarn around the needles, one stitch at a time, stitch after stitch. He admired the intensity of her concentration, her persistence in getting it right, and her confidence that she'd master the craft eventually. She was making herself a winter scarf.

"I'm not sure. Maybe the crazy way it's put together. You dump flour, baking soda, and cocoa powder into the baking pan; scoop out three wells; dump water, vinegar, and oil into the wells; and mix it all together. Then, you bake it."

Jackie's sunny voice with its soothing Georgia drawl was a delight to his ear. He chuckled. "Since I don't know how to make regular cake, I'll take your word for it that this is crazy. Do we get to taste it?"

"Of course." She pulled two plates from the cupboard and two forks from the silverware drawer, cut two pieces from the cake, set them on the plates, and handed him one.

He cut into the cake and stuffed the large piece into his mouth. It was still warm. "Delicious," he mumbled, his mouth full. She giggled.

She sat across from him at the table and sliced into her own piece of the cake. "Say," she said after she swallowed the first bite. "Do you ever hear how Nicholas Tom is doing? Is he still in the burn unit in Anchorage?"

Stephen laid his fork on the table and took a deep breath. "We haven't heard anything for several weeks. It was a very bad burn, and when he leaves the unit, he'll likely spend time in their rehab facility. Poor kid."

"Yeah, he's one of those guys who slams into brick walls that others seem able to leap over with ease. He's basically a good fellow."

Jackie would say that about anyone. She saw only the positive features of people and was able to quickly explain away their rough edges. "How do you know him?" Stephen picked up the fork again and finished off his crazy cake. It tasted like fudgy brownies. He was happy to be the beneficiary of Jackie's interest in cooking.

"His bad luck, and sometimes poor judgment, landed him in the counselor's office from time to time. He was truant too often. His grades were terrible. He got into fights. His counselor asked me to work with him. I found him to be pleasant, funny, and usually kind. He had dreams. He wanted to be a pilot."

"Well, I'm not sure that's a good fit for him."

"Maybe not, but it might work after he matures a bit more. Everyone needs to dream." Jackie took another bite of her cake.

"I wonder what he was doing in that trailer," Stephen said. "Probably not drinking a Coke and reading the Bible."

Jackie smiled. Stephen enjoyed having her in his house. Except for her toothbrush and toothpaste, her Ivory soap in its pink plastic box, the shampoo that smelled like coconut macaroons, and her salmon-colored towel, all of which she kept in the bathroom, she didn't clutter up the place and stowed the rest of her things in the back bedroom. She was quiet and kept to herself. "If you don't tell anyone," he said. "I'll confide that we ran a BA . . ."

The look on her face told him she didn't understand.

". . . ah, a blood alcohol test . . . when he was admitted to our hospital. It showed an elevated level, so he was drinking."

She nodded again. "I'm not surprised. As I said, he makes pretty terrible decisions."

One of the many things he liked about her was her honesty and thoughtfulness. She was young—he thought she'd said she was twenty-three—and refreshingly naïve. And she was handsome with delicate features, bright eyes, and a ready smile. He found the nevus near the corner of her mouth fascinating and wondered if he should talk to her about having the mole removed. It wasn't large, maybe four millimeters in diameter. After removal, she'd have a tiny scar on her otherwise flawless face, but only a tiny one. He didn't dare mention it; she wasn't his patient, and she'd never asked about it. She'd lived with it for years, and undoubtedly, she saw it as part of who she was. His mother would have called it a beauty mark, a better way to think of it than as a medical problem.

"Shortly after Nicholas was transferred to Anchorage, I visited his mother," Jackie said. "That's what social workers do, you know, home visits. I often wish I had time to do more of them, but I wanted Mrs. Tom to know that at least one person at the school was thinking about Nicholas. Their home is standard Yup'ik: crowded, very crowded, with a pile of kids and all their gear. Mrs. Tom was pleasant enough but seemed reluctant to speak about the trailer fire. She kept her eyes on the floor whenever I brought it up. That's the Eskimo way, I know, but her reaction seemed beyond that."

After they both had finished eating, Jackie wrapped the rest of the cake in an old Holsum Bread bag and stashed it in the fridge. "Ah . . ." She paused a moment and then began again. "Dr. Steinberg, I have something to discuss with you."

He studied her face. It didn't look angry or troubled. He couldn't read the emotion within her mind.

"The high school found a decent trailer for me. The art teacher moved into the shop teacher's quarters—they've been a couple for a short while—leaving her place for me."

He held his breath. He didn't want to hear what was coming next.

"It's been wonderful staying here, and you've been so generous to accommodate me, but I'll be leaving in about a week."

He closed his eyes against the reality of her words. When he opened them again, she was staring at him, a worried look on her face. "Are you okay, Dr. Steinberg?"

"Yes, of course. I'm pleased you'll have a place of your own." He swallowed hard. "I've enjoyed having you here, Jackie. It'll be kind of empty without you."

"You are so kind."

"Let me know when you actually leave, and I'll help you move your stuff."

He stayed up later than usual that evening. After Jackie went to the back bedroom for the night, he pulled Sandra's vodka bottle from the freezer, poured two fingers into a water glass, and topped it with reconstituted Tang. He settled into the easy chair in the living room, closed his eyes, and sipped at the drink. Just because she was moving into her own trailer didn't mean he wouldn't see her again. They could still drive the Jeep up and down the frozen river and, after break-up, she could go with him in his boat and for walks on the tundra. But it'd be different with her gone. Lonely. He sighed. Lonely was not a word he liked. He'd been so mad at Sandra when she stormed out that he considered her absence a blessing.

He sat up straight with a jolt and opened his eyes. That bastard Leonard Kills Squirrels had gotten his wish after all, and it was through none of his devious schemes to force Jackie out. Thank goodness she knew nothing about the whole marriage license mess. She'd want Stephen to explain to Kills Squirrels their platonic situation. He wouldn't do that. His personal business was none of Kills Squirrels' business. He shook his head and took a big gulp of his drink.

CHAPTER 20

"**S**o, you're already at thirty-six weeks." George closed the exam room door and shook Mera's hand. "Not long until that baby will be born." Since he planned to do a formal OB-GYN residency after his Indian Health Service commitment was complete, George had become the designated specialist in obstetrics at the IHS Hospital, Bethel. She liked his calm demeanor and his gentle manner.

"Yes," she said. "None too soon." Other than the Braxton-Hicks contractions, this pregnancy had gone smoothly, and Mera was ready for it to end. Too many trips to the toilet in the middle of the night, too much fatigue, too many extra pounds to haul around, and too much worry that she'd also lose this baby. She sat on the exam table, her bulging body dressed in a faded hospital johnny. Her fingers rubbed its soft cotton, which had been worn thin from frequent runs through the laundry. She liked the smooth feel of the limp fabric; somehow it offered a promise of the upcoming birth.

"Lay down, and let's take a look," George said with a smile.

He spread a clean sheet over her, pulled it down below her mountainous belly, and pulled up the hem of her johnny, exposing her bare mid-section. His fingers were warm as they ran over her skin, probing here, poking there. "Nice sized baby," he said.

She stared at his face. He furrowed his brow. She stared harder, trying to read the meaning of the furrow. He kept probing and poking for longer than he had on previous office visits. Something must be wrong. She tried to read his face, to find meaning in his eyes. Her breathing became faster with shallow little puffs. Then, faster yet.

He told her to spread her legs. He probed inside her, fingers to the left, fingers to the right. His brow was still furrowed.

Finally, he backed away from the table and asked her to sit up. His voice no longer had the playful lilt it had earlier. She heaved her gravid body upright and swung her swollen legs over the edge of the table. Her heart raced. Something was very wrong.

"The baby is breech," he said. "Rather than head down, its head is pointed up, so the baby's feet, or rear end, will come out first."

She nodded and took a deeper, shaky breath. When she was pregnant with Marcus, he had been right end up. This baby, however, was situated the wrong way.

"You probably know that delivering breech babies is riskier than normally positioned babies, and we always recommend that kind of delivery be done in Anchorage, where they are better equipped to handle it safely."

She nodded again. Her head felt empty, as if all its blood had drained out. The sink across the room became blurry. So did the soap dispenser.

He continued. "We recommend mothers with breech pregnancies go to Anchorage at thirty-six weeks, so they don't get stuck here in labor because of bad weather."

"That's . . . now," she said. She could hear the terror in her voice. It seemed to scratch at the air.

"You should go in the next several days at the latest," George replied.

Matias had radio clinic that week, so she had to wait until he came home after work to tell him. She wandered around the apartment, her head spinning like Marcus's toy gyroscope. Alaska time became the longest time ever.

When her son begged to play, she lowered herself to the floor and dumped the box of Legos in front of him. He'd have to go to Anchorage with her. She didn't know the housing accommodations for women waiting to deliver there at the Alaska Native Hospital, but surely there'd be room for him. He could sleep in the hospital bed with her. Or if that didn't work, she could always stay in a hotel near the hospital, although a month of that would be expensive.

She started building a little house with the Legos, layering yellow bricks between the rows of red ones. But no matter where she stayed in Anchorage, who would take care of Marcus while she was in labor and then in the delivery room and then in the postpartum ward for several days? Matias couldn't take a month, or more, off work to sit in Anchorage with them, waiting. She knew no one who lived there.

Somebody knocked on the door. It was too hard to get up from the floor, so Mera yelled, "Come in."

Deidre, with baby Daniel in her arms, stepped into the kitchen and looked around. When she spotted Mera on the floor in the living room, she shouted, "Are you okay? What happened?"

"Yes, I'm fine, just too pregnant to jump up very quickly."

Deidre offered her a hand.

"Thanks." Mera rose to her feet and then sank into the sofa.

Deidre held out a pair of green slacks. "I thought you might be able to use these really big pregnancy pants. They were all I could wear in the last month."

Mera took the pants. "Yes, I've grown out of everything and wear these unsnapped." She lifted her kuspuk to show the open zipper of a pair of Matias's jeans. Then she sighed. "I received unwelcome news today."

Deidre looked panicked. "The baby?"

"It's okay, except . . . it's breech." Mera repeated what the doctor had told her and wiped a tear from her cheek with the hem of her kuspuk. "I don't know what to do about Marcus while I'm in Anchorage. It could be a month, or longer."

Deidre pursed her lips and shook her head. "That's pretty ugly. You know that I, or any of us, would happily take care of him. Even at night while Matias is at the hospital. We'd be sure your guys got decent food too."

Mera smiled. Deidre was such a good, generous soul. She looked at her son, still on the floor jamming Lego pieces together. He felt more precious to her now than she'd ever imagined. She hadn't been away from him overnight, ever. She couldn't imagine a month without him. He might forget who his mother was.

A bead of snot rolled out of his right nostril. "Marcus, come here," she called. "Let's wipe your nose." She pulled a sheet of Kleenex from the pocket of her kuspuk and held it against his nostrils. "Blow," she said.

He blew and then looked at Deidre. He patted Mera's protruding belly. "That's my baby in there," he beamed.

WHEN MATIAS WALKED INTO THE KITCHEN from work, he shivered. "Brrr," he said. "It's still cold out there." He stopped with a jolt. "Mera, what's wrong?"

Sobbing, she told him the whole story. As she spoke, he nodded. Again and again, in the distant manner of a doctor. He knew the risks of a breech delivery. He wanted the best for her and the baby, which was, of course, also his baby. She wasn't sure, however, he knew how impossible it all was.

"I'll be okay with you gone; so will Marcus. The other families will take care of us. You know that, right?"

"Yes. But I can't leave him." She continued to sob. "And I can't take him along."

He tried to reassure her even more. She couldn't hear it.

"Well," he finally said. "What are you going to do?"

"I . . . don't . . . know."

She didn't sleep that night. She tossed and turned and dreamed about children that had disappeared, only to be found with missing arms or ears. What if Marcus began to think that Deidre was his mother? What if he hated his real mother, and the new baby, forever, because she left him?

The next day she walked to work at the *Tundra Drums* office and explained to the editor that she would have to go on maternity leave earlier than planned. "We'll miss you," he said. "Do whatever you need to do." As she left the building, he added, "Maybe you'll be able to do a free-lance piece or two while you wait. Maybe something about the pottery classes at the high school, or better yet, something about traveling to Anchorage to deliver a baby."

"Maybe."

HER HEAD CONTINUED TO SPIN; HER thoughts were a tangle. There was no acceptable option. "Have you decided yet?" Matias asked that evening.

"No." She stared over his shoulders at the wall behind him. "What could happen if I stay here for the delivery?"

"Well . . ." He took a deep breath. "See, the baby's head is bigger than its chest or belly or hips . . . Are you sure you want to hear all of this?"

"Yes. Yes, I do."

"With breech babies, when their feet come out first, sometimes the rest of their body comes out without a problem but their head—the biggest part of them—get hung up. Then the umbilical cord is smushed between the baby's skull and the mother's pelvic bones, cutting off the blood supply to the baby. Sometimes the baby's butt is situated to come out first, and its legs are folded against its belly so that the legs plus the abdomen are too big to go through the birth canal. Either way, an emergency C-section would have to be done, and we aren't well-equipped to do that here. The risk of a problem is too high. You don't want that to happen to our baby, Mera."

"What should I do, Matias?"

"Honey, only you can make that decision. I'll be okay with whatever works best for you, but I have to say, I see no other option than you going and leaving Marcus here with me."

She didn't sleep again that night. About three in the morning, she realized she hadn't felt the baby kicking. Was it dead? It was living, with a heartbeat, when George examined her last. That was more than two days ago. She pounded on Matias's shoulder. "The baby hasn't kicked for a while," she said.

He sat up half-way and leaned on his elbow. "How long?" His voice was groggy with sleep.

"I don't know. I haven't really paid attention."

He stumbled out of bed, picked his clinical coat off the chair, and dragged his stethoscope from its pocket. He pulled up her nightgown and lay the stethoscope's icy head on her warm belly. His face was expressionless while he listened. "Great heartbeat," he said. "The baby's fine. Its feet are down in your pelvis, you know, so there is no room to kick now. Try to get some sleep, honey."

THE NEXT DAY, SHE SAT AT the kitchen table eating a bowl of left-over chicken tortilla soup when the noon whistle blared. She reset the clock on the stove, sat back down, and stared out the kitchen window. The snow was mostly gone, except for the mountains of gray-white slush where the plow had dumped its load off the end of the hospital parking lot. Puddles filled the many potholes in the road. The days were long now. The sun wouldn't fall beneath the horizon until ten o'clock that night.

What should she do? Stay in Bethel and risk a dangerous delivery? Go to Anchorage without Marcus? The question echoed through her mind as rhythmic and insistent as a bass drum beat, over and over. Boom. Boom. Boom.

Marcus yelled, "Momá," and toddled to her side. He handed her one of his wooden cars; the front right wheel, made of a slice of wooden dowel, had fallen off.

"Find the missing wheel," she said. He toddled into the hall-way. When he returned, he handed her the lost piece. She pushed it back on the front drive shaft—a piece of coat hanger wire—and handed the car back to him. If only every problem was as easy to fix. She just couldn't leave him in Bethel.

THE TABLE WAS SET FOR THE potluck dinner. It was over a week ago that Mera and Matias had invited the Dorfmans and the Jetterses for supper that night, and Mera thought it would be rude to can-cel at the last minute. "Besides," she told Matias when he asked the wisdom of such a party considering the circumstances, "I need the distraction." Jennifer would bring a salmon casserole, Deidre appetizers, and Mera would serve succotash made of canned corn, canned black beans, canned tomatoes, onion powder, and garlic powder. For dessert, she'd made a cinnamon churros cake. The eve-ning's entertainment would be a slide show of the Maldonados' old vacation pictures.

Mera was arranging an interestingly contorted willow branch to decorate the dining table when David and Deidre, along with baby Daniel, arrived.

"Deidre," Mera said. "We're not going to talk about the baby and the need to go to Anchorage. The Jetterses don't know it's breech. I don't want to tell them until I have a plan. So far, no plan."

"Remember my offer . . ."

"Yes, I certainly will. I just can't leave Marcus."

When John and Jennifer arrived, their twins dashed off down the hallway to join Marcus in the back bedroom. Mera heard Marcus shriek a joyous welcome to his little friends. Those kids had so much fun together. He'd probably love to stay with them while she was in Anchorage. Then, he'd think Jennifer was his mother. She shook her head to dislodge that darkest of dark thoughts.

Jennifer explained that the salmon in the casserole came from the Kuskokwim River last fall. "John caught it right before freeze-up. I hope it isn't freezer burnt. We ate some last week, and it was delicious."

Deidre opened a Tupperware container and set it on the table beside a plate of pilot bread pieces. "My sister-in-law sent me this recipe," she said, pointing to the pale-yellow slurry in the container. "She calls it 'a cup, a cup, and a can.' A cup of mayo, a cup of Kraft grated parmesan, and a can of chopped artichoke hearts. Pretty darn easy and good."

"Where'd you find the artichoke hearts?" Jennifer asked.

"Ordered a case of them from the warehouse in Seattle. We'll probably have to live here for a decade to use them all up."

Mera was setting serving spoons on the table when she heard a CRASH. "Marcus, what was that?" she yelled as she waddled down the hallway, followed by Jennifer.

Silence.

"Marcus, what happened?" In the back bedroom, the dresser lay, drawers face down, on the floor. The three boys sat on the rug, eyes wide open and mouths clamped shut.

"How did the dresser fall over?" Mera asked.

Silence.

"How?"

Still silence.

"Someone was trying to climb up the drawers, right?" Jennifer asked.

The boys looked at each other and then at their mothers. Silence.

"Anybody hurt?" Mera asked.

The three boys shook their heads, vigorously, in synchrony. Marcus was holding his arm against his side at a funny angle. Mera tried to turn his hand over. He started crying.

"Does it hurt?" she asked. She stared into his eyes, trying to read his reaction. Was he hurt or just afraid? His elbow and wrist bent easily but she spotted a tear in his shirt, just below the shoulder seam. Through the hole she could see blood. She gently pulled his arm out of the shirt's sleeve. Again, it moved easily. She kept staring at his reaction. It didn't seem sore. Then she saw it. A scratch snaked down his upper arm and several drops of bright red blood bubbled at one end.

Only a scratch. No broken bones. "Let's wash that off," she said as she led him to the bathroom. While she scrubbed the wound, Marcus sobbed and grabbed at her. He wanted to snuggle.

When the wound was dry, she said, "Marcus, you get to pick the Band-Aid," and held the open box in front of him. He picked the one with an alligator on it, tore open the paper, and Mera plastered it over the cut.

On the way out of the bathroom, he grabbed her leg and wouldn't let go.

"It's okay, Marcus." She picked him up, and he nearly smothered her by clinging to her neck. She peeled away his fingers. "It's okay, honey."

Why was he so clingy? Had he overheard his parents talking about the stay in Anchorage?

They returned to the back bedroom where Jennifer was checking her sons. No damage to either of them. "Okay," Mera said. "We don't need to know who did the climbing. You've done it once and seen what happens. You don't need to climb on the dresser again. Ever. Now, help us set it back upright."

How could she leave him? Mera thought. This was all too much for her.

After dinner, the dirty dishes were piled in the sink and the leftovers stashed in the refrigerator. The guests sat on the couch and in the rocker, Matias sat on the floor behind the slide projector, which was balanced atop two books on the coffee table. Mera lowered herself into the bean bag chair. It felt good to be off her feet.

Matias had decided to show photos of their trip to northern Minnesota. The first slide was the Paul Bunyan and Babe the Blue Ox statues in Bemidji. Next were several pictures of the headwaters of the Mississippi River in Itasca State Park. "It looks so shallow,"

Jennifer said when Matias flipped to the slide of Mera, her pants rolled to above her knees, wading among a pile of rocks.

"It is," Matias said. "This photo is one end of Lake Itasca, the actual source of the Mississippi. That rock bridge marks where the river takes off from the lake."

"I love the pines," Deidre said. "And the crystal-clear blue sky, a far cry from New York City."

Mera felt something weird in her belly. Her insides seemed to be twisting. No pain, exactly, just tumult and twisting. It felt different from those Braxton-Hicks contractions. What was going on? She turned onto her right side. Nothing changed, so she turned back. Now, it felt like an earthquake, a gigantic, roiling commotion inside her. Still no pain. No cramps. Just massive movement. She stifled a groan, turned it into a cough. Then, the weirdness stopped.

While Matias showed pictures of Leech Lake and the huge muskie he had caught there, she pulled herself up from the bean bag chair and slowly walked toward the bathroom. So far, so good. Once inside, she shut the door and checked her panties. Nothing seemed to be dripping out of her bottom. Now she felt fine, no twisting, no abdominal rumblings.

After everyone left, she told Matias about the internal commotion. "Strange," he said.

"I'll check with George tomorrow," she said.

THE CLINIC WAS SLOW, AND SHE was able to see George as soon as she arrived. He listened to her story of the night before, examined her belly, did a digital exam of her vagina.

"Well, that must have been quite the upheaval, Mera," he said. "Your baby turned a somersault. It's now vertex . . . ah . . . it's head is where it belongs, down in your pelvis."

She took a deep breath. Had she heard him correctly? "You mean . . . it's right side up? You mean I don't have to go to Anchorage?"

"Correct. We can deliver the baby right here without any trouble."

Mera danced between the kitchen cupboards and the table as she set out the dishes for supper. She wished she had her wedding china, but it was stored with the rest of their belongings back in Houston. Ditto with her good silver. The tomato-stained Melmac and the cheap dinnerware supplied by the IHS would have to do. Matias's favorite supper, chicken thighs buried in canned mole sauce, was almost done. Homemade mole would be better, but that would have to wait until they moved back to the lower forty-eight. As she folded paper towels to use as napkins, she remembered the candles. Deidre had given her four of the candles-in-soup-cans after the big birthday party. She found them in the storeroom, along with a fist-full of autumn tundra flowers that she'd hung behind the door to dry and then forgotten. Perfect for this celebration.

Matias walked into the kitchen from the entryway, sniffed the mole-laden air, and said, "Wow."

Mera sat on one of the kitchen chairs, held her face in her hands, and began sobbing.

"What's wrong?" Matias's voice was ragged with alarm.

Between sobs, she blurted, "Nothing's wrong."

Matias stooped in front of her and gave her a big hug. "Sometimes babies have to take care of their mothers," he said, laughing.

THEY FOLLOWED THEIR REVISED PLAN FOR the baby's birth, the one that didn't include a trip to Anchorage. When the labor pains—real ones this time—were well established, Matias took Marcus over to the Jetters's where he would stay until the baby was born and his father could pick him up again. Matias had to carry him though because Marcus began screaming and kicking and refusing to go. He wanted to stay with his mamá. "No," he shrieked. "No! No!"

Mera felt awful. Marcus must have realized something big was about to happen, and he didn't want to miss out. Also, it was nine o'clock at night, and not the usual time he visited Brian and Jeff, which probably raised his suspicion even more.

"We're going to the hospital, and our new baby will come out of mamá," Matias said.

"Me too. I want to come too."

"Well, you can't. You'll sleep tonight with Brian and Jeffrey."

"No! I want to come with you!"

His shrieks carried through the evening air as Matias hauled him out the door.

When Matias returned from depositing Marcus at the Jetters's, he and Mera walked, hand in hand, down the boardwalk and across the parking lot to the hospital.

She had forgotten how intense labor pains could be. So much work, but the reward could be huge. Or not. With each round of contractions, a litany of possibilities marched through Mera's mind. A bad tear, like Deidre had when Daniel was born or Down Syndrome like Deidre's sister, or some other congenital abnormality; Matias had told her they numbered in the hundreds when he refused to itemize them. "Breathe easy," the nurse said. "You're doing fine."

George came to the hospital in the middle of the night to examine her. "Looks good," he said. "Only a little longer."

How much longer? Minutes? A month?

"Time to push now," George finally said. She braced her feet against the bed's side rails, took a deep breath, and pushed for all she was worth.

When she opened her eyes, Matias stood at the foot of the bed, his face white as the snow on Three Step Mountain. "Take a breath, honey," he said in a quivery voice.

"I can't push and breath at the same time," she yelled at him. "Right now, I'm pushing!"

"I'll wait outside," he said.

"Good," she gasped.

Later—she had no idea how much later—the nurse threw off the sheet and examined Mera's bottom. "Dr. Gregoir," she yelled for George. "Baby's crowning."

George raced into the room, followed by Matias. George said, "The baby's coming. Hold tight, Mera, this will be cold," and he splashed a basin of disinfectant onto her crotch. "Now push hard, and we'll have a baby."

Tears puddled on the sheet beside Mera's head. Soon it would be over. Soon that baby would come. She took yet another deep breath and pushed. Hard. Then, a sudden rush and the feeling that she'd been stretched open and then emptied out. Her body had taken over and had finished the job. She could see from George's eyes above his mask that he was smiling. "It's a little girl," he said, "and she's beautiful like her mother."

Mera shook with sobs. A beautiful girl. That meant she was healthy, not deformed, not sickly, not dead, but beautiful.

Matias wrapped his arms around her shoulders. "I love you so much," he said. "She's our little Camila." That was the name they had chosen for a daughter.

Chapter 21

The sanctuary at Our Mother of All Saints was the way Virginia liked it, quiet as an ice cave. No singing, no homily, no pages of the hymnals rattling, no feet shuffling on the floor. She liked the peace and the dark. An overhead spotlight lit up the altar; the rest of the room drowned in the shadows. The air stunk like mold. Only a little, but Virginia wished it smelled like candle wax, the way it did when all the candles were lit during Mass.

Marcus, standing beside her, tugged on the hem of her parka. She was watching him while Mrs. Maldonado did some work at the *Tundra Drums.* "What's that?" he asked. His voice rang through the silence like a siren.

Virginia kneeled in front of him and put her finger to her lips. "Shhh," she whispered. "Be quiet. It's a picture of the Virgin Mary."

Marcus stared at the painting. Virginia couldn't tell if he asked about the baby Jesus in Mary's arms or about the thin, yellow halo around the Virgin's head. He seemed satisfied with her answer. When she turned back toward the altar and crossed herself, Marcus watched and then slapped his fist against his forehead and his breastbone. Virginia giggled. He was such a good little boy.

She'd come to the church to pick up holy water for her mother's sister. Aunt Lucy was very old, and she coughed a lot. Virginia thought the water, blessed by Father Brogan, would fix her up. She knocked on the office door. Father Brogan opened it and handed her the water in what looked like a jam jar. "Give her my best," he said.

When they got to the Maldonados' apartment, it was Mrs. Jetters who let them into the kitchen. Mrs. Maldonado sat on the couch in the living room, nursing the new baby.

Virginia studied the child. Camila was her name. Little Camila. She was a pretty child, with black curly hair and skin so light she wondered if she could see her little bones through it.

Marcus raced down the hall to the back bedroom where the Jetters twins were playing. Virginia knew they were there because she could hear them yelling. Those gussuk kids sure yelled a lot. Her own didn't. None of the Yup'ik kids did. She didn't understand it.

"How about some tea, Virginia?" Mrs. Maldonado asked.

"I got it," Mrs. Jetters said as she headed into the kitchen.

The tea warmed Virginia's insides. It tasted good, even though it was gussuk tea, the kind Mrs. Maldonado called Red Rose. She listened to the women talk about the new baby and about the woman named Jackie who didn't live with Dr. Steinberg anymore. "She finally got a place of her own. I'm sure she's happy about that," Mrs. Maldonado said.

Finally, the conversation lulled. "I'll be gone for a couple days," Virginia said. "I'm going to Nunapitchuk to see my relatives. I came to say goodbye."

As she walked the boardwalk back to town, Virginia pushed the hood of her parka back off her head and angled her face toward the sun. It was getting warmer. The rays from the bright sun felt good on her skin. Soon, the ice on the river would break up, and summer would be on its way.

She didn't mind the winter. It belonged to the earth's cycle. Besides, she liked how the tundra looked with snow on top of the dead plants. She liked the way the wind swirled the snow into little designs and the way the icicles hung from the willow branches.

Still, summer was nice too. She was glad it was coming.

VIRGINIA SAT BEHIND HER OLDEST SON on the snowmobile. Her arms barely reached around him, but she was able to latch her mittened fingers together against the front of his parka. His body shielded her from most of the headwind, but it was still cold and uncomfortable when the snowmobile hit the icy bumps in the trail. "Slow down, Quentin," she yelled into his ear.

He turned his head far to the side so that his cheek was in her face. "The faster I go, the sooner we'll get there," he called back. He revved the engine, and they shot forward even faster.

Virginia hadn't seen Aunt Lucy, the aunt she liked best, the one who was nicest to her, for a long time. She hoped she was feeling better. Her cough wouldn't go away. The doctor at Bethel said it wasn't TB, so that was good. Virginia didn't want anyone she knew to get that. Her TB was what made Nicholas so sneaky and difficult. Quentin, the son she now hugged on the snow machine, didn't sneak around or give her trouble. He just drove too fast.

They passed a deserted fish camp on the bank of a frozen slough and then another. She thought it was that second one where her cousins died. The smoke house's roof leaned toward the frozen river, and its door flapped open in the wind. One of the drying racks had collapsed. Either Luther or Morris had been found near those racks. Had he knocked it down when he fell? She tried to imagine them dead there, sprawled on the ground as if they were badly drunk. Maybe that's what killed them.

She remembered playing with them when they were kids. Those boys liked to follow the croaks of the frogs in the sloughs and catch them with their bare hands. They also made rafts out of river debris and floated on them, standing up. They used sticks as oars and sometimes offered Virginia a ride. She was scared of those rafts, scared she'd drown.

The snow machine roared to a stop near Aunt Lucy's house, and Virginia crawled off the seat. She stomped her feet on the frozen river, trying to unkink her stiff knees. She wished they didn't tighten up like that. She climbed the hill to the faded red house and then pulled herself up the two wooden steps to the entrance. She banged on the door, yelled "Aunt Lucy," and walked into the dark room. Aunt Lucy sat on her bed. "Is that you, Virginia?" she called.

"Ee. How are you today?"

Aunt Lucy shrugged. "Okay."

Virginia handed her the bottle of holy water. "Father Brogan blessed this for you. It should make you better."

"What do I do with it? Drink it or rub it on?"

Virginia didn't know. Usually, Father Brogan sprinkled it on people's heads, but Aunt Lucy attended the Russian Orthodox Church in Nunapitchuk. Virginia remembered that during church ceremonies, sometimes those Orthodox people drank it, sometimes they sprinkled it on themselves. She didn't remember if they ever rubbed it on. "Give it here," she said. She unscrewed the top, dipped her fingers into the liquid, and flicked it over Aunt Lucy's head. "There," she said, "now your cough will be better."

Virginia sat on the bed beside Aunt Lucy. They talked about Virginia's kids, about Aunt Lucy's kids and grandkids, about the upcoming fishing season. Finally, Virginia asked about her cousins. "Did Luther and Morris die because they were drunk?" Virginia asked.

"I don't think so. Morris wasn't a big drinker." Aunt Lucy coughed. It sounded like the bark of a seal. She took a deep breath and then continued. "They just died."

"But, they weren't very old."

"Maybe they were thirty." Aunt Lucy wiped her nose with the back of her hand.

"That's young to just die."

Aunt Lucy shrugged. "See that bag over there?" She pointed to a plastic sack on the table under the small window. "Bring it here."

Virginia retrieved the sack and carried it to Aunt Lucy, who untied the top and held it out in front of her. "Have some. Vera Maxie brought it over the other day."

Virginia pulled a finger full of stinkhead mash from the bag.

"Only a little," Aunt Lucy said. "We have to save some for later."

Virginia sucked the last of the fish oil from her fingers. It was good.

Suddenly, Aunt Lucy cocked her head. "A plane," she said, referring to the noise overhead. "Wrong time for the mail plane." They pulled on their parkas and headed outside.

They stood on a knoll above the river and watched a plane land on the frozen water. Others joined them. The plane came to a stop near the clinic. The health aide opened the door and two men inched out to the porch, carrying a third man on a stretcher. With help from the pilot, they loaded the sick fellow into the plane.

A woman walked down the steps from the clinic's porch. Three little kids followed. The lady seemed to be crying, and the children began to tug at her kuspuk.

"That's Vera Maxie and her kids. Who's that on the stretcher?" Aunt Lucy asked Donna Mesak, who was standing next to her.

"Vincent, Vera's husband," Donna said. "He's been sick."

Virginia asked. "What's he sick from?"

Donna said. "He was breathing funny, I think, and his legs gave out. He nearly fell off the boardwalk."

Vincent Maxie was also related to Virginia, the son of her mother's second cousin. Donna said he was on his way to the Bethel Hospital. Virginia wondered if maybe she needed to bring some holy water to him too. What if he died? What would happen to Vera and the kids?

Was someone giving them some kind of poison? Maybe it was poison that killed Luther and Morris. At least, it wasn't Nicholas. For sure, it wasn't him. He was still in the hospital in Anchorage. No one could accuse him of poisoning people now.

FOUR DAYS LATER, WHEN VIRGINIA CRAWLED out of bed, she felt funny. Her mouth was dry as pilot bread. "Mitchel," she yelled to her youngest son, "bring me some water." She took a couple sips, and they felt like they got stuck part way down. She set the water glass on the floor beside her bed. The curtain on the window was blurry; she couldn't see the little white flowers printed on them. She blinked her eyes several times. The oil tank outside the window was even more blurry. She hadn't had any alcohol to drink. What was making her eyes so weird? Maybe yesterday's wind. When she'd walked to the Maldonados' the wind had blown tundra dust into her mouth and eyes. It'd go away soon.

She lay back on her bed, closed her eyes, and waited for the weird things to get better.

Chapter 22

THE BOILED-OVER OATMEAL AROUND THE STOVE's front left burner had the consistency of pavement, a mishap of Jennifer's own doing. She scrubbed it with a wad of grade 00 steel wool, and when that didn't do the job, she took a dinner knife to it. Chip. Chip. Slowly, the pool of dried concrete grew smaller.

Beyond the sound of the scraping, she thought she heard something. She laid the knife on the countertop and listened. It was a knock on the kitchen door, several knocks. A voice from the other side yelled, "River's breaking up."

She pulled on the knob with both hands and after three yanks, the swollen-shut door gave way, and Deidre, with baby Daniel in her arms, spilled into the kitchen. David followed. "The Kuskokwim's breaking up," Deidre said. "You've never seen that and simply must. Come with us. Everyone's gathering near the town dock."

Jennifer's husband wandered into the kitchen and set his hand on her shoulder. "What's happening?" John asked.

"Break-up has begun. Let's go." David said as he headed out the door.

Jennifer and John had been in Bethel for the river's freeze-up last fall, but that wasn't much to see. The ice had started forming in the weedy shallows along the bank and slowly grew like a spreading ink stain toward the center of the river. She had watched small islands of ice float down the narrowing strip of open water until it froze completely over. She'd lost track of the number of weeks before the planes with their duck-footed skis could safely land on the frozen river and the snow machines or dog sleds could safely travel the ice road. Break-up was different, she'd been told.

"The stake started moving sometime last night," David called over his shoulder. Then he stopped, turned, and said, "You may not know . . . The signal that break-up has begun is when the stake, which is painted ruby red and stuck in the river ice during freeze-up, begins to move."

They were a single-file parade—David, Deidre with Daniel, John, Jeffrey, Brian, and Jennifer the caboose—as they headed to the town dock. The snow and ice on the boardwalk had turned to slush, and the tundra had begun to show signs of life. Hints of golden yellow tinted the dark brown mosses and lichens, and Jennifer spotted several emerald blades poking through the wheat-tinted thatch of last year's grasses. Springtime had, indeed, come to Bethel.

They passed the faded blue house where Elizanna Andrew lived. Spotlessly white undershirts and pillowcases were pinned to a rope that ran between the roof and the shed out back. The laundry caught the breeze and billowed like the wings of the cranes that had flown over Jennifer's head last week. Beneath the clean clothes, the ground had turned into a mile of mud. She took a deep breath. In spite of all the muck, the air smelled fresh and new, like a spring morning, like bleach.

When they approached the Andrechecks' house, a different smell, not bleach, not spring, smacked Jennifer in the face as if she'd been hit by a rancid rock. It was fierce and foul. She held her breath, then quickened her step to get past it as fast as possible.

"Ugh," John groaned. "What on earth is that? Something must have died out here." The odor seemed strongest near the dogs that were chained out in the yard.

"Ick. That's poopy," Jeffrey said, and he covered his nose with his mitten.

As they passed, Jennifer watched the dogs in their oil barrels. Their eyes, like shiny black marbles against their white furry faces, followed her. They seemed content, one animal in each barrel. "Why aren't those animals overcome by that stench, whatever it is," John laughed. "Hard to breathe with that in the air."

"I know that smell," David said. "Give me a minute and I'll remember." He took a deep breath and started to cough.

They kept walking, past the Catholic church, past the tiny green shack that housed the *Tundra Drums*. The twins waded in the puddles beside the boardwalk and chased each other with handfuls of dirty snow. Finally, the stench had disappeared.

David stopped abruptly. "Ahh. I remember, stinkheads. *That's* the awful smell back at the Andrechecks' place."

"You never told me you ate that stuff," Deidre said and thumped him on the back.

"I didn't *eat* them, but I smelled them up close. A patient brought some to the clinic, and after he left, I gave it to one of the nurses' aides. We couldn't use that exam room for the rest of the day; had to leave the windows open all night to air it out." He nodded. "Yup, it's stinkheads, all right. Indeed, John, it *is* something dead. Rotten fish."

As they walked toward town, they joined a crowd of people that moved like a lava flow: families, oldsters and youngsters, gangs of teens, and groups of young children who skipped through the sludge on the road and challenged each other to races. The crowd could have filled two school buses. And more kept coming.

Jennifer tilted her head and listened. She heard rolling thunder even though the sky was clear. As they neared the river, the roar grew louder. The closer she came to the water, the more it sounded like boulders crashing down a mountainside. The only mountain around was Three Step, and it was forty miles away. She stared across the river at its triple-humped silhouette. The landmark was still there, far away and shrouded in the mist. "What's that noise?" she asked.

"The ice breaking up," David said. "Eerie, isn't it?"

Eerie was a perfect word for it, Jennifer thought. Mysterious and threatening and strange.

They found an open spot in the crowd along the edge of the Kuskokwim. The murky water churned with huge hunks of gray and white ice that bobbed and collided as they raced to the sea. A cardboard carton sped past, followed by a web of fishing net and several tree trunks, probably from the forests far upriver. Willow sticks, lots of them, floated both between and on top of the swirling, dipping, rolling ice blobs. The Kuskokwim, once serene, was now savage.

Little boys stooped for handfuls of stones and lobbed them into the frenzied river. Ever more people gathered along the bank. That was the noise, all right, the collisions of the hundreds and hundreds of mini icebergs.

Jennifer had never seen anything like that raging river. She'd seen flooded creeks in the California valleys and icy streams high in Yosemite, but they didn't come close to the majesty and terror of the breaking-up Kuskokwim. She felt at one with that river, with its fury, its vehemence. She, too, was angry and vengeful. She, too, boiled inside.

Her sons leaned toward the water, trying to peer into its depths. She gripped their arms. If one of them fell in, the outcome would be unthinkable. She imagined a little snowsuit-clad figure twisting and hurtling among the ice floes all the way to the Bering Sea. Downriver a bit, several boys lay at the river's edge, their upper bodies dangling over the rim of the bank and their skinny arms dangling in the wild water as they tried to catch the willow twigs that washed by. She hoped she wouldn't have to watch any of them tumble in and be swept away.

Others joined the break-up watchers along the shore while some turned away from the river and returned home. David said that by a week after break-up began, the river would be clear enough for boats to travel or float planes to take off and land. Soon, Deidre shouted that she needed to go home to feed Daniel. Jennifer agreed it was time to leave. As she turned her back on the raging river, she spotted Jackie, the school's social worker, and waved. Jackie waved back.

They again passed the Andrechecks' house. This time that awful smell wasn't quite as bad. Jennifer couldn't shake that odor, the scent of decaying fish. How could anyone think of eating it?

They crowded into the Jetters's living room, and Deidre began to nurse Daniel. The twins brought their Lego creations, one by one, to the guests for their approval: a boat, a bird, and several small structures that defied identification. Their young faces glowed with pride.

"What's that?" Deidre asked as Jeff waved a red and blue knobby object under her nose.

"A dog, like Ginger," he answered.

While the Lego display continued, Jennifer couldn't rid her mind of the disorder wrought by the powerful river and the powerful stink of those decomposing fish. "Where do you suppose that stinkhead smell came from?" she asked. She'd not smelled it before on her many trips along the boardwalk. "Inside the house?"

Everyone shook their heads. Then David laughed and said, "If the Yup'ik eat those God-awful things, maybe they feed them to their dogs." Everyone sniggered.

THE DAWN OF SUMMER BROUGHT LONGER days, emerging wildflowers, and returning birds: the snow buntings, arctic warblers, and longspurs. The air was clear as glass and fresh as a lemon. And yet, thoughts of the stinkheads lingered with Jennifer. She contemplated them while scrubbing the bathtub, while stirring macaroni and cheese, while tossing and turning in bed during her many sleepless nights. When she breathed in the crisp, spring air, she contrasted the clean smell of the awaking earth with the stench of the decaying fish. Nothing in the world could persuade her to eat them.

The morning she was hunting for the stapler beneath the clutter on their desk, she spotted Leonard Kills Squirrels's flier announcing last winter's New Year's Eve party. She recalled the cheese ball sans nuts she'd made for the refreshments, the *Unsinkable Molly Brown* movie, the fire in the trailer. *Such a complicated night!* she thought.

At that party, Virginia had told her how stinkheads were made. What, exactly, had she said? Something about digging a hole and lining it with grass. She remembered Virginia's hand gestures that had accompanied her words.

"Mommy," Brian called. "BrianJeff's being mean." That's what their sons called each other now, BrianJeff. John thought it was because they heard their parents call for both boys so often. Maybe. Jennifer sighed. She wished the kids could settle their own quarrels. She glanced at her watch. Almost five o'clock. John would be home soon to help referee their fights. She called, "Brian. Jeff. Does anyone want some raisins?"

"Yeah," they yelled together and raced into the kitchen.

When her sons returned to the back bedroom, Jennifer's thoughts again turned to the stinkheads and their horrible odor. A hole in the ground lined with grass. That was the old way, according to Virginia. She had mentioned a new way. Jennifer couldn't remember exactly what Virginia had said, except there was something about a plastic bag.

After dinner and after the twins had gone to bed, Jennifer and John sat in the living room reading. Someone knocked on the door. It was Stephen.

"So, Leonard Kills Everything Beautiful has finally gone," he said. "I see his dream catcher thing is no longer hanging on the door across the way."

"Yes," Jennifer said. "He packed up his stuff about a week ago and left on Saturday. He was reassigned to the Blackfeet Reservation, somewhere in Montana. He seemed happy about the move." She paused a moment then added, "He never got around to spackling the shot pattern in the ceiling near his door."

"Good riddance."

"Well, he wasn't a bad neighbor, kept to himself and was fairly quiet. The only time he complained to me was when I pinned the boys's Oshkosh b'goshes to dry on the chicken wire around the furnace."

'Well, he lost his stupid war with us doctors."

"Indeed, he did."

"I'm here to borrow a cup of flour," Stephen said. "I've borrowed so much stuff from the Maldonados that I'm embarrassed to ask them again for a while. I want to make some dumplings."

Jennifer poured a cup of flour into a paper towel funnel, folded the ends, and handed it to Stephen. Gussuk foods, like Baskins-Robbins Rocky Road or Dinty Moore Beef Stew with dumplings, were so much better than Yup'ik agudak and stinkheads.

Stinkheads. There was something weird and off-kilter about them, like eating moldy cottage cheese or hamburger meat gone bad.

CHAPTER 23

JOHN, ON RADIO CLINIC DUTY THAT day, was paging through a copy of the *New England Journal of Medicine* when a call came from Anchorage on the satellite phone. It was the neurologist. "Remember the fellow Vincent Maxie from . . . um . . ." John heard pages rustle from the other end of the phone line. ". . . from Nunapitchuk that you guys sent to us several weeks ago? We have a diagnosis."

"Yeah, I remember him. What's he got?"

"Botulism."

John gasped. "Holy cow. Really?"

"Yeah. It's rare, for sure. We couldn't figure out why Mr. Maxie was so weak, so we called a couple neurology colleagues in Seattle. They suggested it. The State Health Department here identified the toxin in his blood. You know, the fatality rate isn't low. It was fortunate that you guys had the good sense to ship the fellow to Anchorage."

John knew it was more dumb luck than good sense. "How's he doing?"

"We gave him antitoxin yesterday, so he'll be improving over time. Takes a while for all the toxin stuck to his nerves to degrade. We'll keep him here for rehab as he improves."

John hung up the phone and dashed down the hall to the doctors' office. Matias sat at one of the desks playing solitaire, and as John started to tell him about the call from Anchorage, Stephen walked in and leaned against the edge of the desk in the corner.

"We have a diagnosis on that fellow Vincent Maxie from Nunapitchuk with the weird neurological symptoms."

Matias and Stephen eyed John with interest.

"Botulism."

"Holy shit," Stephen said.

"No kidding," Matias said.

"No, I'm not kidding. Neuro in Anchorage made the diagnosis, confirmed it with a blood test at the State Lab, and gave him antitoxin, so he'll be on the mend, slowly. Maxie is very lucky."

"You know," Stephen said staring at the ceiling. "I wonder about my hunting buddy Lincoln Egoak from Aniak. Rather than a stroke, maybe he had that too. Now that I think of it, the symptoms might fit."

"And Albert Amos from Nunivak Island," Matias added.

"Hell," John said. "How about those brothers who died at fish camp?

Stephen rose to his feet. "We could have a goddamn epidemic here. Wonder where they picked that up?"

Three weeks later, Stephen appeared at the Jetters's kitchen door.

"I'm here to return this." Stephen handed John a copy of *East of Eden*. "Great read. Thanks for suggesting it. That Steinbeck sure knows how to write a book."

Stephen took a seat at the table and nodded when Jennifer offered him a cup of tea.

"Say, Stephen." John's voice was bright. "About that patient of mine from Aniak who went to Anchorage. You went hunting with him. I saw him in clinic today. He still limps some, but he's pleased to be able to walk."

"Indeed. Glad to hear that. He's a prince of a fellow." Stephen said. "As I recall, he thought he got sick from breathing smoke from a fire of tainted driftwood."

"Yeah." John laughed. "That's hard to believe."

John saw his wife catch Stephen's eye as she sipped her tea. She set the cup on her saucer and took a deep breath. "John told me about the botulism, and I have an idea about that," she said. John and Stephen both stared at her. She sipped at the tea again, slowly. "I've been wondering where Eskimos would get that. Usually, it's from eating poorly canned vegetables."

Jennifer sat straight as a two-by-four while she spoke. She seemed confident and thoughtful, unlike the sad, frustrated woman John had lived with since they moved to Bethel. "If we can figure out where it came from, we can probably prevent it from happening again." She sipped her tea and added, "The Yup'ik certainly don't can corn or beans or stuff like that."

John nodded, with interest in what she said and pride with the way she said it.

She continued. "Virginia told me how the Yup'ik make stinkheads now. Rather than burying the fish in a grass-lined pit in the ground, she said the new way is to wrap them in a plastic bag and let them ripen in there." She looked at Stephen, then at her husband. "Fish can be contaminated with the bacteria that cause botulism, *Clostridium botulinum*, from lake or river water I believe. Recall what you learned in microbiology class—*C. botulinum* are anaerobes and, thus, are readily killed by oxygen."

Jennifer took another sip of her tea. "Keep talking, honey," John said.

"Well, using the old way of preparing the stinkheads, air would circulate down in that pit with the grass, so any of the *C. botulinum* bacteria on the buried fish heads would die."

She paused a moment. Stephen leaned toward her to hear the rest of what she had to say, and John waved his hand for her to continue.

"The other thing to remember is that when those bacteria find themselves in a cold or dry or otherwise inhospitable environment, they form spores to protect themselves. Kind of like bacterial armor. If the conditions improve—become moist or warm—the spores exsporulate."

"Great word, exsporulate," said Stephen. "Back when I thought of such things, I used to envision those little spores as breaking apart like exploding, miniature water balloons that spewed baby bacteria all over the place."

"Right," Jennifer said. "My idea is that when the fish that are aged in those airless plastic sacks warm up, the spores exsporulate, and when the bacteria emerge, they begin to produce their botulinum toxin."

She took a breath. "See, your patients may have eaten fish heads that were contaminated with that toxin."

"Wheeewwweee," Stephen whistled. "Pretty damn good. That's a microbiologist for you. John, do you remember any of that from medical school?"

"Nope." John shook his head. "Not a bit of it."

"Me neither," Stephen said with a chuckle. "Except for the exsporulation part."

Jennifer sipped more of her tea. John watched a sparkle of self-satisfaction spread over her face. She loved thinking about microbiology. She loved talking about microbiology. For her, this was huge fun.

"Oh my God, Jennifer." Stephen's eyes glowed. "I believe you are on to something, here."

John nodded. Indeed, his wife was on to something very important.

"How would you prove that the botulism came from the stinkheads?" Stephen asked. "Do we have to culture something? That probably requires weird culture media we don't have here at the hospital lab."

"It's diagnosed by finding toxin in the spoiled food," Jennifer said. "The state labs use a very specialized test called a mouse bio-assay. They inject the suspected food into mice, and then treat half the mice with antitoxin to neutralize the toxin, if it's there. Thus, if the toxin is present in the food sample, the mice that got the anti-toxin survive and those that didn't die."

"You sound like a microbiology professor," Stephen said.

"Well, that's my dream," she said. A soft smile dawned on her face.

She's so beautiful, John thought.

For him, it was thrilling to hear her speak that way. She knew her stuff; her knowledge of bacteriology hadn't withered as she constantly worried that it had. She was confident. She was smart. A strong surge of pride pulsed through him, deep and fierce.

She paused a moment and then said, "Let me check something."

She walked into their bedroom and returned with *Zinsser Microbiology*. She flipped through the index, paged through the book, and began reading in silence. "Okay," she finally said and then read aloud. "The toxin acts on the myoneural junctions and produces death by respiratory paralysis resembling that caused by curare." She read silently then said, "Um . . . here we go. It says that humans and fish are susceptible to type E toxin, which is found in soil and fish in Russia, Canada, the United States, and Alaska."

"As if Alaska isn't part of the United States," John said.

"You are amazing," Stephen said to her.

John nodded.

"That's what microbiologists do," she said with a seductive tilt of her head. "And, after all, I'm a microbiologist."

"Right," Stephen said. "So, it's a terrific hypothesis, and it needs to be proven."

That night, as they lay in bed, John told Jennifer that she seemed more relaxed than he'd seen her since they'd moved to Bethel.

She stroked his arm. "It's been too long since I thought about microbes and how they make people sick."

John listened to the wind rattle the bedroom window. Jennifer continued. "I love the words surrounding bacteria: spores, toxins, pathogenesis, exsporulation. It's amazing that, while sitting here in our apartment in backwater Alaska, I get to think about *Clostridium botulinum.*"

Her voice wobbled as if she might start to cry. He didn't want her to cry. They were in Bethel on account of him, not her. The sacrifice on her part was probably larger than he had realized. The sting of guilt shot through him.

Jennifer took a deep breath. "I feel like a grad student again, John, surrounded by colleagues—you and Stephen—who can understand the language and concepts of bacteria. So, yes, I feel relaxed, as comfortable as a soak in a warm bath. It's that gentle, wonderful feeling of belonging. And of contributing."

John felt Jennifer stiffen. "Of course," she said with a sigh. "There is the other side of science. Good ideas need to be backed up with facts."

CHAPTER 24

THE AIR IN THE RADIO ROOM was rancid, like stale bread or bad socks. Stephen took a deep breath, smelled the dusty, dead space that surrounded him, and then coughed. He wanted to be outside, under the endless sky, with his boots planted on the awakening tundra. He wanted to wander among the now-blooming spring flowers, the white serviceberry blossoms, and the scrappy pink saxifrages. He wanted to feel the crisp, fresh breeze against his face.

And yet, in this stuffy room, he dealt out his medical advice. His patients depended on him; the health aides needed his guidance. What happened in this room mattered. It mattered a lot. The importance of it kept him nailed to the desk chair in front of the radio.

The last call had been easy: the aide from Tuntutuliak had reported a three-year-old with an ear infection, a fourteen-year-old with a minor laceration on his leg, and a nine-month-old with diarrhea. For now, the radio was quiet. That wouldn't last long.

Stephen looked through the CONTACT sheet and flipped to the second page. There it was, the number for the Alaska State

Health Department. He paused. Was this something he wanted to get into? It was none of his business; it didn't directly affect him or his work at the hospital. The source of the botulism was a public health problem rather than a medical problem. Yet, if none of the doctors at the Bethel Hospital reported these cases, no one would know about them. Besides, the whole thing was so very compelling. He reached for the satellite phone, dialed, explained his question to the State Health Department operator, and finally was connected to someone in the Division of Public Health, who passed the call on to a person in the section of Epidemiology.

The epidemiologist seemed distracted until Stephen mentioned the case of botulism in the Bethel Service Unit. "We suspect there have been others, including two fatal cases," he said.

"Oh, yeah?" Her voice now glistened.

Stephen continued with the details: the dead Uttereyuk brothers and Vincent Maxie from Nunapitchuk, Lincoln Egoak from Aniak, and Albert Amos in Mekoryuk. He mentioned a possible connection with eating stinkheads aged in plastic bags. The epidemiologist asked several questions: where, again, had these cases occurred? How many?

"We're aware of one case of botulism there in the Bethel area," she said. "We're not aware of others."

"Right. The others presented before the case the State Lab confirmed . . . ahh . . . that was Vincent Maxie from Nunapitchuk. The rest of them showed symptoms very compatible with botulism, but that diagnosis wasn't considered at the time, so it wasn't confirmed."

The epidemiologist then said she would transfer him to the veterinarian who was the acting head of the department.

"Mark Ferguson here." The veterinarian spoke in the no-nonsense voice of a leader.

Stephen explained Jennifer's botulism theory. Dr. Ferguson asked several questions. What was the timing of the cases? What were their symptoms? What, exactly, was the story with the stinkheads?

Stephen answered. Ferguson seemed intrigued. He asked if the botulism patients actually ate stinkheads fermented in plastic bags.

Stephen paused. He had no idea if any of those men had eaten stinkheads at all. The connection with the rotten fish was, after all, just a hypothesis, and the notion that the illnesses were related to aging fish heads in plastic was a further hypothesis. "I don't know but will try to get that information," he said.

"Great," Ferguson said.

"And," Stephen added, "I could see about getting samples from stinkheads that are preserved in plastic bags. Would you be able to test for the toxin from them?"

"Absolutely. That'd be terrific."

Stephen thanked Ferguson for his help. When the veterinarian rattled off his direct phone number for a future call, Stephen jotted it down on the back of an envelope that he fished out of the wastebasket.

By the time the radio clinic was finished for the afternoon, Stephen had formulated a plan. He needed a helper from the community, someone who knew the families of the cases well. He found the native people to be very friendly and accepting of the non-natives, but they'd likely be more guarded if a gussuk like him started asking questions about how they prepared their fish. Food was sacrosanct. They'd been drying salmon since the dawn of human history in the Arctic.

He closed down the radio and headed toward the hospital lobby. To his surprise, and delight, the gift shop was open. For the past several weeks, the "CLOSED" sign had hung all day on the shop's locked door. "Mrs. Tom," he said to the lady behind the counter, "I'm pleased to see you. Apparently you were away for a while."

"Ee. I was sick. But now I'm better."

"What kind of sickness did you have?"

"Oh, my eyes were funny. Blurry. And my mouth was so dry I could hardly swallow."

Oh boy, Stephen thought. *That sure sounds familiar.* "Had you eaten any stinkheads before you got sick?"

"Ee. I really like stinkheads. Let's see. I had some at my Aunt Lucy's in Nunapitchuk. They were good."

That was where Vincent Maxie was from. "Do you know Vincent Maxie from there?"

"Of course. I know everyone in Nunapitchuk. His wife gave Aunt Lucy those good stinkheads."

Stephen could hardly believe his good fortune. The story was fitting together very well. "I'm glad you've recovered. I need your assistance."

Virginia was folding knit scarves and piling them on a shelf beside a row of birch bark baskets, sealskin yoyos, and dance fans of woven grass discs surrounded by wolf fur. The scarves were pretty, with intricate designs made of little holes that had been knitted into them. She nodded at Stephen. "What kind of help, Dr. Steinberg?"

"Before we get into that . . ." He lifted one of the scarves. "How much is this? It's beautiful." *And soft*. He rubbed the wool between his fingers. It was silky as newborn baby hair.

"Twenty-five dollars. It was knit by a lady in Mekoryuk, a very good scarf." She explained it was made of muskoxen hair. "Not the scratchy, outer hair, but the soft inner hair. It's called qiviut."

"Qiviut," he said slowly. *Unusual name*, he thought.

"Ee. Qiviut."

Stephen pulled his wallet from his pocket and handed her the cash. He'd give the scarf to Jackie as a house-warming present. She'd like that. Since she'd moved out of his apartment, she seemed very happy in her trailer. It was near the high school. True to her Georgian background, she had disliked the walk in the winter from his place on the hospital compound to her desk in the education compound. The scarf would keep her warm during her now short walk.

Stephen stuffed his wallet back into his pocket. "I've just spoken with the people at the State Health Department about Vincent Maxie. He got sick from a food poison called botulism, and we think other folks around here did too," he said.

"Bot . . . What's that?" Mrs. Tom scrunched her forehead and scratched her head.

"Botulism. It's a sickness people get from eating bad food."

She nodded.

"It can be serious, and we need to get to the bottom of that."

"Ee." Virginia flashed a smile. Her grin was warm in spite of the spaces with teeth missing. Her eyes sparkled. She began wrapping the scarf in bright yellow tissue paper.

"I wonder if those people got sick from eating bad stinkheads," Stephen said. "Do some of the people in Nunapitchuk make them in plastic bags?"

She wrinkled her forehead again. "I . . . don't . . . know," she said slowly, thinking as she spoke. "Maybe."

"Could you find out?"

"Ee." She tucked the wrapped scarf into a paper bag and handed it to Stephen.

He had taken Mrs. Tom to be the town gadabout, and he'd been certain that she was the right person to chat with the folks of Nunapitchuk about stinkhead preparation. "If they do, we'll need to get little pieces of the . . ." He paused for the right word; not rotten, not putrefied. ". . . of the aged fish to test for the poison," he said. "Do you think your relatives would let me do that?"

"Maybe," Virginia said.

"Could you ask them?"

"Ee."

"Great. Let me know what they say."

On the way back to his apartment, Stephen stopped at Jennifer and John's place. "Could I borrow the bacteriology book for several days?" he asked.

"Sure," Jennifer said, and headed down the hallway. Moments later she returned to the kitchen and handed him *Zinsser Microbiology*. "Keep it as long as you need it."

He spent the next hour sprawled on his couch, re-learning about *Clostridium botulinum*, its spores and its toxins and their role in botulism. He knew the bacteria were killed by oxygen and its spores were found in dirt, and he read that, as Jennifer had said, they were also present in river and sea water. He remembered that the bacteria turned into spores under harsh conditions to protect themselves from environmental injuries. As he read, he was reminded that the spores weren't killed by heat and remained dormant for a very long time. The chapter said that the "botulinum toxins are zinc-binding metalloproteases that cleave specific proteins in synaptic vesicles. Motor neuron surface receptors vary for the different botulinum toxins, explaining some of the species' differences in susceptibility to the different toxins." He scratched his ear, wondered what exactly all that meant, and kept reading. When he finished the chapter on Corynebacteria, he shut the book.

He ran his new understanding of the whole process of botulism around in his head. A likely story was that some of the salmon caught by the local fishermen carried the botulism-causing spores from the river. Inside the warm, moist, and low-oxygen state of the plastic sacks, the spores woke up and turned into the kind of bacteria that produced botulinum toxin. When the fishermen, or anybody else, ate the contaminated stinkheads, they also ate the poisonous toxin. The botulinum toxin was one of the most potent toxins around, and ingesting only a few micrograms of it, a minute amount, could kill a person. He closed his eyes and shook his head. Such a nasty germ.

STEPHEN CLIMBED THE WOODEN STEPS TO the entrance to Jackie's trailer. He'd helped move her things from his apartment but hadn't been back since. He banged on the door and wished Bethel had a municipal phone system, so he could ask about good times for a visit.

Jackie opened the door. A giant smile grew on her face. "What a pleasant surprise," she said. "Come in."

She'd cleaned up the place and added nice touches. A pretty curtain now hung on the kitchen window, and a fuzzy black and yellow throw was draped over the orange sofa that belonged to the school district. The stains that had spotted the arms of the easy chair were gone. He pulled off his parka, laid it over the end of the sofa, and sat beside the throw.

They chatted about her job, about spring coming to the tundra. She too had been amazed at the break-up of the Kuskokwim. "We have nothing like that in Atlanta," she said with a chuckle. She asked about Nicholas Tom. "He hasn't returned to school yet, not since the trailer fire."

"That's because he's still in Anchorage, at the rehab facility. He's making progress, I hear, and the skin grafts over his burns have healed well. They're probably trying to provide school there for him."

"I sure hope so," she said. "He's basically a good kid. That was such a terrible fire."

He stood, reached into his parka pocket, and handed her the package. "Here, I brought you a house-warming present."

She unwrapped the scarf, held it up, and beamed. "It's beautiful," she said, her voice soft as suds. She rubbed it against her cheek. "Feels like cashmere."

"Actually, it's called qiviut, the underhair of muskoxen." Stephen crossed his legs and settled deeper into the sofa. "I got it from Virginia Tom at the gift shop. She said it was made by a lady from Mekoryuk." Jackie was studying its pattern of little holes. "By the way, how's your knitting coming?" he asked.

She laughed again and wrapped the qiviut scarf around her neck. "Well, I've made nothing as lovely as this; not by a long shot." She opened a drawer beside the easy chair and pulled out the scarf she had started while living at his place, as well as a pair of mittens. "This is my current project." She held up a set of knitting needles from which dangled half of a little sweater. It looked like it would fit a doll. "It's for my new niece, back in Georgia."

He was proud of her. She seemed to have found her spot in Bethel. As they chatted with ease in the comfort of her new home, he realized, once again, how much he missed having her around.

The next morning, Stephen stopped by the gift shop on his way to see patients in the clinic. Mrs. Tom turned out to be an enthusiastic assistant. She reported that many of her relatives in Nunapitchuk made stinkheads. "It's the men that make them," she said.

"Do they prepare them the old way or the new way in plastic bags?" Stephen asked.

"Usually old way," she said. "Sometimes new way."

HE TRUDGED UP THE STEPS TO his apartment. Inside the laundry room, rather than turning right to the door to his kitchen, he turned left and rapped on the Maldonados' door. Matias opened it and invited him in.

"What's up?" Matias asked.

Stephen snickered at the way Matias accurately recognized this wasn't a mere social visit. Stephen never made mere social visits.

"I've been working on the source for the botulism and need to submit several samples from suspected food to the State Health Department for botulinum toxin testing. We suspect the source is stinkheads stored in plastic bags."

"Wow, what an idea. How did you land on that?"

Stephen explained that Jennifer Jetters, the microbiology wizard, was the brains behind it. Then he added, "I'm going to Nunapitchuk to try to find tainted stinkheads. Want to come along?"

Matias chuckled. "Well, sure."

THEY STOOD NEAR THE TOWN DOCK, waiting for Quentin Tom and his boat. Stephen glanced at his wristwatch. "Virginia said her son'd be here at noon."

Matias patted Stephen on the back. "That, partner, could be any time."

Stephen laughed. "Yeah, that's really right."

"Dr. Steinberg. Dr. Steinberg." Stephen turned and saw Virginia galloping toward them as fast as her stubby legs and big rubber boots could carry her. The hem of her kuspuk fluttered at her sides, and she swiped her wind-blown hair out of her eyes. "I'm going too," she said gasping for breath.

Soon Quentin and his motorboat showed up, and Stephen carried aboard his cooler for ferrying the specimens. He sat on the seat in the bow, Virginia and Matias settled into the middle seats, and Quentin, at the stern, yanked on the motor's starter rope. On the third pull, it sprang to life, and they headed out into the Kuskokwim.

The wind slammed into Stephen's face, and he dipped his chin into the neck of his jacket. The air stung his skin, but it carried the sweet smell of spring. Soon, the ptarmigans would exchange their snowy winter plumage for their spotted brown summer feathers. Soon, delicate flowers would dot the berry bushes, and after that, the berries would emerge.

Quentin's motorboat went much faster than Stephen could row his little dinghy. The riverbanks, lined with budding willow branches and greening tundra grass, sped past quickly. Mist off the bow coated his cheeks, and the waves in the parted water slapped the aluminum hull at his knees.

The motor slowed, and soon Quentin had turned the boat away from the river and into a stream. "Johnson River," Quentin called over the roar of the motor. "It's really a bunch of lakes strung together all the way to Nunapitchuk."

Stephen spotted something standing at the edge of the water ahead. It moved. Looked brown and massive. As they neared, he watched its head slowly rise out of the water. River plants dripped from its mouth, and it shook his head, which carried a huge antler rack. It was a moose. Stephen pointed toward it with an outstretched arm and called to Matias.

When they were about twenty feet from the animal, Quentin swerved the boat toward it. Stephen watched the moose tense its muscles. It turned its head toward them, and the fleshy dewlap under its chin wobbled. Stephen gripped the edges of the bow.

What was Quentin doing? Was he planning to plow into that beast? He took a deep breath and glanced over his shoulder.

In the stern, Quentin, his hand clutching the motor's tiller, laughed. He kept laughing as the boat shot forward. The moose stepped back, grunted, and shook his head again. The boat missed him by about four feet. *Not funny*, Stephen thought. But he'd seen these careless shenanigans before from young Yup'ik men. He supposed it was just like the dumb things young gussak men did back in Philadelphia.

The next time the boat slowed, Stephen saw a cluster of shacks beyond the riverbank. Quentin eased the boat to a rickety wooden dock. Virginia climbed out and began speaking with her son. He nodded and nodded again. "We'll go to Vincent Maxie's place," Virginia said.

Stephen, carrying the heavy cooler in his arms, stepped carefully on the tipsy boardwalk. Slats were missing, and pine rails, where they existed, rose and fell like the runners of a roller coaster. His boots slid on the wet wood. As they neared a small gray house, Quentin called out in Yup'ik. The door swung open, and Virginia spoke in their language to the woman she introduced as Vincent's wife. Vera ducked back into the house and returned with a bulging, black plastic bag. Virginia opened the top, turned to Stephen, and said, "Stinkheads."

Virginia kept talking to Vera in Yup'ik and laid the open bag on the boardwalk.

"What's your mother saying?" Stephen asked Quentin. "Her voice is so stern."

"She's telling them not to eat the stinkheads made in plastic bags. I'm not sure they'll listen to her."

"Dr. Steinberg," Virginia called. "Do what you need to do with them."

Stephen and Matias stuck several cotton swabs into the contents of the sack. The mass inside was mushy. It reeked. Stephen felt a tsunami of nausea sweep over him and swallowed hard. They then put the swabs into a screw-top glass tube and wrote "#1" on it with a black Sharpie.

Virginia led them to seven other houses. At each one, someone appeared with a bag of stinkheads. At each one, Virginia lectured in Yup'ik to the people standing around, using her stern voice. Stephen and Matias took several samples from each bag. Finally, they returned to the boat, and Quentin drove them back to Bethel.

Stephen walked the cooler with the specimens down the hall to the hospital laboratory. As he entered the room, he took a deep breath. Chemical smells, maybe acetone, or carbon tetrachloride, or methanol. Or maybe all of them combined into an organic stew. They reminded him of his job during college in a research lab. He'd liked the job, liked the lab crew and the professor who ran it. He often thought that's why he ended up in medical school.

"Paul," he said to the lab tech. "We need to label these and send them to the state lab." He waved a tube containing a swab coated with gray stinkhead mush toward the technician. On its side, in black marker, was written, "#1."

Paul picked up his pen and turned the page of the specimen book. "Patient's name?" he asked.

Stephen read through his notes. "Let's see. Sample number one is from Vincent Maxie's house."

Paul glanced up. "How do you spell that?"

Stephen spelled out the last name.

"Sample type?" Paul asked.

"Stinkheads."

Paul laid his pen back down on the desk. "Dr. Steinberg, are you shitting me?"

Stephen laughed. "No. We're trying to figure out what's causing all the botulism around here, and the state lab will test these specimens for botulinum toxin."

When Paul had affixed an official label to each tube and completed the test request forms, he said, "Okay, then. I'll pack them up and ship them off. Please write a little note for me to include in the box so they know what it's about. And do you have a name we should direct it to?"

"His name is Ferguson. Dr. Mark Ferguson."

"Got it. The package will go out on tomorrow's plane," Paul said. "I hope."

THE RADIO ROOM WAS STILL STUFFY, and Stephen wondered how they could air it out. Punch a hole through a wall? No. The room was an island in the middle of the hospital, surrounded by the medical records room, the laundry, the pharmacy, and the hallway to the clinic rooms. A hole in the ceiling? No again. Beyond the ceiling was the attic crawl space filled with old equipment and patient records and, above that, the roof.

The radio began to sputter, the receiving light blinked green.

"Dr. Steinberg, this is Denise Kaganak from Aniak. Over."

"Yes, Denise. What can I do for you? Over."

She described a baby with a runny nose. No fever, no cough, no trouble breathing. Lungs were good when she listened with her stethoscope. Eating well. "His older brother has a runny nose too. Over."

"Sounds like a cold to me. Check the baby again tomorrow. Tell the mother to bring him back sooner if he develops a fever or trouble breathing . . ." He was about to say "Over" when he stopped. "Say, Denise. I have a question about Mr. Egoak. The doctors in Anchorage discovered that another patient—a guy from Nunapitchuk—had botulism. That's poisoning from eating bad food. That patient's illness was very similar to Mr. Egoak's. Do you know if he could have eaten stinkheads? If so, do you know if they were aged in plastic bags? Or would he use the traditional method to prepare them? Over."

"Lincoln Egoak's brother is Roland. He lives next to my mother. Lincoln makes stinkheads in plastic bags and stores them under his oil stove. Over."

Stephen again looked up the number for the State Health

Department and dialed. When he was put through to Dr. Ferguson, he told him about Mr. Egoak, the botulism, and the stinkheads putrefied in plastic bags.

"In another day or so you'll get a bunch of specimens from stinkheads from Nunapitchuk that were stored in plastic bags."

"Right on. I'll let you know what we find."

Stephen hung up the phone and sighed. They were on the road to solving the botulism mystery.

CHAPTER 25

"WOULD YOU? COULD YOU? IN A car?/Eat them! Eat them!
Here they are . . ."

Jennifer, flanked by her wiggling twins on the sofa, read aloud.
Jeffrey had chosen the book, *Green Eggs and Ham*, his favorite of
the many they owned by Dr. Seuss. He bounced his foot to the
rhythm of the words and giggled at the rhymes. House, mouse.
Rain, train. Box, fox. Ham, Sam, I am.

"Why are his eggs green?" Brian asked. "That's yucky."

"Because it's a story, and it's not real," Jennifer said. "They're
green to make you laugh."

"Read more," Jeff called.

As she continued reading, she heard the kitchen door open.
Ginger rose from the floor and strutted toward the sound. Her tail
wagged like a copper-colored flag.

"Honey?" It was John. "Stephen has something to show you."

"We're in the living room."

Stephen followed John from the kitchen and handed a piece of
paper to Jennifer.

National Veterinary Services Laboratories
Diagnostic Testing

P.O. Box 844   1920 Dayton Avenue, Ames, IA 50010
515-337-7266

Specimen	Name	Date of testing
Stinkheads	Vincent Maxie	May 12, 1971

Submitted by	Assay
Bethel Native Alaska Hospital	Mouse protection
Bethel, Alaska	

TEST	RESULT
Botulinum toxin	Positive, serotype E

When she reached the last line, she began to smile. "Very interesting." Her voice was as calm as she could make it, but her insides were dancing. She'd been right. Her instincts about the poisoning had been correct, her knowledge of bacteria had led to the answer. And it had been useful! Her understanding of the microbes was useful.

"There are more positive results as well," Stephen said. "Of the twenty-seven samples we submitted from eight bags of stinkheads, twelve of them, from four of the bags, were positive. The state health department is convinced that the new method for preparing stink-heads—in a plastic bag—is the culprit. They now need to organize an educational campaign to encourage the Yup'ik to stick with their traditional methods. The mossy pit-in-the-tundra has passed the test of time. The new ways are . . . well, bad. In fact, sometimes fatal."

"They'll need to be careful with an educational campaign," John warned. "Our help in unearthing the link to stinkheads could be interpreted as criticism, especially surrounding something as basic as native foods. The resistance to such efforts could be huge."

"Sure could," Stephen nodded. "That's why it's a good job for the health department in Anchorage, not us docs who have to work eye-to-eye with the local people everyday."

"Mommy, keep reading," Jeff called and pulled at the sleeve of her kuspuk.

"Boys, your mom is so smart," Stephen said. "She figured out the mystery of the sick people."

Jennifer held her head high and continued to smile. The glow of satisfaction flowed through her, as warm and embracing as a sunny day at a southern California beach. Perhaps she could, indeed, finish her doctoral dissertation. She raised her chin a notch. Yes. Of course she could.

Jeff looked confused. So did Brian. "Read," they said in unison.

THREE WEEKS AFTER STEPHEN SENT THE stinkhead samples to Anchorage, a guy from the state health department arrived in Bethel. John called and asked Jennifer if the fellow could stay in their spare room for several days.

The spare room was also the playroom, and it was a mess. Legos were scattered all over the floor as were the cardboard bricks, assorted pieces of clothing, and the instruments—a triangle, a drum, and a pair of cymbals—Jennifer's mother had sent for Christmas.

"Okay, guys," she said to the twins. "We're having company and need to clean up this stuff." On days like today, she really wished she had a job in a lab and a cleaning lady for the house. She also wished Bethel had a hotel and a restaurant.

SHE LIKED THE YOUNG EPIDEMIOLOGIST WHO walked into their apartment with John. He was friendly, polite, and seemed smart. He explained that the department was planning an educational campaign to inform the Yup'ik to return to their old ways of preparing stinkheads.

"Some of us thought we should just issue a public health injunction against using the plastic bags, but others, myself included, thought that would be a mistake."

"You are very correct about that," John said. "Gussuk laws don't always go over well, here."

"So," the fellow explained to Jennifer, "I'm here to assess the possibilities. Your husband introduced me to several of the Yup'ik folks, and we had nice conversations about how to approach the educational campaign. That woman, Mrs. Tom, was particularly helpful. She's very bright. And opinionated. And outspoken."

Jennifer nodded. "Yes, she's all of those things."

"Tomorrow and the next day, I'll make a few mock-up posters and see how they fly with the Yup'ik advisors. Then, we need to figure out how to spread the word through the villages."

"Consider asking Mera—she's married to one of the docs and is a journalist for the *Tundra Drums*—to write an article for the paper."

"Bethel has a newspaper?" The epidemiologist seemed amazed.

"Well, if you want to call it that. It's more like a periodic newsletter. But Mera is always looking for ideas, and she'll like this one."

John added, "We also have a radio station. The broadcast range isn't very far and doesn't reach all of the villages, but they'd probably be eager for news other than plane crashes, snowmobiles falling through the ice, and drunken fights."

"Ready for supper?" Jennifer asked. "We have baked salmon, canned carrots and peas, pilot bread, and canned fruit cocktail for dessert. It's typical Bethel fare."

The young epidemiologist laughed. "Sounds very good."

TOMORROW WOULD BE ANOTHER DEPARTURE. DEIDRE, David, and little Daniel would leave—headed back to New York City where David would begin a pediatrics residency in several days. Jennifer stared across her dining table at Deidre, whose eyes were darker and more deeply set than usual. She looked tired; she'd probably been up half the night packing.

"I'm happy you can use the leftover food," Deidre said. She had brought two frozen chickens, a loaf of frozen homemade bread, four cans of artichoke hearts, and a half jar of mayonnaise. "We were pretty good at ending our time here with bare cupboards and an empty freezer but not perfect."

Then silence. No one spoke. The quiet between them was heavy as lead. What does one say at such a bittersweet moment?

Deidre perked up and detailed their plans for the next couple days. Her hands flew like swallows as she itemized the schedule:

Ride with Stephen to the Bethel airport tomorrow

Fly to Anchorage

Complete the check-out at the Native Alaska Health Service offices the next day

Fly to JFK the day after that

Stay with her parents until they found a place of their own

"You'll miss Bethel?" Jennifer asked.

Deidre's face softened. She took a deep breath. "Well . . . Bethel is an important, and forever memorable, chapter in our Book of Life. But more than the town or the tundra or the hospital, we'll miss all of you." Her arm swept from her far left to the far right, indicating to Jennifer she meant the entire medical staff and their families.

Deidre remained a mystery to Jennifer. Did she have dreams? Of course she did. Everyone had dreams. *Were they like her own,* Jennifer wondered. Goals missed? Accomplishments rare? Plans for a doctorate dashed—or at least delayed? She hoped not. Deidre deserved a satisfied life. She seemed very settled being Daniel's mother. Her big triumph in Bethel, other than delivering her baby and holding up for the bris, had been the stunningly successful group birthday party. That was Deidre, spreading a celebration to everyone, rather than claiming the limelight for herself. Would she ever see Deidre again? New York was a long way from California. Their lives would be very busy as they all moved onward—new friends, new interests, new goals.

Later that evening, after the dishes were washed and the twins and John were in bed, Jennifer stared out the living room window at the tundra that stretched beyond the swing set on the hospital grounds. The tundra: shifting and changing and seemingly bleak, but at close range, rich and complex. It was a marvel, the tundra.

Her mind wandered. She thought of the soldiers in Vietnam, of the luck of the draw that landed John and the other doctors in Bethel. She and the twins could still be in California, worrying that every phone call was notice of an injury to John, every knock on the door a pair of Marines with news of his death. He could have ended up like her cousin Mike, with his leg blown off, or his classmate Gary, dead in a South Asian swamp.

She watched Virginia Tom trudge along the boardwalk, likely going home from the Maldonados'. As usual, her rubber boots were too big for her little feet. Wisps of her coal-colored hair had escaped her braid and fluttered into her eyes. The breeze blew against the board she carried under her arm, making her a bit unsteady. She stopped, studied the tire tracks in the parking lot's mire as if they carried the answer to a puzzling question, rearranged the board, and then trudged onward again.

For Virginia and the other citizens of Bethel, the changing of the medical guard was like the tundra birds: coming and going, over and over, year after year. Every July, some of the hospital staff left, and new ones arrived; every spring a new crop of pintail ducks flew in from somewhere in the south to breed, and every fall they flew out to warmer weather. Virginia and the other Native Alaskans knew all about Mother Nature and her movements. For them, the comings and goings of the doctors were as predictable as the rhythms of the seasons and the migration of the waterfowl.

They too would migrate in another year. When they left, would the Jetterses be remembered in Bethel? For a little while, but probably not much after that. Still, Jennifer had done an important thing for Bethel, and, as John told her, she should be proud of that.

And she was. Yesterday, she'd seen the signs at the hospital warning against processing stinkheads in plastic bags. "Back to the old ways" they said over a picture of a pile of salmon heads in a moss-lined hole in the tundra. No one else should have to die, or become sick, from botulism—all because of her.

Jennifer heard a little voice from the boys' bedroom. "Get out, Ginger." It was Brian. Ginger had recently taken to crawling into bed with one or the other of her sons. How much of their time in Alaska would they remember? Hopefully at least a little. She didn't want their reminiscences of Bethel to vanish like smoke in the wind. She hoped they wouldn't forget the rush of the river; the kindness of Mrs. Tom; the crisp, refreshing smell of the air in the winter. Even if their memories grew fuzzy, their years in Bethel would be etched into the depths of their being, and that was a good thing.

In several hours, the Dorfmans would leave. George the OB had already gone, headed to Florida for a real OB-GYN residency. Matias had re-upped for two more years, and Stephen would probably stay forever. Then next July, she and John too would disappear from Bethel. Yet the wonders of the place—the smell of the tundra, the roar of the river breaking up, the blazing sunsets and dancing northern lights, the staccato voices of the Yup'ik people, and all the magical gifts of Alaska—would stay with them eternally.

But for now, she had two children to raise, a husband to accompany, and a dissertation to look forward to. Books to read, clay pots to build. Over the next year, she and John would gather many more memories of Bethel to stow in her bank of recollections.

"Mommy. Ginger won't get out." Brian was calling again.

"I'm coming, honey."

Acknowledgements

WITH GREAT GRATITUDE, I ACKNOWLEDGE THE patience and invaluable suggestions of my first reader, Jim, and my longstanding writing group: Marty Calvert, Margaret Nesse, Danielle Lavaque-Manty, Ann Epstein, Cathy Mallet, Cynthia Jalynski, and Hope Haefner. Jennifer McCord and Phil Garrett and their crew at Epicenter Press skillfully transformed an electronic manuscript into a real and beautiful book. Thanks to Cynthia Manson, my literary agent, for her kindness and persistence. And finally, I treasure the Native Alaskans who showed us their magnificent land and ways of living as well as the medical staff at the Native Alaska Hospital, Bethel, for their unending friendship.

JANET GILSDORF IS PROFESSOR EMERITA IN pediatrics and epidemiology at the University of Michigan and teaches in the University of Michigan Medical School's Medical Humanities Pathway. Her memoir *Inside/Outside: A Physician's Journey with Breast Cancer* was published in 2006 by the University of Michigan Press, and her novel *Ten Days*, was published in 2012 by Kensington Books. Her non-fiction book, *Continual Raving: The Story of Meningitis and The People Who Conquered It*, was published by Oxford University Press in 2019, and her novel *Fever* was published by Beaufort Books in 2022.

In 1974 – 1975, she was extremely fortunate to work and live in Bethel, Alaska, the setting for this novel. She currently lives in Ann Arbor, Michigan, with her husband Jim.